THE

THIRTEENTH LEGION

A James Acton Thriller

By J. Robert Kennedy

James Acton Thrillers

The Protocol   *The Venice Code*
Brass Monkey   *Pompeii's Ghosts*
Broken Dove   *Amazon Burning*
The Templar's Relic   *The Riddle*
Flags of Sin   *Blood Relics*
The Arab Fall   *Sins of the Titanic*
The Circle of Eight   *Saint Peter's Soldiers*
The Thirteenth Legion

Special Agent Dylan Kane Thrillers

Rogue Operator
Containment Failure
Cold Warriors
Death to America
Black Widow

Delta Force Unleashed Thrillers

Payback
Infidels
The Lazarus Moment

Detective Shakespeare Mysteries

Depraved Difference
Tick Tock
The Redeemer

Zander Varga, Vampire Detective

The Turned

THE

THIRTEENTH LEGION

A James Acton Thriller

J. ROBERT KENNEDY

ISBN-10: 1530003326

ISBN-13: 978-1530003327

First Edition

10 9 8 7 6 5 4 3 2 1

For Paris.

THE

THIRTEENTH LEGION

A James Acton Thriller

"A fanatic is a man who consciously over-compensates a secret doubt."

Aldous Huxley

"And he bearing his cross went forth into a place called the place of a skull, which is called in the Hebrew Golgotha: Where they crucified him, and two other with him, on either side one, and Jesus in the midst."

John 19:17-18, King James Version

PREFACE

The crystal skulls referred to herein are real and confirmed to be of unknown origin and unknown method of manufacture by top scientists at Hewlett-Packard.

The Home Depot, Forest Plaza Shopping Center, Annapolis, Maryland

"I don't know why we don't just pay someone to do this."

Professor James Acton grinned at his wife, Professor Laura Palmer, as he pushed the large cart containing several boxes of floating flooring along with a few bags of supplies. "You know me, I love working with my hands. Besides, installing a floating floor in the basement is something I've been meaning to do for years."

"You could hurt yourself!"

Acton laughed. "You do realize how many bullets, grenades, knives and vehicles have been aimed in my direction, don't you? If a rubber mallet is what finally takes me out, then so be it." He winked at her. "Just don't have it written on my tombstone."

"Here lies James Acton, beloved husband and son, finally bested by his basement."

Acton laughed, reaching over and squeezing the back of Laura's neck. He leaned in and gave her a quick peck, noticing several beads of sweat on her forehead. "You okay?"

She nodded, but suddenly appeared weak. "Just tired." She placed a hand on the left side of her stomach where she had been shot in Paris. "It still acts up from time to time. It just drains me of energy."

Acton felt his chest tighten at his selfishness. It had been his idea to come here, and he had encouraged her to come along. Then he had travelled up and down almost every aisle of the massive store wanting to get everything he would need in one stop. "I'm sorry," he said, his voice slightly subdued. "I should have come alone, this was too much walking."

Laura reached out and squeezed his arm. "I'm a big girl. I could have said no, or gone and waited in the car." She took in a deep breath, letting it out slowly. "I just need to get home and lie down, I'll be fine."

"Pain?"

She shook her head. "No, just weak."

Acton looked down the long row of cars, their SUV near the end. "Why don't you wait here and I'll get the car?"

Laura gave him half a smile. "It takes almost as much effort to stand as it does to walk."

Acton nodded toward the cart. "Hop in, there's room."

Laura laughed, wrapping herself around one of his arms for support, resting her head on his shoulder. "Don't tempt me."

They continued down the row, Acton pulling out the fob and unlocking the doors. He positioned their cart behind the bumper then opened the passenger side door as tires squealed behind them. He glanced over his shoulder casually. "Asshole, he could kill someone driving like that in a parking lot." Laura didn't look, instead gripping his arm tighter.

She's definitely not well.

The van was a sleek affair, a Mercedes emblem on the front grill suggesting some coin had been spent to purchase it, yet it was being driven as if it had been stolen. As it raced up the lane toward them, Acton stepped around Laura, redirecting her toward her door and away from the van.

Brakes were hit hard, the Mercedes Sprinter shuddering to a stop as the side doors burst open, two men erupting out, covered head to toe in black, both aiming Berettas at them. Laura yelped, her cellphone flying from her hand as she threw her arms up.

"Professors James Acton and Laura Palmer?" asked one of the men as he advanced toward Acton, Acton now pushing Laura behind him as they retreated, the cart forgotten.

Acton said nothing.

The man with the unanswered question extended his arm, placing the gun directly in Acton's face. "You *will* answer the question."

Acton was quite certain the men already knew who they were, and if they were here to kill them, identifying themselves would only hasten their deaths. If they were here to kidnap them then any form of delay, even a few seconds, might get cameras out and people calling police, police that just might happen to be in the area if they were lucky.

"Who wants to know?"

"That kind of talk gets people killed, Professor."

I guess they do *know.*

"If you know who we are then why are you asking?"

Suddenly there was a clap of thunder from behind them and the man was shoved back toward the van, his arms and legs outstretched toward Acton, the other man frozen in place, his jaw dropping in shock.

A second shot rang out, smearing him against the van as tires screeched to their left, a black SUV careening toward them. The driver of the Mercedes hit the gas, the vehicle jerking forward just as a third shot removed him from existence, his head now a red mist filling the cabin.

The SUV came to a halt at an angle behind the van as Acton turned to grab Laura and make a break for it between the rows of vehicles.

"Professor!"

Acton spun toward the voice and his jaw dropped at the sight of his friend, Martin Chaney, reaching for them.

"What—"

Chaney cut him off.

"Come with me if you want to live."

Golgotha, Judea
April 7th, 30 AD
The Ninth Hour

"Sir, we found something you need to see!"

Decanus Vitus wiped his brow, ignoring his underling's excitement, instead staring up at the top of the hill, three solitary crosses standing in the darkness, the daylight gone, a storm like none he had experienced before on land engulfing them.

The gods were angry.

The wind carried the wails of their supporters, though from what he had heard, they were all there for him, the one who claimed he was the son of the Jewish god. It was ridiculous of course, these misguided Jews knowing no end to their arrogance in claiming there was only *one* god, and *he* had chosen *them*.

If he's all-powerful, then why are we the conquerors?

Two soldiers ran down the hill, talking excitedly. "It wasn't a trick! He can see!"

"Impossible. I can't believe it. I've never trusted Longinus. You know he only needs three more months before he earns his retirement. He'll say anything to stay in."

Vitus reached out. "You two, come here!"

The two men froze, their eyes widening in further terror as the skies raged upon the landscape. "Sir!"

"Did you say Longinus can see?"

They both nodded.

Vitus looked up the hill again then shook his head. He flicked his wrist. "On with you."

The men executed two smart salutes before running down the path, away from whatever had just happened atop the hill. For a moment, he thought of ordering them back, he having just realized they were probably abandoning their posts.

Though he didn't blame them.

It *was* terrifying.

It was one thing to face an enemy made of men, another to face the gods. And they certainly seemed in a rage today.

"Sir!"

He finally turned his attention to the young soldier beside him. "What is it?"

"You have to see this, please sir, come!"

He frowned but followed the excited soldier. "What is it?"

"I-I'm not sure, sir. When the earth shook, a large stone tumbled down the slope then split at the bottom. There's something inside it. Something—" He shrugged. "I don't know how to describe it." He shuddered. "I don't *want* to describe it."

"What in Hades does that mean?"

The young soldier continued around the base of the hill, past others fleeing for the walls of Jerusalem and safety from the storm. "When I looked at it, I swear it looked back at me!"

What is he talking about? Some sort of animal?

The man skidded to a halt, his arm outstretched, pointing at a large boulder, a dark chasm wide enough to fit a man's head, forming a jagged line down the center.

"Where is this creature?"

"I'm the one who found it." Vitus turned toward an old man standing nearby, pointing at the rock. "It is in there, but it is no creature."

Vitus stepped forward and peered in the crevice, seeing nothing. He stood back up. "You're imagining—" A bolt of lightning lit the area and for a brief moment he saw something, something strange. A shiver raced up his spine as he stepped back.

"You see it, don't you!" exclaimed the soldier, standing a safe distance back.

"Torch!"

A torch was shoved in Vitus' outstretched hand, its flame battling the wind and rain. He pulled his cloak over his head, creating a barrier between the elements and the crevice, the torch spurting to life as he jammed it inside.

He gasped, his bowels nearly loosening as two red eyes peered back at him.

What in the name of the gods is that?

Salem, Virginia
Present Day, One Day Earlier

Madely stretched then yawned.

"You know, sometimes I wonder why we're here all the time."

His partner, Johnson, looked at him, stifling his own yawn. "Because it's always been done this way?"

"Right, but just because we've always done it this way, doesn't mean it's the right thing to do. I mean, you and I have been on this detail for what, twenty damned years? Nothing has ever happened."

"Well, that's not true. Remember London."

Madely nodded. "True, but ultimately that didn't affect *us*. It was just a precaution that we took it into our safekeeping. In the end it went right back to her, and she knew who we were the whole damned time. Hell, she's even invited us to do our shifts in the comfort of her living room."

"HQ would never go for that."

Madely chuckled. "No, but what they don't know…"

Johnson grinned. "I'm in if you're in."

Madely smiled. "No, no, just wishful thinking." He poured himself another cup of tea from a thermos the old lady had provided them and took a sip.

Best damned tea I've ever had.

He handed it to Johnson who filled his own cup. "Tea and cookies at the beginning of every shift is a nice perk that I bet no one else gets."

"True. I don't know how many more days like this we'll have. She's an old lady."

Johnson frowned, nodding his head slowly as he glanced down the street at the humble home. "She's been looking weaker."

"Yeah, I guess when you think about it, that's why we're here. If she dies, we have to get in there and retrieve it before anyone else does."

A car pulled up behind them, Madely adjusting his mirror. "Huh, they're early." He rolled down his window, turning toward their approaching relief. "Hey guys, you're not due for another hour." Suddenly a gun was pulled, pointed directly at his head. "Hey, wait a—"

A shot fired to his right and he felt something wet hit his face. He spun to see Johnson's lifeless body fall against the dash just as another shot thundered behind him.

Friedrichstrasse, Berlin, Germany

Martin Chaney stood under the awning of the Rossmann Drogeriemarkt, the Scotland Yard Detective Inspector, on an indefinite leave of absence after being shot in the deserts of Egypt, having no business here, his business actually just now emerging from the train station across the street.

Former Detective Chief Inspector Hugh Reading of Scotland Yard, now an Interpol agent.

He sighed.

He hadn't seen Reading in over a year, a man he considered his best friend, at least his best friend outside of the Triarii. Though the Triarii was different. It was a brotherhood formed over two thousand years ago, something you were essentially born into, and by the time you were of age, so indoctrinated into, you could think of no other thing you would rather do.

Though some did.

He had never had any doubts about devoting his life to the Triarii, but life within it wasn't like some cult. He had trained to be a doctor, yet after seeing so many lives wasted in the ER to crime, he had instead turned his attentions to law enforcement, working his way up through the ranks, a good chunk of his career spent working for the man now walking out the doors.

I miss you, old friend.

He stepped out, quickly crossing the street, searching for his friend's shadow. He spotted him, about ten paces behind.

Got you!

He slowed, turning his back so they wouldn't spot him, he not yet ready for his old partner to see him. The sometimes crusty old bastard walked by, oblivious to him being there, Chaney desperate to reach out and say hello.

The shadow passed him and Chaney stepped back into the flow, his hand gripping the pistol in his overcoat pocket. He raised the weapon, took aim, then fired.

There was a loud pop, the noise lost among the din of the busy street, the tiny dart embedding itself in his target's back. The man reached for it, his shoulder blades squeezing together as he gasped in shock, then collapsed slowly to the ground, passing out within seconds.

Somebody shouted for help, a crowd immediately forming around the downed man. Chaney stared at his old partner who turned to see what was happening.

Okay Hugh, do you see me? It's time to talk.

"Let me through!"

Chaney spun to see another man rushing up, pushing the crowd aside then kneeling beside the unconscious man. He then glared directly at Chaney.

Oh shit!

Fear gripped him as he recognized the man, he failing to take into account there might be two watching his old partner. He knew that Reading would be watched, just in the off chance he attempted to contact him, though he had never thought they'd spare two resources.

And he knew this man.

He was a friend.

Rage filled his friend's eyes.

He means to kill me.

Chaney looked at Reading, their eyes meeting, his old partner's jaw dropping in recognition. But there was no time for a reunion.

10

He bolted.

Interpol Agent Hugh Reading stared, his mouth agape, his heart slamming with shock and excitement at the sight of his old friend. They had been partners for years, he the senior of course, but Martin Chaney was a good friend, they spending many an off-hour together.

Until about a year ago, when he had last seen him in Venice.

Then heard nothing since.

He's terrified!

The fear in his friend's eyes was clear, a wave of relief washing over Reading as that meant Chaney had probably disappeared for some good reason. It had pained him that his friend would leave without saying anything, that he wouldn't trust him enough to say something.

Yet he knew the reason.

The bloody Triarii.

It had been a shock to learn where his partner's true loyalties lay, and it had hurt their relationship, the trust having to be earned yet again, but it had. And it wasn't until Venice when they had learned the true extent of the battle raging within the Triarii that he had an inkling of doubt return.

An inkling that had turned into outright suspicion when he had disappeared, putting in for an indefinite leave of absence to recover from his gunshot wound.

And not telling his old partner why.

Chaney turned, running in the opposite direction. Reading rushed after him, his tired bones not as quick to react as they used to, he raising his hand and shouting after him. "Martin, wait!"

Another man cut in front of him, stepping away from the man who had collapsed, and chasing after Chaney. Car tires squealed ahead, an Audi A4 racing toward them on the opposite side of the street, the wheel suddenly cranked as it swung across, pulling a 180 just ahead of the oncoming traffic. It screeched to a halt, the passenger side door thrown open.

Chaney dove in, the tires spinning, the traction control off, before it peeled away in a hail of blaring horns. The other man jumped out into the street, raising a weapon, oblivious to the vehicle about to run him down. Reading slammed into him, they both hitting the ground hard, the gun clattering away before a shot was fired. He spun him over onto his back, his fist raised when he froze.

Wait a minute!

"Rodney?"

He couldn't remember the man's last name, though he had been a guard at the British Museum, a guard who had *fled* the British Museum, rather than face questioning. He was a man he knew to be a member of the Triarii, and apparently a friend of Chaney's.

"What the bloody hell is going on?" He hauled the man to his feet, keeping a firm grip on him as he pulled him out of traffic. "Why are you trying to shoot at Martin?"

Rodney shook his head. "Agent Reading, you don't know what's going on. You need to let me go, now."

"Not going to happen."

Rodney swung his arm in a loop, breaking the grip before placing a foot behind Reading, pushing him off balance and onto his ass.

Reading cursed, glaring up at the much younger man.

A car pulled up beside him, two men jumping out and grabbing the still unconscious man, carrying him to the curb and placing him in the backseat. The car pulled up slightly, Rodney getting in the passenger seat. He pointed at Reading. "Don't get involved, Agent, or someone you care about could get hurt."

Outside Riyadh, Saudi Arabia

Faisal gently pushed his laughing boys inside their almost palatial home. As a member of the Saudi royal family, life was good. Extremely good. He had more money than he knew what to do with thanks to the generous stipends paid out by the family, and though he was far down the line of succession, there was so much money to go around, it meant little whether he was ten times removed or fifteen.

He was rich.

Life was good.

And he had to do little for it, other than run his small corner of the kingdom, with an iron fist granted him by blood.

A good life.

He just hoped the rumors of the treasury being broke within five years due to the low price of oil were just that. Rumors. He knew the reasoning behind it. Saudi oil production costs hovered around $10 a barrel, a price no one outside of the Middle East could compete with. Their aim was to bankrupt shale oil and oil sand production, then lower production, jacking up the price.

But the plan had to work before they ran out of money.

"Safiya! We're home!"

He pulled off his gloves, tossing them to his manservant then dropped in a chair, his boots promptly pulled off. He looked at his servant. "Where is she?"

"I don't know, sir. I had thought she was home."

"Of course she's home, she's not allowed to leave!" He shoved his now bare feet into sandals and dismissed the boys, heading toward their bedchambers.

Perhaps she's asleep.

He felt a stirring down below.

Maybe I'll wake her with a surprise!

He pushed aside the slightly ajar door to their bedchambers and smiled, his wife lying on the bed, a satin sheet covering her. He closed the door, locking it, then stripped naked, his excitement now raging as he grabbed the end of the sheet and yanked it aside.

He cried out.

Two round holes, dripping with blood, were torn through her back, a pool of blood soaking the sheets. He spun toward the far wall, screaming for help, staring at the sheets hanging there, pulled aside. The door to his secret vault lay open and his heart leapt into his throat. He rushed forward into the room, surveying his treasures, the stacks of cash in various currencies and gems of varying sizes and settings, ignored, his eyes seeking what he already knew was missing.

He collapsed to his knees as his servants pounded at the locked door.

It's gone!

Golgotha, Judea
April 10th, 30 AD

Decanus Vitus strode into the room, one of the prefect's assistants, Junius, bowing, holding out his hand and stopping him. "A warning, sire, the prefect is not in a good mood."

Vitus pursed his lips then nodded. "Thank you for that." He held up a small bag. "Perhaps this will improve it."

Junius smiled, his eyes widening slightly. "A gift?"

"You could call it that. A curiosity at the least."

Prefect Pontius Pilate's voice echoed down the halls, his words shouted, though unclear. Apparently, a group of soldiers has pissed off the Jewish elders, they now demanding the men's deaths for blasphemy. Strange things were afoot since the Rabi claiming to be the King of the Jews and the son of their god, had been crucified at the behest of the Jewish elders. Vitus had heard rumors that Pilate had reluctantly agreed, his wife urging him not to, he even giving the crowds the choice between the peaceful man's life, or that of a murderer.

The crowd had chosen.

Vitus thought poorly.

But control of Judea was paramount, and tenuous. Pilate, as prefect of the region, couldn't risk losing control, so in an effort to placate the locals, gave the elders wide leeway in administering their own affairs as long as they didn't interfere with Rome's will.

And in this case, some religious man being executed meant little to them.

15

A group of senior officers marched by, not pleased by what they had heard, a hint of fear in the eyes, Vitus not sure of the source, everyone still on edge after the violent storm that erupted around the time this man called Jesus had gasped his last breath.

The aide held out his hand. "He will see you now."

Vitus strode with confidence into Pilate's office, snapping to attention then delivering a salute. "Decanus Vitus, I have—"

Pilate cut him off with a raised hand. "I understand you were witness to the crucifixion?"

"From a distance, Prefect. I was at the foot of the hill."

"And you witnessed the storm? Did it start as they say, the moment he died?"

Vitus thought for a moment, choosing his words cautiously. "I cannot say with any certainty. The skies darkened I think before he died, but there was a shaking of the earth followed by a much more severe storm, that I do believe began when he died."

"And what makes you say so, if you were so far away?"

Vitus gulped. "I heard the wails of his loved ones just after the ground shook. I heard them before, but they were much more pronounced after."

Pilate nodded slowly, apparently satisfied with this response. Vitus breathed, not realizing he had been holding it. Pilate looked up, though not at him, as if addressing someone else. "These Jews are a difficult people to rule. They believe fervently in their god, and I get the distinct impression merely tolerate us, as if they think they could overthrow us at a moment's notice, as if we were the ancient Egyptians of old. I sometimes wonder if we will have ten plagues visited upon us at some point." He suddenly stared directly at Vitus. "I understand you have something for me?"

Vitus stared blankly for a moment then lifted the forgotten bag. "Yes, something that was found only moments after the ground shook. A large boulder rolled down the hill where the crucifixion took place then split in two. This was found inside." He untied the string binding the bag then reached inside, pulling out the surprisingly heavy object, placing it on the prefect's desk.

A shiver raced up his spine and he noticed that Pilate himself shook slightly as well, rubbing his arms, goosebumps visible despite the heat. "What is it?"

"I'm not certain, Prefect, a curiosity for certain. Please, keep it with the complements of the soldiers who serve you."

Pilate nodded, staring at the object intently before picking it up. "Heavy."

"Indeed."

He turned it, holding it up to a candle burning on his desk, the light playing about it, giving it an eerie glow. "Fascinating." He tore his eyes away, looking up at Vitus. "This pleases me. Thank your men, and give them an extra ration of wine for their brave service."

Vitus smiled. "Yes, Prefect. Thank you, Prefect."

"You are dismissed."

Vitus snapped out another salute then turned, marching from his leader's presence, passing the aide at the doorway, a smile on his face, he apparently pleased his master's mood had improved.

"Junius! Come here!"

The man flinched, obviously the Junius referred to, rushing toward Pilate's desk as Vitus left the room.

But his mood quickly turned, for he was certain he knew whose heads the Jewish leaders were demanding, and they were men under his command, good men, men who didn't deserve to die.

I must warn them.

He glanced back and felt his chest tighten, for if the prefect were to find out, his own head would be added to the pile.

Despite the gift he had just bestowed.

Junius rushed into the prefect's office, his eyes immediately locking onto the object held in Pilate's hands. A chill ran through him, reminding him of the terror he had experienced when the ground had shook and the storm had nearly overwhelmed them. It had been vicious, terrifying, and he had wanted to hide in a corner until it was over.

Pilate had shown no fear, and demanded none be shown by his staff, an order no one dared disobey, he clearly in a foul mood.

"What is it, Prefect?"

"A rather unique sculpture, don't you think?"

Junius stared at it, his hands trembling to reach out and touch it, an action he dared not take whilst the prefect was so engaged. "It-it is that. I don't think I have ever seen anything like it."

"Nor I. They claim it was inside a stone, broken in half when that Jew was crucified."

Junius bowed repeatedly, unsure of what to say, it sounding fantastic to him. He didn't believe in the Jewish god, though he had to admit his faith had been shaken enough to hedge his bets, directing a silent prayer to him. And if this sculpture were related to what had happened, then their god's power was truly great.

And perhaps he was more real than any of his own gods.

I've never had a prayer answered, at least not one I could say wouldn't have happened anyway.

Suddenly Pilate placed the object on his desk. "Take it."

"Yes, Prefect." Junius reached forward, lifting the object and turning it toward him, it seeming to stare back at him. He gasped, an uncontrollable shiver rushing over his body, he nearly dropping it.

"Be careful, you fool!"

"Y-yes, Prefect." He carefully placed it back in the bag the Decanus had brought it in, tying the string around the top. "Wh-what should I do with it?"

"Take it, put it somewhere. I don't care. I don't have time for it."

"Y-yes, Prefect."

He turned to leave when Pilate barked a final command at him.

"But don't dispose of it! I may have use of it someday."

"Y-yes, Prefect."

Junius rushed out of the room, gripping the object tightly to his chest, heading toward his own modest office. He placed the bag on a shelf carved into the wall then sat, taking several deep breaths as he tried to get control of his frazzled nerves.

There was a knock at the door, sending his heart racing once again.

"Enter!"

The door opened and an old man stepped inside, closing the door behind him. But *was* he an old man? He appeared frail, yet his posture was good, his stride and motions strong. If Junius were to see him walking in the dark, merely a dimly lit shadow, he would swear he was half the age he appeared to be.

"What do you want?"

The man nodded toward the shelf with the sculpture.

"My name is Ananias, and I have come to speak to you about your new acquisition."

"It was strange. He looked scared."

Professor James Acton's eyes narrowed as he looked at his wife, Professor Laura Palmer. Their friend, Hugh Reading, was on speaker, Acton's cellphone sitting on the couch behind them, they having one of the more riveting conversations he could recall having, at least recently.

"Scared of *you?*" asked Laura.

"That's what I thought at first, but then like I said, someone started chasing him. He got in a car and the guy was going to take a shot but I stopped him."

Acton shook his head. Their friend, for he did think of Martin Chaney as a friend, had been missing for over a year. They weren't as close with him as Reading, though they had spent social time together, Chaney even coming to one of their digs in Egypt. It was there that he had been shot, trying to protect some of Laura's students.

And it was there that things had descended into a mysterious spiral that deepened with each ongoing day. Chaney had slipped into a coma then came out of it, appearing in Venice when they had found an artifact the Triarii for centuries had been searching for.

And then had disappeared.

It had deeply troubled their good friend, Reading, the two men very close. Reading was a bit of a loner after his divorce many years ago, he and his son estranged until only recently. And he had found love once only to have it tragically ripped from him, the poor soul swearing off ever falling in love again.

It pained both him and Laura, knowing what their friend was going through.

And it had thrilled them when Reading had called, his excited utterance of "I saw Martin!" momentarily giving them hope the two would be reunited.

But it wasn't to be so, apparently.

"And you said it was Rodney who tried to shoot him."

"Yes."

Laura leaned toward the phone. "Are you sure? He seemed like a nice young man when I met him."

"Same here," agreed Acton. "He was clearly indoctrinated into the Triarii, but then again, so was Martin."

"Exactly!" exploded Reading. "They're both members of that damned cult! And remember what we were told, that there's some sort of split in the Triarii. Clearly Rodney is on the other side and has been after Martin."

"Maybe that's why he disappeared? He's afraid for his life?"

Reading grunted. "Could be." He sighed. "Things were never really the same after London, you know, when we all met."

Acton laughed. "How could we forget? You two spent your time chasing me down as a multiple murder suspect."

"I didn't arrest you, did I?"

Laura dropped her chin. "You arrested me!"

"Nooo, I merely took you in for questioning."

"Huh, not how I remember it. It was come in voluntarily, or I'll arrest you."

Reading laughed. "Sounds like something I'd say. But after I found out Martin was part of this Triarii, and was more loyal to them than the Yard, it just wasn't the same. He tried, I know, to patch things up, and I think we were headed there, but after he disappeared…" He growled. "A man can't have two masters."

"Agreed," said Acton, "but he did help save Laura."

"Yes, but in doing so, betrayed his oath. He could have just as easily got her killed."

Acton squeezed his wife's shoulder. "But he didn't."

"True, but he should be a copper first, cult member second."

Acton glanced at Laura, they both sensing the pain their friend was in. He could only imagine how he would feel if his best friend, Gregory Milton, were to disappear without a trace, but not before telling the university he'd be leaving.

It meant Chaney had disappeared of his own free will. It may have been self-preservation, yet if he had time to submit the paperwork to leave his job temporarily, surely he could have called his supposed best friend.

"Well, you saw him today, and I don't believe in coincidences, so I think that means he wants to see you."

"I think you're right. He looked directly at me, so he knew I was there."

"Are you going to keep looking for him?"

"Absolutely. If he's in trouble, he needs my help."

Laura pursed her lips then spoke. "Maybe you need to talk to the Triarii directly."

"That's exactly where I'm heading now."

Hope Trailer Park, New Mexico

Leroy flipped the black-tailed jackrabbit on the grill, the aroma filling his nostrils, causing his eyes to close so he could focus his ecstasy on the one sense. The secret was the marinade, a combination of herbs, spices, oils, and a hint of lighter fluid he and his wife had come up with over years of experimentation. There was nothing that could blacken a piece of meat faster than a combustible liquid. Sure, the government bureaucrats and their Bilderberg masters said it was dangerous, but he didn't believe a thing they said.

If the government says something is bad, then they don't want you to know how good it actually is.

He avoided all modern medicines and genetically modified foods, and that included pretty much anything in the meat department. He trapped and hunted his own food, had been for years, and he was as healthy as they come, not that he'd trust a doctor to confirm his assertion.

Fit as a fiddle, his wife would say. He was in good shape, could see for miles, and his hearing was fantastic.

He opened his eyes, the sound of a vehicle approaching pushing his enjoyment of his dinner to the side. Peering at the dark SUV, too fine a vehicle for anyone living in these parts, he immediately became suspicious. He flicked aside a latch on the barbeque platform, positioning his foot for what might be about to happen, thankful his wife was visiting friends down the dusty dirt road.

I'm ready for you bastards.

The government had finally come, tired of him challenging their lies on the Internet, calling them out on their deception of the American people.

But he was prepared.

Four men stepped out, weapons raised.

He pressed his foot down.

The barbeque slid forward, its solid metal front easily absorbing the bullets fired at him. He jumped down the escape hatch hidden under the barbeque, hitting the ground then pulling on a lever that reset the entire contraption built years ago. Unless those government agents could figure out how to work it, he was safe.

He sprinted down the tunnel, it extending for several hundred feet, taking him deeper into his property and farther from the road. Yanking on another lever, he was suddenly flooded with light. He climbed up through the hood of a Jaguar he had discovered abandoned roadside a few years ago, several gunshot blasts to the engine telling him the pissed off Texan who had owned it had learned the hard way you don't travel long distances in one of these.

He stepped out onto the ground, the destroyed engine long since removed, then gently closed the hood, the gunfire having ceased. Peering out from behind the large rock concealing the Jag from the roadway, he spotted the four men leaving his trailer, the SUV soon departing in a cloud of dust.

He waited for them to disappear then sprinted back to his home, rushing inside. He glanced about, nothing out of place, but he knew what they had come for. He threw open the door to his small office and punched the wall, his safe open, his most prized possession gone.

"Bastards!"

Golgotha, Judea

36 AD, 6 years after the crucifixion

Prefect Pontius Pilate sat at his desk, his wife behind him, massaging his shoulders, she sensing his tension. He had been recalled to Rome, they not happy with how he had dealt with the Samaritan uprising. He had tried his best, of that he was certain, yet his best hadn't been enough.

But that couldn't be the reason.

He was good at his job, he was more than capable, yet everything that could go wrong had gone wrong.

And he couldn't understand it. He was certain he had somehow annoyed the gods, they having forsaken him years ago. His wife was convinced it was because he had allowed the crucifixion of the Jewish Rabi, Jesus. He had to admit the thought had crossed his mind. Over the years, story had become legend had become myth, many of his subjects convinced the man had been reborn, resurrected from the dead, even some of his own troops having deserted, they yet to be found.

These followers of Jesus were becoming a bigger problem every day.

But it was no longer his problem.

Junius entered the office then froze. "Oh, I'm sorry for interrupting, I didn't realize—"

"It's okay, Junius, I was just leaving," said Pilate's wife, a wife he realized more now than ever, he loved, she having stood by his side, unwavering all these years. She would never let him know how much she had hated it here in this desolate, remote land, so far from the Rome she loved.

She was a good wife.

And he was certain she now worshipped this man Jesus.

25

He watched her leave then turned his attention to Junius, a loyal aide if there ever was one. He was going to miss him, his successor Marcellus having requested he remain for continuity.

"Prefect, I was wondering what you wanted to do with this?"

Junius held up the sculpture found so many years ago and Pilate felt a shiver radiate up his spine and outward.

Then his jaw threatened to drop.

He pointed at the eyes staring back at him. "*That* is the cause of all our problems."

Junius' eyes narrowed, puzzled. "Prefect?"

"From the day that damned thing graced these walls, things have gone badly for us. Get that thing out of my sight!"

"So you're not taking it with you?"

"Absolutely not! Let my replacement deal with the evil that this thing brings. I for one will be happy when it is in my past and forgotten to time." He sighed, giving the sculpture one last look. "I swear it is staring into my soul, judging me in some way I cannot understand, to some measure no man could possibly meet." He flicked his wrist, dismissing Junius. "Do with it as you please, but make certain it never reaches Rome."

Grunewald, Berlin, Germany
Present Day

Martin Chaney sat in a rather comfortable, high back chair, the sumptuous leather, generously padded, wrapping itself around him. He closed his eyes, it the first chance he had had all day to relax.

"So what happened?"

He opened his eyes, his joy killed by their Berlin contact, Dietrich, as he entered the room, two tall glasses of beer in hand. He passed one to Chaney.

"Thanks." He took a long drag, savoring the brew, Germans having mastered the formula centuries ago. He rested the glass on the arm of the chair. "There was a second tail that I missed."

"Who?"

"Rodney Underwood."

"Sheisse." Dietrich raised his glass slightly. "You are lucky. I have heard he has become what you Brits might call a nutter."

Chaney nodded, a frown creasing his face. He knew Rodney, had known him for years. He was a good man and good friend, and to have him as an adversary was heart wrenching.

But that's what happens in a civil war.

Friend against friend.

Brother against brother.

And he considered Rodney both.

The rift that had existed in the Triarii for eight hundred years was finally coming to a head, and there could be only one winner. In the end, either the crystal skulls they had been entrusted with to protect would be united, or they would remain separated, the fear of what might happen if they were brought together dividing the ancient organization since the disaster in London in 1212, the Great Fire levelling much of the city, three united skulls sitting in the epicenter, unscathed.

"It's too bad, he's a good man, but now that they've seen me, they know I'm trying to make contact with Hugh, so they'll keep an extremely close eye on him from now on."

"You knew that could happen."

Chaney nodded, taking another drink. "I know, you plan for every contingency, but you don't necessarily expect it to actually happen. I never would have guessed that they'd have two men on him. We thought their resources were spread pretty thin what with their funding problems."

Dietrich grunted. "Each side still has a lot of money." He sighed then drained his glass. "And when you think about it, how many people are they actually watching? You didn't—don't—have a lot of friends outside of the organization."

Chaney pursed his lips, doing a quick mental tally of the people he'd consider friends outside of the Triarii, and he had to admit it was a pretty thin list. There were many at the Yard that he thought of as work friends, though other than Reading, rarely spent time with them outside of special occasions.

And then there were the professors.

"So what are you going to do now?" asked Dietrich, eyeing his empty glass, it apparently looking like another.

"There's one more attempt we can make."

Dietrich's eyebrows rose. "Who?"

"The only other two friends I can think of." He leaned forward, putting his glass aside. "But now that they know I'm trying to make contact, they'll have increased their surveillance of them, I'm sure."

Banks of the Seine, Paris, France

Henri smiled. It was a perfect day, the sun gently kissing his skin, a nice breeze taking the edge off, the beautiful city he loved going about its business, as if in defiance of the tragedy that had occurred only weeks ago.

Love must go on.

He gazed at the beautiful creature sitting next to him on the bench, the walkway along the bank of the Seine filled with young lovers. He didn't know her well yet, in fact, didn't even know her name yet, the darling not having succumbed to his charms.

But she would.

They always did.

His problem was sealing the deal, something always seeming to get in the way, not the least of which was his thin wallet.

A life devoted to the Triarii didn't pay well, not in his position as a janitor at the Museé du Quay Branly. Some of his fellow Triarii held government or corporate positions, though he wasn't so lucky. He didn't mind. The Triarii did provide for him, extra funding so that he could live a decent lifestyle, though it was still modest, especially since he had to maintain his cover. A janitor pulling up in a Mercedes at work would appear suspicious, as would inviting friends for dinner to find he lived in a luxury apartment.

No, he reserved his extra money for small indulgences. A better bottle of wine, a finer cut of meat, a more expensive block of cheese.

Indulgences easily hidden from those around him.

He lived well, and he loved the life chosen for him, a life where he served the Triarii, his assignment a high honor.

Protecting one of the thirteen known skulls.

"Come on, ma chérie, at least tell me your name."

She didn't look up from her phone, a frown spread across her face. "Please, sir, leave me alone."

"Sir? You make me sound like your father!"

This elicited a look. "You're old enough to be him!"

That actually hurt, his chest tightening slightly, the beginning of a pit forming in his stomach. He caught his reflection in her sunglasses and nearly gasped.

You are *old!*

It was as if he were seeing it for the first time, he denying it all these years. He had crossed forty long ago, fifty was far too close. And no matter how much he wanted to deny it, he was lonely. He had chosen the life of a bachelor, it something many in his position did, not wanting to have to lie to a woman he loved about what he did, not wanting to try and explain why he refused promotions or continued to work in a low wage job at his age when he had a family to support.

The single life was easier.

Though it wasn't better.

"I'm sorry, I didn't mean to hurt your feelings."

He felt a hand on his arm, squeezing gently. He looked down at it then back up at the young woman who had removed her glasses. He patted her hand then leaned back on the bench, stretching his arms out, tilting his head to absorb the sunlight. "It's okay, my dear, you're right. I'm an old, lonely man who has to grow up or he'll be alone forever."

She twisted toward him, hooking her leg up under her so she could face him. "Why don't you find a nice woman, one closer to your age?"

His head lolled to the side and he smiled at her. "It's complicated."

She laughed. "That's a choice on a social website." She paused, her eyes narrowing. "Are you gay? Perhaps you need—"

Henri's eyes shot wide open and he sat upright, waving his hands at her. "No no no! I'm not gay, it's just my job, that's all."

"Ahh, too busy to find a woman."

"Something like that."

He positioned himself to face her, smiling. "You know, I think you're the first woman I've talked to in a long time. I mean, really talked to, without playing some game."

"You mean, without trying to get me into bed."

He grinned. "You don't know what you're missing."

She gave him another look. "Don't ruin this, Henri."

He laughed, patting her knee. "I like you. It's too bad I didn't meet you twenty years ago."

"I'd have been four."

"See, now I know how old you are!" He winked. "Just kidding." He sighed. "Ugh, I just realized I'm twice your age."

She smiled. "Don't worry, you don't look it."

"I know, I know, I look older." He did the quick mental math. Age divided by two, add seven.

I can't date a woman under 31 without looking like a creep.

"Do you have any older friends? Say, thirties?"

"Yes, but none I'd set up with a perfect stranger who tried to pick me up on a park bench."

His phone vibrated in his pocket. "I *really* like you," he said, fishing out his phone. "You're going to keep a good man on his toes, one day."

She held up her left hand, a diamond solitaire now plainly visible. "Already done."

"Oh mon dieu! I wish I had seen that." He answered. "Oui?"

31

"Thirty-two. Sixteen. Oh Seven. Condition Omega."

His eyes opened slightly wider. "Understood." He hung up then took the young lady's hand, giving it a gentle kiss. "I'm afraid I must go."

"The job?"

He smiled as he stood. "Yes."

"If you don't want to be alone, Henri, then you should seriously reconsider your priorities."

"Somethings are easier said than done." He bowed slightly. "I enjoyed our conversation."

"As did I."

He briskly walked toward his car, a beat up two-stroke Citroën that impressed no woman, especially a class act like the young girl he had just met. He climbed in his car and headed for the museum, almost on autopilot as their conversation replayed itself in his mind. She was right. If he didn't want to be alone, he'd have to reconsider his choices.

But leaving the Triarii wasn't an option.

Was it?

It was definitely something he had never considered, so it was something he had never asked. Could he leave? Could he simply ask to retire? Surely they allowed that. It wasn't as if the Triarii was some cult or gang you couldn't leave, though he had never heard of anyone leaving.

Except for those Deniers who had split away. And even they still believed in the doctrines they had grown up with, they simply wanted to reunite the skulls and tap their power. Even he had to admit he was curious about what would happen, but he knew his history, he knew what had happened in London and how the Deniers claimed it had changed their chosen path from one of finding and gathering the skulls together, to one of finding and keeping them separate.

Yet though he was curious, he would never betray the organization he had devoted his life to.

He arrived, waving to the guard in the booth, his face never leaving his paper. "Bonjour Jacques."

"Bonjour Henri, you should get that engine checked, I think only one of those horses is running now."

"I know, I know, but life on a janitor's salary—"

"I left my sympathy in the same garbage can you tossed your last promotion offer in." He flicked his paper, straightening out the pages. "Have a good day."

"You too, mon ami."

He headed straight for the storage room, bypassing his normal routine of changing into his official garb and sticking to his cleaning schedule.

This was a Condition Omega situation. He had never had one before, though he knew it meant the council thought the skull was in danger of being stolen. He swiped his pass, unlocking the storage room.

"Henri, is that you?"

He frowned, his partner, Stéphane, beating him there. "Oui. Is everything okay?" he asked, rounding the tall storage shelf of the row the skull was kept in. One look at Stéphane's face and he knew the answer.

"Non." Stéphane pointed at the empty box on the floor. "They beat us to it. We're too late."

Henri stared at the empty box, shaking his head.

"They didn't even leave a fake."

"These people don't care about maintaining the secret. They only care about uniting the skulls."

Henri sighed. "Okay, close it back up while I get the fake from the car. We don't want anyone here knowing it's missing. We still might be able to recover it."

Stéphane agreed. "Okay."

Henri left the room, his mind racing.

If the skull is gone, and I have nothing to protect, perhaps I can retire.

Domus Tiberiana, Rome
July 18, 64 AD

Junius bowed to his emperor, Nero, waiting for the all-powerful man to acknowledge him.

He didn't, instead washing his hands in a bowl held by one of the many slaves, another then drying them. Nero finally turned to Junius, giving him a once over. He didn't appear impressed. "You are the aide to Antonius Felix, Prefect of Judea?"

"Yes, sire, and I come with a gift for you."

"What is it?"

"A curiosity, sire." Junius rose slightly, still partially bowing, then snapped his fingers. Ananias appeared, the old man who had entered his office over thirty years ago slower now, though still far spryer than a man his age should be. On a cushioned tray in Tyrian purple, he carried the sculpture of a skull, carved from a single piece of quartz crystal.

He shivered, its eyes glaring at him as if angry to be in Rome.

Nero's jaw dropped slightly, his eyes wide, a noticeable shiver rushing through his body as he stepped toward it, his hand outstretched. "I've seen nothing like it in all my years!"

Junius bowed again. "Nor have I. It was discovered at the site of the crucifixion of the man they called Jesus."

"The leader of these damned Christians?"

"Yes, sire. When the ground shook as he died, a large stone rolled down the hill and split in two. This was apparently inside." He motioned toward Ananias. "This man was there when it happened."

Nero considered him. "You saw this happen?"

35

Ananias bowed. "Yes, sire."

"What have you to say about it?"

"Only that it is a great honor to have this in one's possession. It is from a time long ago."

"And how do you know this?"

Ananias smiled, bowing deeper. "I am an *old* man."

Nero frowned. "And rave like one, too." He snapped his fingers, two of his slaves leaping forward. "Put it in my chambers. I will examine it later."

The slaves bowed and took the skull from Ananias, he staring after it almost longingly. "Sire," he said, "if it is your pleasure, I will remain here rather than return to Judea, should you have any questions regarding the skull."

Nero, already returning to his chair, dismissed him with a flick of his wrist over his shoulder. "Fine." He dropped into his chair, looking at Junius. "It is an odd thing, that."

"It is, sire. I find myself strangely drawn to it."

Nero agreed, his eyes following the slaves as they left the room. "If our enemies could see that, they might just surrender without a fight."

Junius smiled. "It is a terrifying spectacle."

"It is indeed." He waved them toward the door. "You are dismissed. Give my thanks to Antonius."

"I shall, sire."

Junius backed out of the room at a bow, Ananias doing the same. Out of sight, he turned, striding swiftly down the corridor, his heart heavy as if he were leaving behind a child. He looked at Ananias.

"I wasn't expecting you to ask the emperor for permission to stay."

Ananias smiled slightly. "My place is with the skull."

Junius stopped, holding out an arm to halt the man who had become his friend over all these years. "There's a secret you've been keeping from me, isn't there?"

Ananias looked at him, his smile spreading slightly. "And it is a secret I will keep to my dying breath."

Fleet Street, London, United Kingdom
Present Day

Hugh Reading walked up the steps to the massive wood doors of a building he had hoped never to enter again.

The Triarii Headquarters.

It was a well-kept secret, he one of the few people who knew where it was outside of the membership, and he had doubts about how many of them knew. The last time he had been taken here, it had been against his will, his longtime partner and friend, Martin Chaney, having shot him with a tranquilizer dart.

He had never completely forgiven him for that.

Yet now, here he was, about to willingly enter the lair of a cult he felt didn't always have the best interest of those who were not members, at heart.

His eyes narrowed, a new sign on a brass plaque to the right of the door.

Social Interactions International Inc.

"What the bloody hell is that?" he muttered.

It must be a new cover.

He tried the door, expecting it to be locked, but not wanting to appear the fool by knocking, just in case the cover was indeed a real business.

It opened.

Interesting.

He stepped inside and his jaw dropped at the difference. What had once been a plush, comfortable lobby, littered with old leather couches and rich wood highlights surrounding a marble floor, had been replaced with sleek modern furniture and dozens of suits crisscrossing the area and holding impromptu meetings.

It had all the appearance of an actual company.

Including the smiling receptionist who looked at him expectantly.

He walked up to her, pulling out his ID. "Agent Reading, Interpol." He paused. "Umm, this is going to sound like an odd question, but is this the"—he lowered his voice to barely a whisper—"Triarii Headquarters?"

She looked at him with a dumb smile, as if humoring an old man. "Sorry sir, this is Social Interactions International. We develop consumer apps for the mobile market. Perhaps you've heard of one of our dating apps?" Her eyes widened. "You know, we've got an app just for seniors like yourself."

Reading felt himself turn red. "Seniors? I'll have you know, little lady, that I am *not* a senior."

The young woman paled, clearly flustered. "Oh, sorry, sir, well, you just remind me of my granddad, I mean—"

"Before you taste-test your shoes any more, tell me how long you've been here?"

She sucked in a quick breath, apparently happy the subject had changed. "Next week we're celebrating one year."

Reading frowned. It fit in with the timeframe, it about the same time that Chaney had disappeared. If the entire Triarii went into hiding then things must be far worse than any of them suspected. "Do you know where the previous tenants went?"

She shrugged. "No idea. To be perfectly honest, I've never heard anyone mention who they were. And oddly, no one ever comes here looking for them." She shook her head. "Maybe that's why they went out of business?"

Reading glanced at the elevators. "Do you occupy the entire building?"

"Yes, sir, all four floors."

Reading's eyes narrowed. "Four?"

"Yes, sir."

"What about the lower levels?"

Her eyes popped slightly, the old-man-humoring smile returning. "There *are* no lower floors, sir."

"Ahh, okay." Reading bowed slightly. "Thank you for your time."

She flashed a smile and gave him a wave as he turned around. If these people didn't know about the lower levels then there was a chance the Triarii were still here.

Or...

He turned around, returning to the desk.

"Yes, sir?"

"One more odd question."

"What's that?"

"Can I see your wrist?"

The Himalayas, Nepal

Chen knelt on the cool stone floor, surrounded by his fellow monks, the Buddhist temple at the top of the mountain the most peaceful place he could imagine in this world. In his youth, he had travelled for several years to discover his true path, and to join the organization his mentor had, passing their rigorous training and taking the oath generations of monks in his order had.

The crystal skull kept at this holy place had been here for hundreds if not thousands of years, no one really knew.

It had just always been.

The stories told by the elders were that a white man had come almost a century ago, excited to find it, then had asked for volunteers to teach him the history of the skull, and to share in the knowledge he himself possessed.

Their lama had apparently volunteered, returning two years later, making no mention of what he had learned or experienced, simply resuming his duties.

He had been but the first of this temple to join the order protecting a worldwide network of skulls.

The task to protect the skull had been passed down generation to generation, and it was now his turn, and eventually, it would be the youngsters in the rear of the room.

The doors behind them opened with a bang, cold wind sweeping inside causing the torches to flutter. He ignored it, it most likely ignorant tourists who had braved the long climb, thinking their unique effort afforded them uninterrupted attention.

Then the purposeful sound of boots marching on the stone echoed through the chamber and he turned to see who the new arrivals were.

He cursed.

Gunfire sprayed across the ceiling, disintegrating small chunks of the roofing in puffs of dust as someone yelled for everyone to remain where they were.

But he was already on his feet, sprinting toward the side chamber where the Crystal Oracle was held, and where he had spotted two of the attackers heading.

"You!"

He looked and saw a gun swing toward him. He dove, headfirst through the sliver of a doorway, tucking his head toward his chest and executing a perfect summersault, immediately leaping to his feet as the two men arrived through another entrance. His foot snapped out, catching the first one under the chin, lifting him from the ground and launching him into his partner.

Both fell in a heap.

He immediately rushed forward, two quick jabs to the throat leaving both gasping for air, their windpipes crushed. Two more rushed inside, startled to find their partners down. Chen stepped forward, grabbing the first man's AK-74 and pulling it toward him, the barrel aimed at the wall. Chen slammed his forehead into the man's nose, the attacker crying out as the satisfying crack left no doubt as to the condition of his appendage. Chen spun the distracted man around, aiming the weapon at his partner and squeezed the trigger, several rounds spurting out the barrel and into the target's stomach.

A fifth man, backed up by several more, strode confidently into the room, a Beretta raised and aimed at Chen. Chen spun the man with the broken nose, using him as a human shield as he backed away, toward the skull.

"You can't win."

Chen nodded at the three men on the floor. "I wouldn't be so sure."

The leader smiled. "You need to be willing to do whatever it takes."

He squeezed the trigger, killing his own man, the body slipping from Chen's arms, leaving him exposed.

Then the gun belched lead again, a searing pain radiating from Chen's chest, sending him stumbling back toward the Crystal Oracle that had been his responsibility for so many years, before collapsing to the floor.

The leader stood over him while the others took the skull, placing it carefully in a specially designed case.

They must be Deniers.

He stared up at the man who now towered over him, struggling for breath. "What do you intend to do?" he gasped.

"Discover the truth."

Chen drew a final breath, shaking his head. "You mustn't, it's too danger…"

The world went black as the sounds of receding footfalls echoed in the small room, his last thoughts of how he had failed in his duty, and how his failure had put the entire world at risk.

Domus Tiberiana, Rome
July 19, 64 AD

Emperor Nero bolted upright in his bed, the voices quickly receding, now only a dull whisper, as if he stood in the center of a large gathering, everyone else hugging the walls in polite conversation.

It was driving him mad.

"Are you okay, my love?"

He glanced over at the woman who had asked the question, searching for her name.

He came up empty.

Another rose to his right, resting her chin on his shoulder. "Can't sleep, darling?" She gave him a devilish smile. "There's a cure for that, you know."

He lay back down and both women draped themselves over him.

But he wasn't interested.

Something had woken him. He had been uneasy all evening and he hadn't slept well. He had shown the girls a good time, he a talented lover if he did say so himself, it always a pleasant romp in the evenings when his wife was in Antium.

But tonight had been different.

What's changed?

He ran through the day's events, it one of constant meetings as they usually were, running an empire so large not at all the glamourous life he had dreamed.

Maybe I shouldn't have killed mother.

At least she had done most of the mundane work, but he was pretty sure she had planned on killing him. To what purpose, he wasn't sure. It was not as if she could become emperor, and any successor would have tossed her to the lions.

Perhaps she was as innocent as she claimed.

He did have to admit he felt some regret, he now realizing that everyone around him was plotting against him, though he had no evidence of it. Yet. As soon as he did, he would have them all staked to crosses as examples to anyone who thought they could defy him.

He was emperor.

Of Rome.

He was all-powerful.

A living god.

The voices laughed.

"Shut up!"

The cooing girls, one servicing him, unnoticed to this moment, halted their efforts.

"Do you wish us to leave?" asked the one who had been nibbling on his earlobe.

He shook his head, realizing he was feeling pretty good. "No, resume."

And they did.

It *was* a good life.

"Fire!"

He ignored the voices.

"Fire!"

The girls didn't.

"Don't stop."

"But, sire, there's a fire!"

He sat up, realizing that it wasn't the voices after all. Footfalls pounding toward the room had him swinging out of bed and throwing on a robe. His aide entered, breathless. "Sire, there's a fire!"

Nero strode toward the windows, noticing the strange orange glow for the first time. "Where?"

"Everywhere!"

He reached the window and gasped. For as far as the eye could see the city burned, easily several districts engulfed in flames.

"What should we do?"

Nero leaned out, the air heavy with a smell he had always loved—burning wood. Cries in the distance told him his citizens were terrified, and that this was his opportunity to prove to any doubters, especially the voices, that he was the right man at the right time.

"Call up all fire brigades and the reserves. Evacuate all people at risk to the public buildings in safe districts and send for additional food and water. We can't risk the people starving should the food stores be destroyed or the aqueducts damaged."

"Yes, sire."

"And wake the Senate. I will be going to personally survey the scene at first light."

"Yes, sire."

His aide hustled away as his two bed companions stood whimpering at his sides, terrified. He put an arm around each of them. "Calm down, ladies, you are perfectly safe here." Heads buried themselves into his chest. "What can I do to convince you?"

The raven-haired beauty who was one of his favorites stared up at him. "Play us a song?"

He smiled, eyeing his lute sitting nearby. "Very well. One song, then I must go. We can't have people thinking that their emperor fiddled while Rome burned."

Fleet Street, London, United Kingdom
Present Day

"They're gone."

"What do you mean they're gone?"

Reading shrugged to no one, his phone pressed against his ear. "I mean they're gone. The Triarii headquarters is now some hi-tech company that makes dating applications for old people."

"Did you sign up?"

Reading glared at the phone, wishing Acton could see his face. "Sod off."

A burst of laughter and static responded.

"Now there's one thing she said that has me curious."

"What's that?"

Reading continued down Fleet Street at a brisk pace. "She said there were no lower levels."

"Really? There were several, weren't there?"

Reading nodded. "Absolutely. Now, when Martin was shot, you said you guys came out some sort of tunnel with a ramp at the end. Do you remember where it came out?"

"No, I was busy tending to him. Hon? Any idea?"

Laura's voice joined the conversation. "It's a blur, but I know we travelled a couple of hundred meters maybe, enough to get you perhaps a street or two over, then we ramped up, a garage door of some type automatically opened and we were in an alleyway. I continued forward until we came to a street then we turned...umm...right, I think."

"Do you remember the street?"

"No, but my next turn put us back on Fleet, and if I remember correctly I could see the police in the rearview mirror."

Reading stopped, looking about. "Wait, you came out, turned right onto a street, then your next turn was onto Fleet, with the Triarii HQ behind you."

"Yes."

"Do you remember if you turned left or right onto Fleet?"

"Oh God, Hugh, umm, wait. Right. No, left. I'm so confused. Americans all drive on the wrong side of the road—I've been away too long. No, I turned left, because I didn't have to try and cross the traffic."

"Excellent." Reading glanced behind him at the building that had once housed the two-thousand-year-old organization, then the traffic flowing next to him. "Okay, I think I know what street you came out on." He briskly walked toward the next intersection then turned left. "I'm guessing you came out on Farrington."

"That could be right, now that I think about it."

He continued down the sidewalk and stopped at the narrow entrance of Bride Lane, a large delivery door fifty meters from the street. "I think I may have found it. Give me a minute."

He began to jog toward the door then thought better of it, he quickly losing breath, silently making another commitment to hit the gym. He reached the door and examined it, it large enough to fit a four-by-four with little problem.

"I'm here. I think this is it."

"Can you get in?"

Reading shook his head. "I don't see any handles or any type of keypad, bell, anything. Just plain walls."

"They were probably controlled by transponders in the vehicles," said Acton. "I don't think you're getting in there unless they want to let you in."

Reading hammered on the door, the resulting din making him cringe as it filled the narrow lane.

"I don't think that's going to work. Remember, they did everything with codes."

Reading nodded. "Yeah, and they were very security conscious." He looked about, trying to spot anything out of the ordinary.

He smiled, a CCTV camera under a balcony catching his eye. "I think I'm being watched. Just a second." He eyed his surroundings and spotted a good-sized piece of cardboard lying on the ground. He picked it up, fishing a pen out of his pocket, then quickly drew two straight horizontal lines, followed by a third line, slightly curved upward. He added his cellphone number then held it up to the camera.

His phone vibrated almost immediately.

"Bloody hell!"

He held the phone to his ear.

"Jim, I'll call you back."

Unknown Location, London, United Kingdom

The Proconsul of the Triarii, Derrick Kennedy, watched the former Scotland Yard detective as he stood in front of the sealed escape tunnel that led to their former headquarters. They had been forced to abandon the location a year ago after the rift became too much, and it had been the greatest humiliation of his life.

But necessary.

"Can he be trusted?" asked one of his team manning the security station.

Kennedy pursed his lips. "His loyalties lie with his friend. He can be trusted as long as he thinks he's helping him."

"And if he were told the truth?"

"They were partners for years. He wouldn't believe us."

The door opened and Rodney Underwood stepped inside. "Sorry I'm late, sir."

"Look!"

They all turned toward the screen the security tech was pointing at. Reading was writing something on a piece of cardboard.

"What's he doing?" asked Rodney.

Kennedy remained silent, knowing the question was about to be answered as Reading flipped the finished product around.

It was the symbol of the Triarii and a phone number.

"I think we better see what the man wants."

The Home Depot, Forest Plaza Shopping Center, Annapolis, Maryland

"Take them out."

"Sir?"

Chaney held the phone closer to his mouth. "Take them out! That's an order!"

"Yes, sir."

Chaney stared through the window at the two professors he considered friends, their hands slightly raised as two armed men confronted them. He knew from Professor Acton's history that he was plotting his escape, the man the luckiest unlucky bastard he had ever met.

The first gunman dropped, then the second, then the driver.

His chest tightened and his stomach flipped, it always a sad day when his fellow Triarii had to die.

"Let's go," he said, his voice subdued. Their vehicle surged forward, toward the scene then screeched to a halt as he threw open the side door, reaching out to the two terrified professors. "Professor!"

Acton stared at him, startled. "What—"

"Come with me if you want to live!"

There was a moment's hesitation then Acton grabbed his wife by the hand and pulled her toward the door, helping her inside then jumping in himself.

"Go! Go! Go!"

The van peeled away as Chaney slid the door shut, turning toward his friends. "Give me your phones."

"Huh?"

"They can be tracked." He motioned with his fingers. "Hurry, now."

Acton pulled his phone from his pocket, handing it over as Laura searched her handbag then pant pockets.

"I must have dropped it."

Chaney put the phone on the floor and smashed it with the butt of his gun.

"Hey! That's expensive!"

Chaney rolled down the window and tossed the phone out as they pulled onto the main road. "Sorry, necessary. We can't risk that they're tracking you." He turned to Laura. "You're sure you lost it?"

She nodded. "I had it in my hand when those men arrived. I must have dropped it."

"Okay, fine." He leaned forward toward the driver. "Take it easy, we don't want to draw any attention."

The man nodded, the van immediately slowing.

"Who were those people?"

Chaney frowned, looking at Acton then Laura. "I'm afraid they were Triarii. Or at least, used to be." He sighed. "A lot has happened since we last saw each other, Professors."

Laura reached out and took his hand. "It's been so long, we've been worried."

Chaney squeezed her hand, smiling. "I've missed you guys too. And Hugh? How's he been doing?"

Acton sighed. "Not that good. He fell in love."

"What! I don't believe it!" Chaney noticed the gloom on their faces and his eyes narrowed. "What went wrong? She didn't leave him, did she?"

Laura shook her head, her eyes glistening. "She was"—she took a quick breath—"killed." Laura's hand darted to her mouth and she closed her eyes, shaking her head, unable to go on.

"He met her in the Amazon. A native girl. He fell hard for her and they spent a spectacular few days together, but there was trouble and she was shot." Acton stared blankly out the window. "She died in his arms."

Chaney bit his finger, fighting back his own tears. "My God, the poor bastard."

"He took it hard. Really hard." Acton sighed, turning back toward Chaney. "He's sworn he'll never love again."

Laura rested her head on Acton's shoulder, wiping her tears away with a tissue retrieved from her purse. "He's missed you, you know."

Chaney frowned, guilt sweeping over him at the thought of not being there for his best friend in his time of need. "I know. It wasn't by choice that I disappeared."

Acton put his arm around Laura. "He said he saw you in Berlin and Rodney tried to shoot you."

Chaney closed his eyes for a moment, his head bobbing. "Hard to believe it, but it's true. Rodney and I have been friends for years. But that's what the Triarii has come to."

"But why?" asked Laura, returning the tissue to her purse. "Aren't you all Triarii? Or is he one of the Deniers you told us about? The ones who want to take all the skulls and bring them together, to try and harness their power?"

Chaney sighed. "Professors, I'm ashamed to tell you that the Triarii has been taken over by the very people we've been fighting for years." He looked at them both. "We're all in danger."

Bride Lane, London, United Kingdom

Reading took the call.

"Hello?"

"Hello, Agent Reading."

"Who is this?"

"This is the proconsul of the Triarii. How can I help you?"

Reading looked about, finding himself still alone. He tossed the cardboard in a bin, staring up at what was now confirmed to be a monitored camera. "We need to talk."

"About?"

"Martin Chaney."

"Phones are so unsecure, Agent. I suggest we meet."

"Where? I'm at your old headquarters but it seems to be abandoned."

"That was unfortunately necessary after recent events."

"What events are those?"

"All will be explained when you come in."

Reading frowned, his eyebrows rising slightly. "Come in? There's no way I'm coming in. We'll meet somewhere public."

"I thought by now we could trust each other."

Reading grunted. "You have Martin call me and I'll trust you."

There was a sigh. "I'm afraid I can't do that."

"Why?"

"Because your former partner has betrayed us all. He's no longer part of the Triarii."

Leaving Annapolis, Maryland

"What? But I thought they were a small splinter group?" Acton glanced at his wife who appeared equally shocked, then back at Chaney. "And why were they after us?"

"The Proconsul turned. Apparently he's always wanted to reunite the skulls, only none of us knew. He was just waiting for the thirteenth skull to be found."

"How did you find out?"

"When we were returning from Venice we got word that he had put out a hit on us. I had suspected something might happen, I just had never imagined it would be him. We immediately went into hiding and have been on the run ever since."

Laura squeezed Acton's hand, her fingernails digging into his palm. "So why are they after us?"

"To get to me. They've been watching everybody I know in the hopes I might make contact seeking help. We're desperate, with nowhere to go. And now he's given an order to take all the skulls."

Acton's eyes narrowed. "I thought they were all hidden around the world and only two people on the council knew where any one skull was for security purposes."

Chaney nodded. "This is true, but unfortunately half the council split with him. And, as you well know, many of the skulls are actually in public. They only needed to know where a few of the more hidden ones were to get them all."

"And he has them?"

"We believe so. We're hearing rumors on our secure networks that there have been hits all around the world." Chaney's head lowered. "Many are dead. Many good men and women." He looked up. "He needs the thirteenth skull to complete his plan."

"Of uniting all the skulls."

"Yes."

"Which you believe is a bad thing."

"Yes, absolutely. We've seen what just three did to London in 1212. The resulting blast almost wiped out the city, killed thousands."

Acton glanced at Laura. "Again, so you say."

Chaney glared at him, a little frustration creeping into his voice. "Yes, so *I* say!" He held up a hand, closing his eyes. "Sorry, Professor, but these are tense times. Me and my team have been on the run since you found the thirteenth skull in Venice. I've had to stay in hiding, unable to contact my friends or family lest they be used against me."

"Yet you reached out to Hugh. Why?"

"I need his help."

Acton's eyes narrowed. "How can *he* help?"

"I was hoping he might be able to help me find the new location of the Triarii."

Acton chewed his lip for a moment. "We were just talking to Hugh, really just minutes before you arrived. He called us while we were in Home Depot. He said he went to Fleet Street and they weren't there."

"He did!" Chaney shook his head. "Well, that means he's been compromised." He sighed. "They moved about a year ago, after I contacted them that the thirteenth skull had been retrieved. The Proconsul moved the headquarters to a secret location he had apparently been preparing for some time, then dismissed any of the council he knew would oppose his plans, replacing them with people who would support his cause. We need to find this location and retrieve the skulls so they can be returned to their rightful resting places and this coup can be put down once and for all." Chaney slammed his fist into his other hand. "The Triarii has been split since 1212, though it has always been a tiny minority that want to unite the skulls. It was only three skulls in London, and look what happened! Now the arrogance of modern man believes it is time to unite all thirteen! Whether you believe or not, these are bad people who will stop at nothing to achieve their goals."

Acton's eyes narrowed, thinking back on his dealings with both sides, tranquilizer darts almost always used. "I thought both sides abhorred violence?"

"Professor, dozens have died in the past several days as the Deniers have moved to retrieve the skulls. Our policy of non-lethal force has been abandoned. This is an all-out civil war, and in the end, only one side will be left alive."

Farrington Street, London, United Kingdom

Reading hesitated as the door was thrown open to the SUV that had just pulled up, its tinted windows allowing no view of those inside, or of him to those outside, once he committed.

Rodney's face appeared from the darkness, smiling. "If you would, please?"

Reading frowned then climbed inside, closing the door behind him. His chest was tight, his heart thumping hard as he realized he might be about to die. Though if these were indeed the Triarii he had encountered before, they didn't kill.

Then why had Rodney tried to shoot Martin?

Rodney handed him a dark hood. "If you don't mind."

Reading pursed his lips, drawing a breath as he eyed the hood, the vehicle already in motion.

Rodney smiled, patting what Reading assumed was a shoulder holster. "I can always tranquilize you if you'd prefer."

"Uh huh."

Reading took the hood and placed it over his head, the claustrophobic feeling immediately taking hold as his breath, hot and moist, quickly dampened his face. "Where are we going?"

He could almost sense Rodney's smile. "That would defeat the purpose of the hood."

Reading rolled his eyes, a wasted action. "That's not what I mean. I mean, are we going to your headquarters, or somewhere else?"

"Somewhere else. It's a place we use for these types of meetings. Private and secure, nothing of value. Except our staff, of course, who are always valuable."

"You didn't seem to think so in Berlin when you were going to shoot Martin."

"Martin is no longer one of us, and *his* people drew first blood. We're in a fight for our lives, Agent Reading, and this fight that has been brewing for eight hundred years is finally going to end, one way or the other, in the coming days."

Reading closed his eyes, taking in a slow breath, then sighed.

Lovely. And once again, I'm caught in the bloody middle.

He had been stunned that there was actually a two-thousand-year-old organization, descendent from the Roman Empire, that worshipped and protected crystal carvings of skulls. In fact, he wouldn't have believed it if his own partner hadn't been a member, and he had seen the violence surrounding trying to obtain just one of them.

Laura was a scientist and had studied them most of her career, and she swore she couldn't explain them. He knew what his own research on the web had told him, most saying they were fake, others claiming they were from aliens or lost civilizations. He dismissed the fantastic, though with the Triarii themselves admitting to swapping out the genuine articles with fakes whenever sent for testing by the likes of the BBC, it did explain why the mainstream scientific community now dismissed them.

But Laura he trusted, and he knew she wasn't daft. She was highly intelligent and didn't go spouting off crazy theories. All she would admit to was that they were of unknown origin and method of manufacture. He had held one himself, feeling its perfectly smooth surface, a feat apparently quite remarkable even now, and these skulls definitely predated modern times.

Apparently, a large tech company in the United States had tested one in the seventies, and couldn't explain how they had been carved.

According to them, and confirmed by Laura, each were carved from a single piece of crystal quartz, and stunningly, they were carved *against* the grain, which no modern sculptor would do, it almost guaranteed to shatter. Even modern lasers couldn't duplicate their construction. And the smoothness was also unexplainable pre-twentieth century, Laura having suggested the only way to get them so smooth would be a combination of sand and water running over the surface for hundreds of years.

They were a mystery.

That, he was willing to admit to.

But magical powers?

No.

Though someone believed.

Otherwise, he wouldn't be in a strange vehicle, blindfolded at gunpoint.

Leaving Annapolis, Maryland

Acton was trying to process the data dump still ongoing, he not sure anymore who were the good guys and who were the bad. He knew Chaney, had known him for several years, and Reading had known him for far longer. If there was somebody he was going to trust, it was going to be Chaney. He had to. At least until he had some time to think things over. His eyes narrowed as something occurred to him. "If they were watching us, hoping to get to you, then why would they try to kidnap us?"

Chaney gripped the door handle as they swung into a parking garage, the driver taking them quickly up several levels. "They think they can use you to get to me. That's why they were following Hugh. I took one of them down but there was another one I didn't spot in time."

Laura frowned. "Rodney."

"Yes. Once they stopped me from seeing Hugh, he was immediately safe."

"Because they assume you won't try again."

Chaney nodded at Laura. "Exactly. So I immediately came here because you are the only two other people I'm close to that might actually be able to help."

Acton's brow furled. "How can we help?"

"You've got money. They presume I'm going to ask you for some at some point."

Acton nodded slowly. They had money. A lot of it. Laura's late brother had been an Internet pioneer, selling his company for hundreds of millions, and leaving it all to her. They were rich, stupid rich, and the Triarii obviously knew it, and by extension, so did these Deniers.

"*Are* you asking for money?"

Chaney smiled at Laura. "Not at all."

Laura seemed unconcerned with the answer, she always generous with her money, never hesitating to help those truly in need, though Acton had no impression that Chaney was waiting to ask.

"But why try to take us?" asked Laura.

"It's a change in tactics, for sure. I'm guessing they were hoping to hold you and force me to give up the thirteenth skull to save your lives."

Acton frowned, squeezing Laura's hand a little harder. "So what you're saying is that they could try it again."

Chaney nodded. "Absolutely. I can think of only one way to make sure you remain safe."

Acton wasn't sure he was going to like what he was about to hear. "What?"

"Hand yourselves over to them."

Acton's eyebrows shot up, he not expecting that answer. "Umm, you expect us to turn ourselves over to these murderers?"

Laura shook her head. "Are you daft?"

Chaney smiled at Laura. "Probably. But as long as they think they can use either of you against me, you're in danger."

Acton was still shaking his head in disbelief. "How will us walking into their headquarters and waving 'hi', make them want to use us any less? Wouldn't they just toss us in a room and put the word out they'll kill us if you don't turn yourself in?"

Chaney shook his head. "Not if they think you betrayed me."

Acton's eyes narrowed. "And how are we supposed to make them think that?"

Chaney grinned.

"You're going to steal the thirteenth skull from me."

Domus Tiberiana, Rome
July 21, 64 AD

Everything burned.

His wife, his concubines, his home.

All of it.

It raged through his body, through his nightmares, through every waking moment.

It all burned.

And the voices continued to taunt him, the cacophony of madness in his mind almost overwhelming, the voices laughing at him, whispering in corners just out of sight, gone before he could catch a glimpse of them.

But when he was out with his people, fighting the fires at their side, searching the rubble for survivors and directing his men personally, they were silent.

Almost.

It made him feel like a man, something he wasn't sure he ever had experienced before. He had power, certainly, and men feared him, of that there was no doubt.

But he had little self-respect.

At least until the fire had begun.

His city was being destroyed, though its sacrifice was giving him a confidence that had eluded him for years, his position and his own arrogance usually carrying the day.

"Sire, wake up!"

He bolted upright in bed, immediately shivering, his body drenched in sweat. He had left the concubines to their chambers, his wife returning from Antium to join him in the fight.

She was exactly who he needed in times such as these, she a calm, wise woman whose council he valued.

I wonder what mother would think of all this.

"Report."

"The situation remains dire. Three of the fourteen districts are completely destroyed, another seven damaged."

"And the additional hands?"

"Volunteers are pouring in from all the neighboring cities. We have the manpower and we now have the water. We will win this fight, sire, thanks to your quick actions."

Nero ignored the nose embedded firmly in his ass, instead throwing on his robe and stepping out into the balcony, it still dark, morning light barely cracking the horizon. More of the city now burned, though much of what had in previous nights now smoldered.

He strode along the balcony, past his bedchambers then paused, turning toward his private office, a place few people were ever allowed to see.

And frowned.

The crystal skull, the gift from Antonius Felix in Judea, sat on a pedestal, angled to face his bed in the next room.

The voices raged, the whispers almost loud enough to make out.

Then a stabbing pain behind his eyes sucked the energy away as he gasped, dropping to a knee.

"Sire! Are you okay!"

The pain eased, slightly, and he glared back at the skull, a rage filling him. He held out his hand and his aide helped him to his feet, Nero steadying himself on the balcony railing. He stared at the skull, a sudden realization causing him to gasp, his aide flinching as he anticipated another collapse.

"It all started when that damned thing arrived."

"Sire?"

It had been found the day they had killed the man called Jesus, the man these blasted Christians all worshipped, their spread like a disease upon the land, causing too many of Rome's citizens and territories to abandon their true gods, instead worshipping this single, fictional apparition who had no statues built in his honor, no name to pray to.

It must be cursed!

And he realized what the voices all along had been trying to tell him. The gods were angry. They were angry with the people turning away from them, and they were demanding he take action to stop the spread of these Christians and their one false god.

He glanced at the skull then stormed into the room, grabbing it from its resting place and raising it high above his head. Looking up, his eyes met those of the sculpture, a battle of wills suddenly underway, the voices screaming unintelligibly, the stabbing pain returning as he tried to find the strength to smash it into a thousand pieces and end the curse that had befallen his people and his city and his empire.

He fell to his knees, the skull still gripped in his hand, then dropped to his side, it rolling from his outstretched fingers.

"Sire!"

His aide's pleas went ignored as he realized destroying the vessel of their torture might make things far worse than they already were.

If bringing it here caused this, then removing it should end it.

He forced himself to his knees, closing his eyes, refusing to look at those of the skull that bore into his sole, the uncontrollable urge to shiver in its presence one he refused to give into anymore.

66

THE THIRTEENTH LEGION

"Get me the legate of the Thirteenth, now!"

Unknown Location, London, United Kingdom
Present Day

"They've killed dozens and have stolen all of the skulls except Jupiter and Zeus, and the skull Professor Acton found in Peru."

Reading couldn't care less about the stolen skulls, though he found the body count very concerning. The Triarii, even its splinter group known as the Deniers, rarely killed, tranquilizer guns their weapon of choice.

The problem was, he wasn't sure whom to believe. Rodney had raised a very real gun, about to shoot at Chaney, and now the Proconsul, who Rodney worked for, was claiming it was the Deniers that were doing the killing, and Chaney was one of them.

He eyed Rodney for a moment then returned his attention to the Proconsul, the man older than he had expected, yet somehow exactly as he had expected. Wise looking, with an air about him that commanded respect, *expected* respect. "How did they know where the skulls were?"

"Each member of the council knows where the skull they are responsible for is located, and who protects it. They also know where one other is hidden, though they have no responsibilities for it unless the primary dies or is otherwise incapacitated. After the thirteenth skull was finally found after all these years, a schism happened almost immediately, with the council split. Those who supported the Deniers—unbeknownst to me up to that point, obviously—immediately seized control of their own skulls, and those they were backups for. At least that's the prevailing wisdom among those who remain, but it doesn't explain everything."

"What do you mean?"

The Proconsul shook his head. "To be honest, I think some did betray us, but after they were able to so efficiently seize all the skulls, I had our security double-checked, and taps were found on our secure lines. I believe one of our senior security staff, who is now missing, placed the taps, perhaps years ago, allowing the Deniers to monitor the secret conversations between our council members and their teams."

Reading pursed his lips, nodding. "So they'd know where everything was hidden, who was protecting them, and how."

"Exactly. They already had the Smithsonian skull that President Jackson stole when he was a member, they have the thirteenth that you found with the professors, and now they've managed to steal eight others. Unfortunately we only have the original two now, the Oracle of Jupiter, found in Golgotha, and the Oracle of Zeus, found years later in Greece, plus the skull Professor Acton discovered in Peru." He sighed. "I fear the other ten may be lost to us forever."

"Are the three you have secure?"

"Yes. Very." The Proconsul scratched his chin, lowering his voice slightly. "Listen, this has been an ongoing feud among us for almost eight hundred years, beginning in 1212 after the disaster in London. Now blood has been spilled on an unforgiveable scale, something that has never happened before. We know they want them, and they will kill to get them."

"How will you stop them?"

"We've moved the three remaining skulls to a location known only to a handful of people, and they are under heavy guard. Unfortunately, I fear it may not be enough."

Reading asked the question that had been gnawing at him since yesterday. "Why were you following me?"

The Proconsul smiled slightly. "Because we know you two are friends, and we were hoping he might reach out to you at some point. We've been following you and the professors for over a year, ever since Martin failed to report back with the Venice skull."

"Do you think Jim and Laura are in danger?"

The Proconsul frowned then nodded. "Most definitely."

Reading pointed at Rodney. "Give me my phone. Now!"

Rodney looked at the Proconsul who nodded. The phone was produced.

Reading called Acton's number, it going directly to voicemail.

His gut flipped, his cop intuition telling him something the facts hadn't yet.

Something's wrong.

Outside Annapolis, Maryland

Acton stared at Chaney, his eyes wide. "Excuse me?"

Chaney chuckled. "It's really quite simple, Professor. I will give you the skull, you'll call a number I give you, tell them you have it, and want to meet. They'll arrange it, and as you American's might say, Bob's your uncle."

Acton looked at Laura. "Do we say that?"

She shrugged. "You're asking the wrong person."

Acton turned to Chaney. "Won't they ask how we got it?"

"Of course. You tell them that I showed it to you when I tried to recruit you. You then realized that I must be working for the wrong side, and stole it. With your history of getting involved in things that don't concern you, they'll absolutely believe it."

Laura leaned a little harder against Acton. "I'm not so sure about that."

Chaney smiled at her. "Listen, your reputation is one of always doing the right thing. Keeping this skull in the hands of the Triarii is the right thing, even if you don't believe in their power. And once they see you actually have it, they'll believe any story you tell them."

Laura's eyes narrowed. "But I thought giving them the thirteenth skull was exactly what you *didn't* want?"

Chaney nodded. "It is, but eventually they're going to catch us, and when they do, they'll have all of them anyway. This way, we have a shot at getting our hands on all of them."

Acton leaned back, his head tilting to the side, his eyes narrow. "How?"

"Easy. We'll place a tracker with it."

Acton gave him a look. "It's a *transparent* crystal skull. Won't they notice something sticking to it?"

Chaney chuckled. "We'll bug the case you'll be carrying it in, that way we'll know exactly where it is at all times. Once we know their location, we can hit them and take the skulls back."

Laura inhaled sharply. "Hit them? You mean attack them?"

"Yes."

"That didn't work out so well when the Delta Force tried it. What makes you think *you* can?"

Chaney smiled, holding up a finger, counting off his reasons. "First, we were expecting them, and it wasn't us that stopped Delta, it was the armed police unit that just happened to be outside our doors that ultimately stopped them, and, as you know, they only surrendered because they knew their mates were going to spring them. Also, their mission parameters were different. They were ordered to kill everyone in the building because we were all terrorists, remember? If they had been after a specific target like we are, I'm pretty sure they would have succeeded. In our case, we'll have the element of surprise, and some private help that is well-trained."

Acton didn't like the sound of that. "Private help?"

Chaney spread his hands, palms up. "As you know, Professor, we're not killers. We will kill if we have to, but we've contracted a private firm for the takedown. We have men training with them now, and they're ready to hit anywhere in the world whenever we give the word."

Acton frowned. "Mercenaries."

Chaney's head bobbed. "I'm not happy about it either, but what choice do we have? These renegades have killed dozens already, and are about to unleash a destructive power unlike anything the world has ever seen."

Acton sighed.

Chaney as well. "Look, I know you don't believe, Professor, but I do, and so does every single member of the Triarii. If there was something you believed that others didn't, would it stop you from believing, or simply make you realize you're on your own, with a duty that remained?"

Acton said nothing, the answer obvious.

"And I'll ask you one final thing before you dismiss the skulls so quickly."

"What?"

"What was your reaction when you looked at it the first time?"

"Huh?"

"Did you shiver?"

Acton's eyebrows slowly rose at the question, he leaning back slightly as he thought back to Peru. His eyes opened wide. "Yes, as a matter of fact, I think I did."

Chaney smiled. "So did I."

Acton shrugged. "So what? It's an instinctual response at seeing something creepy."

Chaney's smile spread. "Or is it?"

Unknown Location, London, United Kingdom

"Hey Greg, it's Hugh."

"Oh, hi Hugh. God, this is a strange coincidence. I was just about to call you."

A pit formed in Reading's stomach. Gregory Milton was Acton's best friend. They had known each other since college, and Milton was dean of the university Acton worked at, a sometimes strenuous relationship when boss and employee clashed, yet outside of the halls of learning, they were tight.

Very tight.

Reading's relationship with Milton however was casual, purely through Acton.

And Milton had never found a need to call him in the past.

"What's wrong? Has something happened to Jim and Laura?"

Milton sighed. "I'm afraid I've got some bad news."

The pit deepened. "What?"

"It looks like they've been kidnapped. There was a shooting outside the Home Depot here, and I'm not sure what happened yet, but it looks like they were both abducted. I just got the call and was about to call you before heading for the police station."

Reading took a deep breath, glaring at the Proconsul and Rodney who stood on the opposite side of the room, talking in hushed tones. "Okay, I'll be on a plane as soon as I can."

"Good. Use the emergency fund, I'm sure she'd want you to."

Reading frowned, turning his back to the others and lowering his voice. "You're probably right, but I hate doing that."

"Which is exactly why she gave you access."

Reading chewed his cheek. Laura was rich. Beyond rich. Hundreds of millions of dollars rich. He hated taking advantage of that, always feeling guilty when they would fly him places, though he eventually had been able to rationalize it by doing the math. A plane ticket to her was like buying a coffee to him.

And he wouldn't think twice if she or her new husband bought him a coffee.

"Okay, fine. I'll make the call. I'll be there as soon as I can. Talk to you soon."

"I'll keep you posted with what I find out. Goodbye."

Reading ended the call and spun on the others in the room. "Jim and Laura have been kidnapped," he said, striding quickly toward them, rage in his eyes. Rodney stepped in front of the Proconsul, sensing Reading's desire to tear out someone's throat. "Did you have anything to do with it?"

The Proconsul shook his head. "Absolutely not." He turned to another guard standing near the door. "Get me the Maryland detail, now!" The guard nodded and left, returning only seconds later with another person who rushed into the room with an outstretched cellphone.

"Sir, it's for you, urgent!"

The Proconsul took the phone, his side of the conversation mostly grunts before he hung up. He handed the phone back then turned to Reading. "I'm afraid you're right. Our agents that were tailing them report an attack."

Reading felt himself turn purple as anger and concern consumed him. He glared at Rodney.

"Get me to my flat, now!"

Motel 6, Annapolis, Maryland

"This is the case."

Chaney handed Acton the rather heavy case, everyone now crammed into a too small motel room on the outskirts of Annapolis. Acton rested it on his knees and slid the locks aside, the case opening with a hiss. Gently lifting the lid, his eyes widened and he felt Laura shiver beside him as they gazed upon the skull they hadn't seen since discovering it in Venice over a year ago.

It still gave him the heebie-jeebies.

"As you can see, it's form-fitted for the skull, so we're hoping they'll just use *it* rather than transfer it to their own case."

Acton snapped it shut. "Unlikely."

"Perhaps not. Each skull is a little different, and since they've never seen this one, they won't have a case that fits as well. They'll want to keep it as safe as possible, so they could very well use it."

"They'd be fools if they did. They'll know you'll try to plant a tracking device inside."

"Oh, absolutely, they'll scan for tracking devices, but it will be turned off. When you arrive, they'll open the case to confirm its authenticity. When that happens, a timer will be activated. Ten minutes later the tracking device will be activated unless the case is closed, at which point the timer will reset to another ten minutes."

"Why?"

"Just in case they leave it open, we want the tracker to activate so we at least know where you are. Our hope is that they will use the case, so we want to delay the activation to give them time to scan it for signals."

Acton nodded. "I see. If they find one, they'll know we're working for you."

"They won't find it. The tracker will be turned off, but if something goes wrong and they do find it, just plead ignorance. If you stole the case from us, then it's a very plausible story that you wouldn't know it was bugged."

Acton glanced at Laura. They hadn't yet had time to talk about it, to come to some sort of agreement on whether they should actually go through with this, or to simply wash their hands of the entire affair and hunker down until the Triarii and the Deniers figured things out among themselves.

Yet they could be in danger. If the Deniers were now killing, and they thought they could use them to get to Chaney and the thirteenth skull, then there may be no escaping getting involved and helping to bring down the Deniers. It might put an end to the Triarii in their lives.

Laura squeezed his hand, he knowing her well enough to know she was having the same thoughts. He turned to Chaney. "Okay, so the case is bugged. They'll scan it for signals then hopefully decide it's clean and use it to transport the skull, you hope to the location where they have the others."

"Exactly."

Laura leaned forward. "But what if they scan the case again?"

Chaney smiled. "They'll have to get lucky. The tracker will only activate for a thirty-second interval every five minutes. After a few scans, I'm sure they won't bother."

Acton let out a long sigh. "So you're hoping to get lucky."

Chaney's head bobbed. "Yup."

"And what happens with us?" asked Laura.

"They should take the skull, hear your story, then let you go. There's no reason to harm you, and at that point they won't care about me anymore, so there's no point in following you. They'll have what they want."

"Let's hope you're right."

"So you'll do it?"

Acton looked at Laura, who nodded slightly.

"Brilliant!" Chaney handed him a phone. "Time to make the call."

Nubian Desert, Egypt, University College London Dig Site

Cameron Leather peered through his sunglasses, the glint of light in the distance exactly where he expected it to be. He raised his binoculars, the image of an Egyptian soldier immediately popping into focus. The man waved, Leather returning it before continuing his patrol.

It had been quiet here since the attack on the camp by extremists hell bent on destroying anything they considered blasphemous. Good men had been lost, including from his own security detail, though the children, the students, had been saved.

As a soldier, he had seen a lot of death, especially in the British Special Air Services. He had retired a Lt. Colonel and formed his own company, mostly hiring ex-Special Forces from around the world to provide private security to the rich, powerful or famous.

Though never the infamous.

He had his standards.

Laura Palmer, who fell solidly in the 'rich' category, had hired him several years ago to provide security after an incident in London, with a stipulation in the contract that he had been reluctant to agree to, it meaning he'd be out of the action, action he thrived on.

She wanted *him* to provide the security whenever possible. She felt since she was hiring *his* firm, she should get *him*. He had refused, but the remuneration she offered had been huge.

And he had been wrong about the action.

The woman had a propensity to get herself in trouble along with her new husband. It had meant he'd been in more intense firefights than he had ever dreamed of after retirement, so he was more than happy to stick where she wanted him.

He was rarely bored.

Things were still slightly tense here at Professor Palmer's archeological dig site. Students from her former school of University College London worked the dig expertly, grad students Terrence Mitchell and his new wife Jenny running it when Laura was away. She was supposed to have returned by now, but a gunshot wound in France had taken her down and mostly out for a while, she not yet fully recovered.

He looked forward to her return.

Then there might be some action.

Though he doubted it.

Their little patch of the desert attracted little attention, and with a permanent Egyptian military guard stationed less than a kilometer away, funded by her, he had little doubt things would remain quiet.

I wonder who's richer, the Queen, or Laura Palmer.

He had a funny feeling it would be the latter, with most of it being liquid assets.

His satellite phone vibrated on his hip. He extended the antenna and took the call. "Go ahead."

"Colonel? This is Agent Reading."

Leather's eyebrows rose slightly, his spine tingling as he sensed he was about to get in on some of the action he and his men were so desperately craving. "Hello Agent, if you're calling me, I assume there's a problem?"

"Yes. Jim and Laura have been kidnapped."

Leather froze, then began to jog back to the dig. "From where?"

"A mall parking lot in Maryland."

"Any ransom demand?"

"Not yet, and there won't be. It looks like it's a breakaway sect of the Triarii known as the Deniers."

Leather frowned. "Christ, those bastards again?"

"It looks that way."

"Okay, do we have any idea where they might be headed?"

"No, but my money's on London."

"Why?"

"Because that's where three of the skulls they want are located, and they're the only ones they don't have."

"Okay, I'm leaving inside of ten minutes. I'll meet you in London, but it's going to take me almost a day to get there."

"That's fine. I'm getting on a plane now to go to Maryland to see if I can track down any leads from that end."

"Understood. I'll contact you as soon as my team arrives."

"Good. And colonel?"

"Yes?"

"Be prepared for a firefight. These people are armed and dangerous and possibly large in numbers."

"Understood, we'll be ready."

Leather ended the call as he arrived in the camp, his men joining him.

"Problem?" asked his second-in-command, Warren Reese.

Leather grunted. "Isn't there always?"

Reese laughed. "I love this gig."

Motel 6, Annapolis, Maryland

Acton read the coded sequence on the back of the card Chaney had given him, his chest tight, his stomach in knots as he was once again about to be thrown into the fray against his will. Triarii business had tortured his life and that of his wife's over the past several years on too many occasions, and after retrieving the thirteenth skull for them, he had assumed it was over.

Until the man across from him had disappeared.

Then he had known, someday, somehow, he'd be pulled back into it.

It was just the way his luck seemed to go.

His life had always been fairly routine, at least for an archeologist. He loved going on digs, spending weeks or months on his hands and knees digging the dirt to unlock the secrets of the ancient world. He loved shaping young minds, teaching them about the past so they might better understand the world today and where it was headed, as their leaders seemed to ignore the lessons learned at such a high price, sometimes only decades ago.

He had never anticipated being in regular gunfights. He glanced at Laura as he heard the call being put through, his code accepted. Part of him might link her to his bad luck, though the discovery of the skull in Peru was before he had ever met her. If anything, *he* was the unlucky one.

She just made it bearable.

God I love that woman.

He gave her a quick wink when a voice was finally heard. He tapped the screen, putting it on speaker.

"Professor Acton, this is an unexpected surprise. Are you okay?"

Acton frowned, glaring at the phone. "Yes, no thanks to you."

"I'm not sure what you mean."

Acton shook his head. "Listen, I know what's going on. Martin told us everything."

"Did he now? And are you certain he told you the truth?"

Acton glanced at Chaney, suddenly wondering if putting the call on speaker had been wise. "He had no reason to lie to me. Either way, I want out from under this. He saved my life, you're trying to take it."

"We're trying no such thing—"

"Stop. I don't want to hear it."

"Then what is the purpose of this call?"

"I have something you want."

"And what is that?"

"The thirteenth skull."

There was a pause. "I'm sorry, I don't understand. *You* have the thirteenth skull?"

"Yes."

"How, may I ask, did you acquire it?"

Acton looked at Chaney, the man nodding with a smile, urging him on. "Martin trusted us and showed us the skull. I realized that the only way to protect my life and that of my wife's was to prove to you that I'm not a risk, so I took it from him."

"How?"

"I'm well-trained, so is my wife, you know that."

"Yes, Colonel Leather has done an admirable job with you both. So what now?"

Acton inhaled. "I want to meet and give you this damned thing, then we part our ways. You'll have no reason to be after us since Martin will never trust us again, so will never be found near us, and he's a good man, so he won't take revenge on us." Acton glared at the phone. "I want the Triarii out of our lives once and for all."

There was a pause, Acton beginning to wonder if the signal had been lost.

"Professor Acton, I think that can be arranged."

British Airways Flight 289, London, United Kingdom

Reading buckled his lap belt, trying to get comfortable, it an impossible achievement with his long legs and the ridiculously inadequate legroom found on most planes today. He could have gone first class, hell, he could have chartered a private plane and Acton and Laura wouldn't have questioned it for a moment, but that wasn't him.

He felt guilty enough having paid a ridiculous amount for a last minute flight.

Why do they feel they can jack the last minute fares when they have the seat available? Don't they want it filled?

He growled slightly, the young girl sitting beside him staring at him curiously. He winked at her. "Might have been my tummy."

She giggled, burying her head in her mother's side.

He stared down the aisle, his right leg stretched out in it, giving at least half his body some reprieve as he continued to obsess over the cost of his ticket. Why was it when the price of jet fuel went up, ticket prices went up, but when fuel prices dropped, the ticket prices remained high? It was the same with gasoline for the car, groceries, or any other bill nowadays.

But he knew damned well why it was happening.

Consumers had shown they were willing and able to pay the inflated prices.

He didn't fault companies for raising their prices when their own expenses went up. The problem was they no longer seemed to pass on the savings when things changed. Now they would lower the price slightly then edge it back up to the full price consumers had been forced to pay previously.

It was highway robbery.

He wasn't anti-one-percenter, anti-capitalist, or overly political, but it cheesed him off every time he ordered something and there was a fuel surcharge that hadn't been there before, or a delivery charge when none had existed before oil prices had run up.

He had taken to lowering his tip, he feeling a bit guilty about it at first, his own son delivering food part time for some extra spending money. But he told the delivery boy every time what was going on. "I tip ten percent less any surcharges. Talk to your boss about getting those included in your tip."

They never went away happy, and he sometimes wondered if his food was spit on the next time he ordered, but he didn't care.

It was the principal.

He was being ripped off, and he was going to fight back in some little way.

Like when gas prices spiked the first time. He had refused to pay it, instead putting five or ten quid in the tank, and immediately switching to regular from premium, a mechanic buddy of his telling him modern cars didn't need premium, even if the manual said they did.

It's a hedge against the car being driven in the third world where the octane is very low.

He hadn't used premium in almost a decade and his car was none the worse for it.

And it had saved him thousands, meaning the gas companies had lost thousands. If they hadn't tried to rip him off in the first place, he'd have kept pumping premium.

But no more.

He was one man in an ocean of consumers, but he was doing his part to fight back against the unchecked greed that seemed to be the norm today.

He often thought of some of the "lectures" Acton would give about history, and how what was happening today in many instances echoed the collapse of many an empire throughout it, not the least of which was the Roman Empire. It was Acton's opinion that Western civilization as it was today was on the decline, and risked disappearing this century if voters and their leaders didn't smarten up.

And it wasn't corporate greed behind it.

That was just a symptom.

Society had changed from trying to build something better, to trying to get its share of what had been built.

Reading pulled his laptop out of the pouch of the seat in front of him as they reached altitude, putting his hand on the top of the seat, pushing gently so the person in front of him couldn't lean back. The man poked his head around to see what was going on, though not before Reading removed his hand. The man sat back down, trying again, Reading's hand already blocking the seat.

The man's head whipped around again, Reading opening his laptop.

"Are you pushing on my seat?"

"No mate, I guess it's just not working. Mine isn't either, but I don't believe in making the person behind me uncomfortable for an eight-hour flight. Do you?"

The man glared at him but said nothing, returning to his seat.

He didn't try again.

The mother sitting at the window grinned at him, leaning closer. "I wish I had the courage to do that. For the life of me I don't understand why they allow these things to recline, not with the tiny amount of space they now give you."

Reading motioned toward his knees, his left one pressed against the seat back. "Sometimes it's necessity, not bravery."

She smiled, her daughter suddenly occupying her lap, peering out the window at the lights below. Reading turned his attention to the latest reports on the kidnapping. The FBI was treating it as a kidnap for ransom since Jim and Laura were wealthy. He didn't bother mentioning that it was probably a breakaway sect of a two-thousand-year-old cult descendant from the Roman Empire behind it because they thought once again the Actons might be able to help with a missing crystal skull.

It just didn't sound believable.

He snapped the laptop shut, returning it to the pouch, then popped his shoes off, the trick to comfortable air travel given to him by probably the best friend he had left in the world.

A friend he was worried sick about.

Domus Tiberiana, Rome
July 21, 64 AD

Flavus stood at a respectful distance, his stance straight and respectful, his eyes fixed on a distant point and not at any of those present.

For staring at the emperor could be dangerous.

His legate, Quintus Caesennius Catius, had selected him to join him when summoned by the emperor, the palace a place he had never been, nor imagined he ever would. He was young, ambitious, though too close to a commoner ever to hope to gain any real rank. He was a Roman citizen, which counted for a lot, yet as in any empire, there were the rich and there were the poor. His service would guarantee he'd end up somewhere just above the bottom, though if he could rise far enough in rank, his share of any bounty his legion may earn would increase, affording him a more luxurious retirement.

In twenty-five years.

His best friend, Valerius, had promised him a position when he himself had the power to do so. Valerius would be a force to be reckoned with, he of a more noble station, especially with Pliny having taken him under his wing.

It's all about the connections.

Yet as he watched the proceedings in front of him, he took some satisfaction in knowing his friend had yet to visit the palace, and had yet to be in the presence of the emperor.

"Follow me."

Flavus followed the emperor and Legate Catius into another room, Flavus battling to keep his eyes under control at the sight. Dozens of seers surrounded what appeared to be a skull carved of glass, all on their knees praying to various gods for forgiveness and protection.

"It is this that is responsible for the fire."

How in the name of the gods did this piece of glass cause these horrendous fires?

Catius had more tact. "I don't understand."

"Since its arrival it has spoken to me," explained Emperor Nero, Flavus clamping his jaw shut, battling a shiver that rushed up and down his spine as he stared at the skull, its eyes glaring at him in a red rage, the torchlight surrounding it reflecting off the smooth surface.

Stop looking at it!

He tore his eyes away, redirecting them to the smoke filled vista out the windows, the fires still raging in some districts.

"Spoken to you? How, my emperor?"

"I cannot explain it, nor can any of these ineffectual imbeciles. But I am certain Jupiter himself came to me in a vision demanding the skull be removed from Rome lest it cause even more destruction."

Catius kept remarkable control. "A vision from Jupiter is indeed a great honor. It should be heeded."

"Which is why I called you. I want this cursed object removed from Rome and taken as far away as possible."

"Yes, sire. Where would you have us take it?"

Nero flicked his wrist. "Some place far. Britannia perhaps. Those heathens deserve it."

"It shall be done."

"Good. I knew I could count on you."

"Who should we deliver it to when there?"

Nero wagged a finger. "No, I think you misunderstood me."

"I beg your forgiveness."

Nero ignored the apology. "The Thirteenth Legion will deliver the skull to Britannia, and remain with it, ensuring it never again returns to Rome."

"Remain? For how long?"

Flavus broke into a cold sweat at the response.

"For all time."

Approaching London, United Kingdom
Present day

Laura sighed, peering out the window as her homeland sped past. She loved living with James and adored her new home, his old, though she missed England and she missed her university. She had managed to get a job at the Smithsonian in Washington, DC, which had meant she could commute from their home, thus spending much of the year together, instead of splitting time between two continents.

It had been the right decision.

Though tough.

"I think this is the only time I haven't looked forward to coming home."

Her husband leaned closer and took her hand, squeezing it gently as they both stared out the window at London below. "I hear you. I love London, but not today."

Laura drew in a breath, leaning back in her chair and closing her eyes. "I have a really bad feeling about this."

"Me too. I know you want to go with me, but I don't want you to."

Her eyes flew open. "James! We already discussed this, I'm going!"

James shook his head. "No, if this goes bad then I need you on the outside, taking care of things." He held up a finger, cutting off her protest. "I don't like the fact they insisted on no phones and their own plane. At least if Hugh knew where we were then I'd feel better, but right now nobody we trust knows where we are and why."

Laura looked at her husband, latching onto the last thing he said. "You don't trust Martin?"

"Not for a second. A year ago? Implicitly. Now? No way. This is a cult we're dealing with, no matter what side of their own internal debate he falls on. That means they put the cult first, everyone else second or worse."

Laura's head slowly bobbed as she thought about it. "We're the infidels."

"Exactly, great analogy, but let's not go there. You know how I tend to ramble." He flashed her a grin and she smiled, patting his hand.

"Yes, you do on occasion."

He squeezed her hand. "When we land, I'll insist you be allowed to go on your own. If they don't agree, we'll just leave the skull, turn around and walk away."

"And if they stop us?"

"Then we know they were always going to go back on their word and we're in the same position anyway. If all they want is the skull, then handing it over should be enough."

Laura frowned as the wheels touched down. "We should have just let them pick it up in Maryland. We'd be done with this already."

James shook his head. "Martin would have never given us the skull if that were the case. Insisting it be handed directly to the Proconsul is the only way to ensure it has a chance of being tracked back to the others."

Laura peered out the window. "Regardless of what's going on, I think Martin is right."

"I agree. The only way to keep us safe is to make the other side think we're not on Martin's side, and that he's now our enemy."

Laura felt her chest tighten as they pulled up to the private terminal, a dark SUV waiting for them. "Isn't that Rodney?"

James leaned over her, peering out. "Yeah."

She could tell from his voice that he was concerned. Hugh had said that Rodney was carrying a real gun, not one of the tranquilizer weapons, and he had been prepared to use it.

Is he prepared to use it on us?

They deplaned, Rodney bowing slightly. "Professor Palmer, Professor Acton, it is good to see you again." He nodded at the case. "Is that it?"

James stepped forward, putting himself slightly between her and Rodney. "Yes."

"Very well. As agreed, it is to be opened in the Proconsul's presence. You will permit us to scan it of course, to make certain there are no tracking devices or explosives?"

"Of course."

"Excellent." Rodney opened the rear door. "Please, I think we'll all feel safer when we're not so exposed."

James shook his head. "I'll be going, my wife won't be."

Rodney frowned. "That wasn't part of the agreement."

"I'm changing the agreement. You want the skull. You don't need her."

"You may be right, but those weren't my orders. I must insist you both come with me."

James placed the case on the ground and took her hand. "Then we're done here. There's your skull."

Rodney moved his suit jacket aside, revealing a shoulder holster filled with a very genuine looking Beretta. "I'm afraid I really must insist."

Laura felt her chest tighten and she wrapped herself around her husband's arm. He looked down at her and she frowned. "I guess we have our answer."

James nodded and they climbed into the back of the SUV, the doors slamming shut, Rodney getting into the front with the case. He turned back.

"Sorry about this."

A panel slid up, separating them from the front, a hissing sound immediately heard. James reached for the door but it was locked. She tried her side without success. Holding her breath, she watched James hammer his elbow repeatedly into the glass to no avail, his face turning red before he finally gasped for air, a cough immediately taking over as she too expelled her lungsful of carbon dioxide, breathing in the gas as her world slowly went dark, her husband still slamming against the glass, the dull thuds fading away.

To nothing.

Baltimore/Washington International Thurgood Marshall Airport, Baltimore, Maryland

Reading waved at Acton's best friend, Gregory Milton, as he stepped through the doors, having cleared customs a little quicker than the others, his Interpol ID greasing the wheels.

"Hugh, good to see you," said Milton, shaking his hand.

"Good to see you too. Thanks for picking me up."

"No problem." Milton motioned at Reading's carry-on. "Let me get that for you."

Reading shook his head. "The day you carry something for me is the day *I* was shot in the back."

Milton chuckled. "Fine, fine. Eventually though, playing the handicapped card is going to wear thin."

"Enjoy it while you can. You're lucky to be walking, let alone feeling good enough to carry people's bags."

Milton flicked his wrist. "Bah, I expected you to say no. If you had accepted, you'd be a heartless sonofabitch if there ever was one."

Reading tossed his head back, laughing. "Ahh, I missed that strange American sense of humor." As they walked, the conversation turned to the situation at hand. "Any word? I've been out of the loop for too many hours."

Milton shook his head, frowning. "Not much. According to the police, their credit cards haven't been used, and with the exception of your ticket, none of their accounts have been touched. None of the numbers that might be called to make a ransom demand have been called except by known numbers." He threw his hands up in frustration. "There's been nothing!"

Reading nodded. "That's because this has nothing to do with ransom, and everything to do with the damned Triarii."

Milton glanced at him then pushed through a revolving door. "You're certain of that?"

"Without a doubt. While I was meeting with their Proconsul, he received a call from their people on this end that witnessed the abduction. They said it was Martin's people."

"Martin Chaney?"

Reading nodded, his chest heavy with the admission.

"I thought you two were best friends?"

"So did I."

"Do you believe the Triarii? I mean, do you really think he might harm Jim and Laura?"

Reading shrugged. "If you had asked me that yesterday, I would have said no. No question about it. But if he truly was saving them from the other group killed in the parking lot, then why haven't we heard from them?"

Unknown location, United Kingdom

Acton woke to a pounding headache and a high-pitched tinnitus-like buzz in his ears. He opened his eyes slightly, the world around him humming as if he were listening to it from the bottom of a swimming pool.

He tried to swim for the top.

Yet it was no use.

He was simply too tired.

Something pungent hit his nostrils and he was suddenly jolted awake to find his arms bound to the chair he was sitting in. His senses reset themselves in a horrific cacophony of noise and light before settling down. He spotted an elderly man standing nearby, Rodney at his side.

Laura!

He twisted in his chair, first to his right, then his left, breathing a sigh of relief as he saw a young woman administering the same smelling salts to his wife who flinched, looking around in confusion before spotting him.

"James!"

He desperately wanted to reach out, straining uselessly against his bonds.

He glared at Rodney. "What the hell is going on? We had an agreement!"

The elderly man stepped forward. "Calm yourself, Professor Acton."

Acton's eyes narrowed, his fury redirected at the man obviously in charge. "Who the hell are you?" But he already knew the answer. He recognized the voice from their conversation after the confessional in Coventry several years ago.

"I'm the Proconsul of the Triarii. We spoke before."

Acton let out a loud breath. "Yeah, I recognize your voice." He stared at the man then sent daggers at Rodney. "I thought we had an agreement."

The Proconsul smiled. "We did. And you broke it."

Acton felt his chest tighten. "What do you mean?"

"The case has a tracking device in it."

Acton shrugged, trying to keep up the act. "If it did, it's news to me."

"Perhaps, perhaps not. Either way, I don't know if I can trust you anymore."

Acton shook his head, leaning forward in his chair. "Listen, didn't it occur to you that Martin might have put a tracker on it just in case it was stolen?"

"Perhaps. But this was a clever one. It had a delayed signal."

Maybe they know where we are!

The Proconsul flicked his wrist. "Remove their bindings."

Rodney stepped forward, cutting the zip ties binding both of them then stepped back. Acton massaged his wrists then reached out for Laura's hand. He gave it a squeeze then looked at the Proconsul, holding up his free hand, displaying the effects of the ties.

"Why?"

"Because, Professor Acton, you aren't a danger to us. You were restrained merely for your own protection."

Acton gave a vigorous harrumph.

"If you hadn't been, Professor, can you honestly say you wouldn't have gone on the attack the moment you woke?"

Acton frowned, the man right. His instinct would have been to leap from his chair and launch himself at Rodney. He nodded. "What now?"

"Well, if you are assisting Mr. Chaney, then his aim is to find our location. If you aren't, and the tracker was merely installed just in case of a theft, then he knows our current location regardless."

Acton tilted his head slightly to the side. "I can't believe you'd be stupid enough to bring us anywhere important without being *very* certain the case wasn't bugged."

The Proconsul smiled. "Professor, you don't last two thousand years by being a fool. This location is of no importance. Where we will go now, is."

"Let me guess, we're coming along?"

"Absolutely. If you are working for him then he won't risk hurting you. If you aren't, then you might be in danger if we let you go. Either way you're safe with us until he finds us."

"How will he find you if you've turned off the tracker?"

"He'll find us, Professor, because we haven't turned it off."

Acton's eyebrows rose. "Excuse me?"

"Professor, I intend to have Mr. Chaney and his men find us, and deal with him and his group, once and for all."

Annapolis Police Department, Taylor Ave, Annapolis, Maryland

"Why's Interpol interested in this case?"

Reading flipped through the case file, it rather thin, not bothering to look up at FBI Special Agent Foster, it the eyes that always gave away the lie. "We've been monitoring a group involved with archeological thefts, so when it came across my desk that two preeminent archeologists had been kidnapped in a shootout, I naturally took an interest." He finally looked at Foster, waving the file. "These two have been on our radar before, so I thought I better come and see if I could be of any assistance."

Foster didn't appear pleased. "I can assure you we can handle things ourselves, but you're welcome to attend our briefings."

Reading bowed slightly. "That would be more than enough. I assume I can look over the evidence?"

Foster chewed his lip for a second, considering Reading. "Sure, why not." He pointed to a box on his desk. "Help yourself."

Reading removed the top and began to rummage through the very few items inside, all in evidence bags—shell casings and a smashed cellphone, the case it was in one he recognized instantly as Acton's. He held it up. "How'd this happen?"

Foster shook his head. "We're not sure. A witness says it was tossed out of the vehicle as it sped away."

"This is Jim's. Where's hers?"

Foster dropped the file he was reading on his desk. "Now how the hell would you know that? And why are you calling him Jim?"

Reading flushed, his lack of sleep and adrenaline fueled energy causing him to make mistakes. He said nothing, already hating himself for lying.

"Listen, buddy, are you holding out on me? Do you know these two?"

Reading sighed, nodding. "They're two of my best friends, and I'm willing to do anything to make sure they're safe."

Foster pointed at the door. "Get the hell out of here before I report you."

Reading nodded. "I'm sorry I lied, but they're my friends."

Foster lowered his hand then his voice. "Look—Hugh was it?" Reading grunted. "This is my job, day in and day out, and I'm good at it. We'll find your friends. I've got your number. If anything comes up, I'll let you know, but for now, you need to get out of here before someone starts to ask questions about why Interpol is here, and you and I both lose our jobs. Understood?"

Reading smiled slightly, extending his hand. "You're a good man, Special Agent."

Foster chuckled and shook his hand. "I'm an asshole if you ask my ex-wife and those I work with."

"But you're my kind of asshole."

Foster tossed his head back, laughing. "Now what movie was that from?"

Reading shook his head with a shrug. "No idea, but I know someone who'd probably be able to tell us right away."

"Well, you find out and maybe we'll have a beer after this is all done."

"Sounds good."

Reading left, in a bit better mood now that the truth was out, though a new pit was already forming, he about to betray the trust granted his position by default.

He climbed into Milton's van.

"So? Anything?"

Reading nodded. "Yup. Where's the police impound?"

102

Lucius Valerius Corvus Residence, Pompeii, Roman Empire
July 22, 64 AD

Flavus leaned back on the comfortable cushions, his legs stretched out to his side, a bowl of grapes and a glass of wine within reach as slaves waved large fans, taking the edge off the heat. Across from him was Lucius, his best friend of many years.

It was a tough visit as it could be their last.

"You're certain you heard him correctly?"

Flavus nodded. "Absolutely. We're not to return. Ever."

"But that makes no sense! I've never heard such an order given. Yes, a legion can be sent to a location to potentially be permanently stationed there, but the troops are rotated in and out on a regular basis." Lucius speared a grape with his dagger. "That *must* be what he meant."

"That's what I thought as well, but Legate Catius disagrees."

"You spoke to him of this?"

"More like *he* spoke to *me*."

Lucius laughed, pulling the skewered grape off the blade with his teeth. "That's senior officers for you." He jabbed the air between them with his dagger. "Learn from him, he's a good man."

"He is, indeed."

"Either way, you've got a long, difficult mission ahead of you. Those barbarians in Britannia are proving to be a challenge. They seem to resist civilization to their core. I've heard talk of wiping them out rather than attempting to pacify them."

"Seems extreme."

"It's just idle talk, I'm sure. They're an island of barbarians that will never amount to anything. We'll be sending a lot more troops there soon to try and gain more control. Perhaps then you'll be able to return."

"Let's hope."

Lucius took a long swig of his wine then leaned closer, lowering his voice. "You didn't hear this from me, but the emperor has gone mad. I don't think he's long for this world. Either the gods will claim him, or the Senate. And when his madness no longer rules the land, you'll be free to return, I'm certain."

Flavus shook his head. "I don't know. I hope you're right, but I have a bad feeling about this."

"Stick close to Legate Catius. Follow his orders and you'll survive."

"I've been named to his personal guard so I'll be safer than the poor souls on the frontlines."

"Ahh, then you'll be protected by the best. Maybe someday you'll be honored with admittance into their ranks."

Flavus felt goosebumps race across his body at the idea. "It would indeed be an honor to become one of the third and final line. Should it come to pass, I would die a happy man. I can imagine no greater honor for the son of a blacksmith than to serve Rome as a member of his legion's Triarii."

London, United Kingdom
Present Day

"Is everyone in position?"

"Yes, sir."

Chaney nodded with satisfaction as he watched the various camera angles available from the back of their van parked less than half a kilometer from the last known location of the tracking device. It was still randomly transmitting yet hadn't moved. If it had been discovered, he would have expected them to disable it, which had him hopeful their ruse had worked.

But it had been over half an hour and there was no way this was their final destination. He was already five minutes past the cutoff he had given himself for going in.

It was time.

"Sir, look!"

Chaney leaned forward, the dot clearly having moved from the last update five minutes ago. He smiled at the others, backs slapped and fists bumped. "Looks like they were a little too trusting."

"Probably can't believe the professors would betray them."

Chaney tossed his hands up, shrugging. "Who cares? Whatever the reason, it worked. Let's stand down and follow them. I want to hit them as soon as they reach their destination."

Police Impound, Annapolis, Maryland

Reading lay sprawled across the driver seat, searching the glovebox then the floor, coming up empty. His Interpol ID had given him access to the police impound lot along with directions to Acton's seized vehicle, it now evidence. The poor attendant had been flustered with Reading's lack of paperwork, but his persistence and continued waving of the Interpol credentials had quickly pressured her into giving him access.

I'm going to lose my badge if I'm wrong.

"What makes you think it's here?"

Reading glanced at the rear, Milton searching the cargo area. "Jim's phone was tossed from the vehicle, smashed beforehand, but Laura's wasn't. They wouldn't let her keep it if they wouldn't let him keep his."

"So you think she left it in the car?"

"Could have. It wasn't found at the scene and it wasn't at the house. It was ringing a few times before going to voicemail, but now it goes straight through."

"So the battery's probably dead." Milton gasped, a sound Reading recognized as pain. He glanced back at the man, bent over and searching, one hand gripping his back. He had been shot and left for dead, but was now nearly fully recovered, though his stamina was low.

"Why don't you let me finish—"

"These are the two best friends I have in the world. I'm not going to let a little pain stop me when there's a chance I could help." He paused, looking at Reading. "Wouldn't the police have traced it?"

Reading shook his head, his hand fishing under the driver's seat. "No, they didn't have her number until I gave it to them. By then it was no longer ringing. She's still using a phone registered in the UK, so when her name was run through the system, nothing showed."

"Christ, her roaming charges must be nuts."

"It's nice to be rich." Reading felt his fingers hit something under the passenger seat, it sliding away. He reached deeper, his fingers finding it once more. He gripped it and knew immediately what it was. "Got it!" He pulled his hand out and grinned with triumph at the sight of Laura's cellphone. He crawled back outside, showing it to a wincing Milton.

"Just what good is this going to do? It's not like we now know where she is."

Reading closed all the doors, locking the vehicle. "We need to break into this thing," he said as they walked toward the security station with the keys.

"Why, what's on it that's so important?"

He pointed to Milton's van. "Get ready to leave quickly."

Milton shook out a nervous nod, walking a little too eagerly toward his vehicle, the engine roaring to life as Reading handed the keys over, a spare set apparently found at Acton's home. "Interpol thanks you for your cooperation. I'll be sure to mention you in my report"—he leaned in, reading her nametag—"Officer Bartlett."

The woman beamed, mumbling out a confused thank you mixed with a you're welcome and have a nice day.

Reading climbed into the van and Milton hammered on the gas, nearly tossing him out the side, he not yet having a chance to close the door. "Bloody hell, take it easy, this isn't a getaway."

"Sorry." Milton eased off the gas and Reading pulled his door shut then yanked his seatbelt on. "Where to?"

Reading pulled out the phone. "Like I was saying, we need to break into this thing."

"Why?"

"It's got a phone number on it that I need to call."

"You've never heard of the white pages?"

Reading chuckled. "This is most definitely an unlisted number."

Milton's eyes widened. "Ohhh, I think I know who you mean." He nodded at the phone as they turned into traffic. "If you give that to the police, will they give you the number?"

Reading shook his head. "Highly unlikely, and besides, I can't exactly tell them who it belongs to and why we want to talk to him."

A smile spread across Milton's face. "If we're going to do this unofficially, then I might have an idea on who can help us."

Reading stared at Milton. "I'm listening."

St. George's Hill, Weybridge, Surrey, United Kingdom

The convoy of three vehicles pulled off the road and through a set of wrought iron gates, a long straight drive leading to a large estate, dimly lit, it barely visible from the road.

"Why do you think they're letting us see this place?" whispered Laura in Acton's ear.

He shook his head slightly. "I was thinking the same thing." And it was true. There had been no blindfolds, no knockout gas, nothing. They had left the location they had woken up in, left London, and now, about an hour later, were arriving at what he assumed was their destination, a destination supposed to house at least several crystal skulls, the Triarii's most secret and prized possessions.

They intend to kill us.

Laura latched onto his arm. "I have a bad feeling about this. Martin was right, these *are* the bad guys."

Their SUV came to a halt and the door was opened. Acton climbed out then helped Laura to the ground as he quickly surveyed the area. The grounds were teeming with armed personnel, there no non-lethal tranquilizer weapons here. This was clearly a stronghold, perhaps even *the* stronghold. It made sense. They were away from the city, the grounds were extensive and cleared with good lines of sight in all directions, and the structure itself was large and built of solid stone.

How the hell does Martin think he can take this place?

Their vehicle pulled away, disappearing around the rear of the estate, the Proconsul greeted by two men rushing down the wide steps leading to the main entrance.

"Sir, I'm relieved you made it."

The Proconsul merely nodded then motioned toward the case containing the skull. "We have it and its being tracked. Prepare for an assault, almost definitely tonight."

A shiver raced through Acton as he felt Laura's hand squeeze his.

"Yes, sir, we're ready. Are you expecting lethal force?"

"Absolutely. They've killed dozens in the past few days. They're here to wipe us out."

Acton cleared his throat. "They can't possibly think they'll succeed. I thought you were all over the world?"

The Proconsul turned toward them. "We are, but if they get the final skulls and go to ground, what remains of our organization will have no way to find them."

"Are the other skulls here?"

"Those that remain, yes."

"But why risk them? Haven't you just led your enemy straight to what they want?"

The Proconsul smiled.

"You don't last two thousand years without a plan."

St. Paul's University, St. Paul, Maryland

"So you think you can get into the phone?"

Tommy Granger looked up at his dean, Gregory Milton, and grinned. "Already done."

"Jesus, that quickly?"

Tommy leaned back in his swivel chair, crossing his arms. "When you're good, you're good." He winked at Mai Trinh, eliciting flushed cheeks and a giggle from his girlfriend and exile from Vietnam, she now persona non grata after helping the professors and a Delta Force member escape her former home. He pointed at the computer screen. "I've got everything here. What do you need?"

Reading leaned forward, peering at the display. "A phone number."

"Called, received, or stored?"

"Huh?" Reading's eyes narrowed as he processed the question. "Oh, stored."

A few clicks and Tommy began to scroll through a list of contacts.

"Stop." Reading pointed at the screen. "That's the one."

"Dinner, Kraft? Is this some kind of joke?"

Reading ignored the young man, scribbling down the number then double-checking it. He stood back up and pointed at the screen. "Now delete everything on your computer and give me the phone."

Tommy unplugged the phone, handing it to Reading. "Why? What's so important about this Kraft Dinner guy?"

"None of your concern. Just delete everything."

Tommy continued to do nothing, the impetuous idiocy of youth on full display. Milton cleared his throat and Tommy turned his head, his dean giving him a look that had a couple of shades leave the young man's face. Milton raised a finger, pointing at him.

"*Everything*. If I find a copy has been kept or there's any chance of retrieving the data, there'll be hell to pay."

Tommy nodded, turning back toward the computer, his fingers flying across the keyboard, open windows disappearing, then a program started that Reading recognized from his training sessions that wiped data from hard drives by repeatedly overwriting it. Tommy spun in his chair as the program finished its work, facing the two men. "Happy?"

Milton nodded. "Very."

"Jeez, you hack one DoD mainframe and nobody ever trusts you again."

Mai's chin was on her chest, the tension of the past few minutes apparently causing the young, shy woman to recede into her own cocoon. "I trust you," she whispered.

Tommy beamed a smile at her that had the chin lifting about an inch. "That's because you took the time to get to know me."

Reading scowled at him. "Listen, lad, I don't know you enough to *not* trust you, but there are people who will kill to get this number. By making sure you don't have it, I'm protecting your life." He nodded at Mai, someone obviously important to the naïve young man. "And hers as well."

Tommy's eyes bulged slightly then he turned back to the computer, running another program.

"Just in case."

"Uh huh." Reading followed Milton from the room, the door sighing closed behind them.

"Do you think he'll be able to find the Triarii?"

Reading nodded. "If anyone can, Dylan Kane can."

Southern Gaul, Roman Empire
September 12, 64 AD

Flavus followed his legate, trying to hide the horror he felt as they walked through the encampment, the moans and cries of brave soldiers in agony heart wrenching. A battle was being fought here behind the palisades, and too many good men were losing.

Dysentery.

It had swept through the ranks swiftly, a seemingly unstoppable scourge that had taken most of the frontline troops and their commanders down, as well as much of the legate's inner circle.

Flavus had been quickly promoted, Legate Catius having taken a liking to him, and more importantly, displaying a trust in him.

"How many?"

Flavus cleared his throat. "The latest report shows almost one third of our men are sick and unable to fight."

Catius shook his head, a deep frown creasing his face. He paused atop a slight hill, giving him a view outside the palisades, scanning the forest that surrounded them. "And the Gauls?"

Flavus felt his stomach flutter at the thought. "Our scouts report a buildup to our west. Their assessment is that an attack is imminent."

"The Gauls have always been trouble, but nothing like this. To gather a force strong enough to attack a legion is almost unheard of."

"It *is* unusual."

Catius looked back at his tent. "It's that damned skull. It's cursed. It cursed Rome and now it curses us!"

Flavus said nothing, though he felt his legate was probably right. The emperor himself had said as much, the message delivered by Jupiter a powerful omen not to be ignored.

We must get this abomination as far from Rome as possible!

A sharp breath burst from Catius' nose as his head slowly shook, his attention returned to the neat rows of tents hiding the ill. "If we stay here, we're dead."

Flavus' eyebrows shot up. "But we're Romans! We don't surrender!"

Catius chuckled, looking at the young man. "No, we don't, but we can't win every battle, not when the gods themselves are against us."

Flavus' head dropped as his eyes cast down on the mud at his feet. "I'm sorry, sir, you are correct, of course."

"Chin up, soldier. You won't find the enemy between your toes."

"Sorry, sir." Flavus raised his head, his eyes slightly wide. "What will we do? If we're too sick to fight…" He wasn't sure what else to say without sounding defeatist.

"We load the sick into the wagons and send them south, back to Lugdunum. Send enough healthy men to protect them, but they must leave now, no delay."

Flavus nodded. "And the rest of us?"

"We head north, and try to avoid a fight I fear we cannot win."

Sana'a, Yemen
Present Day

"So, how's your day?"

CIA Special Agent Dylan Kane—Kraft Dinner to those secretly storing his number on their phones—peered through the scope of his sniper rifle, sweeping slowly from left to right, trying to find his target, his phone positioned near his mouth, an earbud keeping private the conversation with the woman quickly occupying more of his thoughts. "Nothing special. You?"

Lee Fang sighed, a burst of static filling his left ear. "You know me, trapped in this apartment." She paused. "I miss you."

Kane felt it in his chest and his stomach. It was a horrible feeling, yet a wonderful one. He had never missed anyone in his life, and now here he was, in the middle of yet another shithole, talking to a woman he was pretty sure he loved—another first—and he could *feel* the pain of separation.

It was fantastic.

He had never told a woman that he loved them before, at least not sincerely. Lines were delivered to seal the deal on occasion, and he had felt guilty lying, though sometimes on this job you did what you had to to get the job done.

Even if hearts were broken.

He had yet to tell her how he felt, he not yet ready, and he was terrified of putting it out there to just get silence, or worse, a "thank you", in return.

"I miss you too."

"You're sure? There's no woman there with you?"

From his prone position, Kane glanced over his shoulder at the rooftop. "Pretty sure. Besides, they'd be head to toe in black if they were."

"That narrows down where you are."

"Hey, no guessing."

"Sorry."

She truly did sound apologetic, and the pain he was feeling for her grew. The poor woman was living in exile, under an assumed identity provided her by the United States government as a thank you for her helping thwart a recent coup attempt. Yet in doing so, she had been forced to kill a top ranking Chinese general, and the former Beijing Military Region Special Forces Unit soldier was now in hiding, considered a traitor by her country, and forbidden by her adopted country to work in any job that might utilize her old skills.

She was bored.

Colossally bored.

Just as you'd be.

He had sensed the mental anguish she was going through and had offered to try and be a friend to her, he one of the few people in the world who knew her true predicament. A friendship had blossomed, then a romance, this the first real relationship he had ever been in, his history of wham, bam, thanks for the slam, now a thing of the past, assuming things with Fang worked out.

Having no track record in these things, however, he had no idea whether they would.

He just knew which outcome he was hoping for.

She's incredible.

She was gorgeous, his type definitely Asian, and she was the first woman he had ever slept with that he was pretty sure could give him a run for his money in the ass kicking department, should he ever cross her.

The woman had skills.

She just couldn't use them.

He stopped his slow scan of the crowd, moving the scope back slightly. "There you are."

"Who?"

"Sorry, babe, gotta go. I'll see you soon."

"Don't make promises you can't keep."

Kane chuckled. "You know me too well. Bye, babe."

"Bye."

He ended the call and squeezed the trigger, twice, putting two bullets into Aziz Kanaan, the mastermind behind the New York City attacks. Scrambling back from the edge of the roof, he rolled to his feet, dropped his weapon down a vent for later retrieval by a CIA lackey, then rushed down the back stairs to the street below as his special-issue Agency watch sent an electric pulse to his wrist. Pressing the buttons in a coded sequence, a message scrolled across the face.

Reading?

A pit formed in his stomach as he realized there was only one reason the Interpol agent would be contacting him.

Something's happened to the professors.

St. George's Hill, Weybridge, Surrey, United Kingdom

"Is everyone in position?"

Chaney watched through binoculars as the teams sounded off in his earpiece, then receiving the final confirmation, he gave the signal. "Proceed."

Immediately the exterior guards began to drop, one, two, sometimes three at a time as several sniper positions surrounding the estate opened up on men he had once thought of as comrades. He closed his eyes for a moment, tears threatening to cloud his vision as the last of almost two dozen went down, not a shot fired by their enemy.

For there had been nothing to fire at.

He stepped into the four-by-four, closing the passenger door as his teams raced through the gates, the lock blasted the moment the assault began. The long drive left nowhere to hide—they were sitting ducks if their enemy decided to retaliate, but no one did, the only sound their tires skidding on the gravel, then their boots on the same as they jumped out and rushed toward the main doors, other teams continuing to the sides and rear of the building.

And still, nothing.

Suddenly an alarm sounded and floodlights bathed the entire area in a harsh glow, a glow that only lasted moments as the sniper teams took out the bulbs, quickly plunging them back into darkness, one finally locating and eliminating the last speaker blaring the warning.

An eerie silence settled over the area, faint emergency lighting and a full moon providing the only illumination.

He motioned toward the door. "Let's go."

Small charges fired at the windows, detonating on impact as two men rushed the doors, carefully placing explosives on the lock then taking cover. Chaney delivered a hand signal and the charges detonated. Stun grenades fired through the shattered windows, several tossed through the gaping doors, the resulting explosions deafening, even from outside.

And still not a shot fired in response.

Something's wrong.

Acton sat in a chair set against a wall, Laura beside him. The control center they were in had dozens of monitors and about half a dozen men, including the Proconsul and Rodney, the action outside unfolding before them like a reality show. Occupying each of the four corners were crystal skulls, the Oracles of Jupiter and Zeus, the skull he had found in Peru, and the thirteenth skull he had just delivered.

He shivered.

Maybe he's right.

He interrupted the Proconsul's hushed conversation. "Shouldn't you be moving those?"

The Proconsul turned toward him. "Pardon me?"

"The skulls, shouldn't you be moving them?" He nodded toward the monitors. "It doesn't appear to be going well for you."

"No." The Proconsul turned back to the monitors, his conversation resuming as if never interrupted.

Acton turned to Laura, lowering his voice. "Mighty confident, aren't they?"

Laura leaned closer, their heads touching. "They don't seem to be putting up much of a fight. I don't understand. They don't seem concerned at all."

Acton cleared his throat. "Why aren't you fighting back?"

119

"Give it time," said the Proconsul, not bothering to face Acton. "How many?"

"We've counted twenty-four," replied Rodney, Acton straining to hear. "Twelve inside, the rest outside, surrounding the building."

"And the sniper teams?"

"They've already repositioned inside the grounds."

The Proconsul turned toward Acton, smiling.

"Activate the automatic external defenses."

Klaus Becker gripped his MP5K submachine gun tightly, his eyes watching the perimeter like a hawk, this operation going far too smoothly, the complete lack of response running contrary to all the briefings they had received. He and his men had been training these civilians for months now, teaching them self-defense, weapons and tactics—essentially everything they'd need for this very night.

Yet so far, it appeared there had been little need. His sniper teams had done the work so far, with his clients simply standing back and watching the action.

Until Martin Chaney, their leader, had ordered Becker's men to remain outside.

A mistake.

If ever there would be a place their foes would defend, it would be the interior of the building. The lack of resistance had him wondering if anyone was actually inside, perhaps all the defenses placed outside.

Though that would be foolish.

And he didn't think his enemy was foolish.

He wasn't so certain about his clients.

These men seemed normal, except for the fact they didn't think in terms of surviving their mission. They seemed only to think in terms of the mission succeeding, apparently unconcerned with their own survival.

They simply wanted to retrieve an item, even if it meant only a single man surviving.

And it was an item he had no intel on.

It might as well be a black box.

But he had to admit he didn't care. So far, there hadn't been a single casualty among his men, and their time was handsomely paid for. In this business, you didn't ask too many questions.

Something moved from the corner of his eye and he cursed.

"Take cover!" he shouted, leaping through the blown out window beside him as hidden machine guns popped out of the ground and opened fire. He heard the cries of his men as they were mowed down, the gunfire intense but brief, the sudden silence indicating the automated defense system had finished its job.

His men dead, his clients all safe inside the building.

A rage built within him.

"What the hell was that?" asked Acton, leaping to his feet to get a closer look at the monitors, the dozen men outside made quick work of by something or someone.

"Sentry guns. They eliminate anything that moves," explained Rodney.

"Jesus, I hope they don't malfunction." Acton's eyes narrowed as he turned his attention from the monitors to the Proconsul. "Why didn't you use them when they arrived?"

The Proconsul stared at him for a moment. "You keep forgetting, Professor, that we have a plan."

Laura took Acton's hand. "Where are the other skulls?"

"What other skulls?"

"The other skulls. I thought you had all thirteen now?"

The Proconsul stared at her, his eyes slightly narrowed. "It would appear you have been misinformed. These are all the skulls that remain under our protection. The others have all been lost to Martin Chaney and his Deniers."

Acton's jaw dropped slightly as he looked at Laura.

Are we on the wrong side of this?

Chaney surged forward, his weapon raised in front of him as he and his team advanced deeper into the large building, Becker reporting over his comm what had just occurred outside.

But there was nothing that could be done about that.

"We'll disable the defenses when we take the control room."

"Copy that, sir. Our drones' infrared are still showing only a few hotspots above ground. It's most likely in the basement."

"Agreed. We'll clear the upper levels first before we attempt to take the lower."

Someone rounded the corner and Chaney squeezed off a round, taking the surprised man out.

He sighed.

I'm sorry, old friend.

Acton jabbed a finger at the monitors. "You have to evacuate! They're slaughtering them."

The Proconsul glanced at him then returned his attention to the screens. "Everyone here today volunteered for this. If we don't put up a good show they'll realize what our plan is."

Acton paused, processing what the Proconsul had just said. "I thought it was to end this once and for all?"

"It is."

Acton shook his head, throwing his hands up in exasperation. "Well, it doesn't look like you're succeeding."

The Proconsul turned to him, smiling. "Looks can be deceiving."

Chaney stepped behind the corner as a rather large charge blasted open the doors to the control center. His team surged in, he directly behind them, several shots heard through the haze.

"Cease fire!" he shouted, slapping down the two nearest weapons, both aimed at the professors. "They're not the enemy."

"But you appear to be."

Chaney glanced at Acton, ignoring his statement, then strode to the center of the room, Rodney glaring at him, the Proconsul simply looking disappointed.

In him.

He had to admit the disappointment in the old man's face hit home, this a man he had looked up to for years, a man who was now his enemy.

Perhaps when this is all over…

Chaney pointed at the skulls. "Get them ready." He pointed at another one of his men. "Disable the automated sentry guns then destroy the equipment."

Acton stepped forward. "I thought you were supposed to be the good guys."

He turned to the defiant professor. "We are."

"You just slaughtered a bunch of people—"

"As they would have done to us if the roles were reversed."

"I'm not so sure about that."

123

Chaney sighed. "Professor Acton, what do you think happened here today?"

"I think your breakaway group has managed to destroy the Triarii from within."

Chaney shook his head. "No, Professor, the Triarii as you have known it *is* the breakaway group." Acton's eyebrows leapt and Laura gasped. "Our mission, the Triarii's mission, from the beginning, as given to us by our greatest sage, Ananias, was to seek out and find the skulls in order to discover their power. He told us there were thirteen, so we sought them out. It was only when the third was discovered and united with the first two that we had the disaster in London." Chaney glanced at the Proconsul. "That was when we lost our way. Instead of continuing our search to bring the skulls together, we let fear rule us, instead finding them so we could keep them apart.

"A few of us through the centuries, however, continued with the original mandate, in the hopes that one day man would reach the technological level to harness the power the skulls are capable of. We were labelled renegades, spoken of with derision, the membership taught to believe we Deniers were going against everything the Triarii stood for. But nothing could be further from the truth."

The fact Acton wasn't interrupting him suggested he might just be getting through to the man, so he pressed on, something deep inside him hoping that if he could convince Acton of the truth, then he would pass this message on to his friend, so Reading would realize he was still a good man, not the traitor he feared his old partner now thought of him as. "Do you know why they call us the Deniers?"

Acton shook his head slightly.

"It is not because we deny that there is any risk to uniting the skulls as they would have you believe, it is because we deny that the current mandate of the Triarii is its genuine mandate. Everything we have done is to return us to the old ways. *We* are the true Triarii, not the people led by this false proconsul."

Acton's voice was slightly subdued. "So you now have all thirteen skulls?"

Chaney nodded. "Yes."

"So it was you who killed to get them?"

Chaney felt his chest tighten, his eyes staring at the floor for a moment as a wave of shame swept over him. "Unfortunately it was necessary. Everyone we have killed has been a brother to us, and it pains me deeply that so many had to die, but we had no choice."

The Proconsul's voice suddenly boomed. "Your arrogance is unbecoming. We have witnessed the destructive power. We have long said that until we know what the origin of the skulls is, we are not ready to understand their purpose. Before we have the answers to even the most basic of questions, we are not ready to harness their power." He pointed a finger at Chaney. "And you're selective with your history. Our scrolls tell us that our mission was to remove the original skull from Rome and keep it as far from there as possible. The sage you speak of was considered a fool by many, a curiosity by the rest. He was well liked, yes, but his final words were recorded merely because they related to the skulls and were curious in nature. Yes, we sought out the other skulls he referred to, but not until the accidental discovery of a second one in Greece, centuries later. You conveniently cherry pick phrases from the scrolls to suit your belief system. You've co-opted our original, noble purpose, and twisted it into a dark quest to seek a truth we may not be ready to learn, risking all of mankind to do it."

Chaney drew a deep breath, pursing his lips as he considered the Proconsul and what to do with him. He exhaled, a decision made. "I see there is no convincing you." He raised his weapon, aiming it at the Proconsul.

"No!" Rodney leapt in front of the Proconsul, a burst of gunfire erupting from Chaney's left, Rodney dropping to the floor, clutching at his chest.

"No!" cried Chaney, shoving the shooter toward the door as Laura cried out, rushing to Rodney's side, Acton stepping in front of the Proconsul. "Take the skulls to the vehicles, I want everyone out of this room, now!"

Acton glared at him. "You've got what you came for. Enough people have died, so why don't you just leave?"

Chaney nodded slowly, his eyes glued to Rodney's as the man gasped his last breaths. "He was one of my best friends before this all started." He looked at the Proconsul. "I truly am sorry." He held up his weapon. "Tranquilizer darts. I could never kill you. You've been my mentor for over a decade, a man I admire. If you could just see past the beliefs you've been indoctrinated with and join us, we could discover the truth together."

The Proconsul said nothing, though his anger was clear, Laura glancing up from Rodney and shaking her head. Chaney knelt at his old friend's side, gripping the man's shoulder and squeezing it. "I'm so sorry," he whispered. He looked up at the Proconsul. "Sir, please, you are welcome to join us to witness what we are about to do. You've always been our leader, and I will always think of you as such. I don't blame you. *You* didn't lose your way, that was lost eight hundred years ago and you've merely continued the mistake our ancestors made."

The Proconsul stared down at Rodney then at Chaney. "You have all the skulls, and your people have drained most of our accounts. We are but a shadow of what we once were. I have failed in my duty, and am the leader of what is now nothing. Take what you came for. We are done."

Chaney's heart slammed hard, the words painful to hear, the tone they were delivered with suggesting a finality that indicated there would be no changing this man's mind. "As you wish." Chaney stood, turning to Acton. "Coming?"

Acton's eyebrows popped. "Huh? Of course not!"

"I'm afraid I must insist."

Laura rose and Acton placed himself in front of her. "Why?"

"Because as long as you are with us, they won't try anything that risks your lives. They're like that to a fault."

"You used to be."

"And will be again. Professor, if we succeed, the world we live in tomorrow will not be the same one we live in today. Don't you want to be witness to that?"

Acton's head dropped slightly as he drew a breath, his eyes focused like lasers on Chaney's. "Of course I do. But the reality is that I expect you to put thirteen balls of glass next to each other then wonder why you went to all the trouble to recreate a disco!"

"James!"

Chaney laughed. "Oh, Professor, I've missed you. You are right, of course, to doubt. We don't know what will happen, but we do know that three unleashed enough power to reduce half of London to rubble eight hundred years ago. We also know that the Great Fire of Rome began the night the first skull arrived there. It nearly destroyed the greatest city the world had ever known to that point. Don't you want to know why you shiver every time you look at one of them? The Triarii have refused to study them, considering it almost a sacrilege. *We* will test this. *We* want to know the answers to the questions *they* don't dare to ask. Come with me, Professor, and help us discover the truth."

Acton sucked in a breath, Chaney sensing he was winning the notoriously curious man to his side. "And what if nothing happens?"

"What do you mean?"

"I mean, if nothing happens, and this all turns out to be for naught, what will you do?"

Chaney shook his head. "That won't happen."

"But if it does?"

Chaney sighed. "Then our life's purpose will have been for nothing."

"Will you return the skulls to the Triarii?"

"*We* are the Triarii."

Acton gave him a look. "You know what I mean."

Chaney smiled slightly, glancing around the room then at the Proconsul. "Should we fail, then yes, we will surrender the skulls to you, Proconsul, return your funds, and you will never hear from us again."

Acton turned to the Proconsul. "Satisfied?"

The Proconsul shook his head. "Not at all. You forget, Professor Acton, that I believe in their power. He's only agreeing because he knows he *will* succeed in unleashing their power. The difference between him and I is that he thinks he can control this power, I do not. I fear *when* he succeeds, he will destroy everything around him, including perhaps the world itself."

Chaney felt a tightness in his chest as his cheeks flushed, the frustration of the old arguments coming back to the fore. He turned to Acton. "Professor, we are not fools. If we detect anything going out of control, we will stop the experiment immediately. We believe we have the technology to harness the power, but should we not, then we will stop and await a time when we shall, be that ten years, a hundred, even a thousand years from now. Eventually the secrets of the skulls will be revealed. *I* feel it will be tomorrow." He tilted his head forward slightly, staring at the professor he had so much respect for. "One last time, Professor, will you willingly join us?"

Acton looked at Laura who shook her head slightly. "Somebody has to be there to stop this if it goes wrong."

Her eyes popped wide. "Surely you don't believe?"

Acton inhaled slowly. "I didn't, not for a second, until he mentioned the shiver. Didn't you feel it too?"

Laura frowned, her reluctance in admitting to the truth undeniable. She nodded. "Almost every time I looked at it."

"Could it actually be something other than an emotional response?"

Laura closed her eyes and nodded. "I don't want to believe, but you know I've devoted a huge portion of my career to the study of the one I had access to. We couldn't determine how or when it was made, and we now know why the televised and reported studies claimed they were fake."

"The fakes the Triarii substituted."

Laura nodded. "I can't explain them, and that has always made me think there was something special about them."

Acton stared into her eyes, crouching slightly. "You want to go, don't you?"

Laura looked up at him, a sheepish smile spreading. "I'm gobsmacked that I'm saying yes, but I do."

Acton gave her a peck on the forehead then turned to Chaney. "If we go, I man the kill switch."

A rush of adrenaline flowed through Chaney as he smiled.

"Absolutely."

Milton Residence, St. Paul, Maryland

Reading's phone vibrated on the kitchen table, everyone flinching, even Milton's young daughter, Niskha. Her mother, Sandra, quickly led the little girl from the room as Reading swiped his thumb across the display, putting the call on speaker so Milton could hear.

"Hello?"

"Hi, is this Hugh?"

"Yes."

"This is Dylan. How are you?"

Reading breathed a sigh of relief. There weren't a lot of young whippersnappers that he had faith in, he one of those that felt today's generation was a lost generation, though Dylan Kane was one of the exceptions. "I've been better."

"I guess so. Has there been any word since your message?"

"Negative, but I'm out of the loop on this one. The FBI was humoring me and now have cut me off."

"Any thoughts on who took them?"

Reading leaned back in his chair. "Those two have pissed off so many people around the world, it could be anyone—"

Kane chuckled. "Too true!"

"—but we're pretty confident it's an offshoot of the Triarii, the so called Deniers."

Kane sighed. "I see. Well, I can't do much from where I am, but I'm going to make some calls. You should be hearing from trusted friends shortly."

It was Reading's turn to sigh. "Glad to hear it, Dylan. Thanks."

"No problem. Now I've gotta go, but keep me posted."

"Will do."

The call ended and Reading turned to Milton.

"Trusted friends?"

Reading smiled. "If it's who I think it is, we're in good hands."

Lee Fang Residence, Philadelphia, Pennsylvania

Fang sprinted, hard, screamo music blaring in her ears, it an excruciating experiment never to be repeated. Sure, it pissed her off so much that she did indeed run faster, but it also took any joy out of the workout.

Tomorrow, disco.

Her phone beeped in her ear and she lifted her arm to read the call display. She grinned, hitting the stop button on her treadmill then pulling the phone out, she recognizing the spoofed number of her boyfriend.

Boyfriend!

That was a word she had been certain was relegated to distant memory after her exile, and even in her wildest fantasies she never thought she would be attracted to a white guy. But Kane was different, different from any Caucasian she had met before, and surrounded by them now for over a year, she realized a lot of her misconceptions and prejudices were based upon propaganda inflicted on her by her former government.

Kane was incredible.

Americans were nice people.

Life was looking up.

"Hi!"

"Hey there, how are you?"

She felt goosebumps at the sound of his voice. "Sweaty and breathing hard."

"Ooh, just the way I like you!"

A wave of embarrassment washed over her. "You're so bad!"

"Listen, I can't talk, this is fast. You up for some potential action?"

Fang's grin spread as her heart slammed for an entirely new reason. "Absolutely!"

Kane's charming laugh had her eyes closing as she pictured his face. "Thought you might be. The professors are missing."

"Acton and Palmer?"

"Yes. Hugh Reading is in St. Paul now with Dean Milton. I want you to take the go bag and join them. I've sent details to your secure account."

"Ok. Who do you think took them?"

"We're not sure, but we think it might be some cult. The details are in the email. I'm going to get Chris involved so we can start to get some intel, but people are dead, and it's been over twenty-four hours with no word."

"From what you've told me, those two have annoyed quite a few powerful people."

"Yes, so you might need more firepower."

"Who?"

"I'm going to give BD a shout, see if he can shake loose a few of his team to help you. Laura also has her own ex-SAS team that is ready to deploy the moment they have a target."

Fang frowned as she wiped her forehead with a towel. "Lots of guns."

"Yup. That's what has me worried. If it's outside the country, you can't go, it's too risky. Just act as liaison here for Reading. Hopefully Delta and the SAS guys can take care of everything else."

"You can count on me."

She could almost see his smile. "I never had any doubt."

The Stone Manor, Luray, Virginia

CIA Analyst Supervisor Chris Leroux gripped the back of his girlfriend's head, tight, his fingers intertwined with her hair as he pressed his lips against hers, their tongues exploring each other, the real action taking place below the roiling surface of the hot tub.

He moaned.

"That feels good," he whispered, CIA Agent Sherrie White's expert hands suddenly releasing him then tugging his bathing suit bottom off, the decision to wear it clearly a mistake.

"You ain't seen nothin', yet." Sherrie repositioned herself, straddling him, their hips grinding together under the water. She groaned, her head dropping onto his shoulder. "This was such a good idea," she gasped as he grabbed her shoulders, pulling her down hard. "Whenever I visit your parents, I feel like I need to unwind."

"Me too," gasped Leroux as he struggled for control.

"Yeah, but your mother isn't judging you every second of the day. Me, I'm always under the microscope."

"That means she likes you."

"Christ, I'd hate to see what she's like if she didn't. That must have been horrible for your high school girlfriends."

Leroux pushed her back slightly so he could see her eyes. "You *do* know who you're talking to, don't you?"

Sherrie laughed. "Yeah, somebody who's now looking forward to his high school reunion."

He grinned, thrusting his hips and lifting her out of the water, rivulets running down her naked skin, her exposed breasts sending another rush through him.

And she was right. He *was* looking forward to his next reunion. He had skipped the last one, the nerd-dork-geek crowd rarely showing up unless they had become insanely successful and wanted to rub it in the faces of their former tormentors.

But he hadn't become successful.

At least not in a way that he could boast about.

He was CIA, doing a job he couldn't talk about. Yes, he had probably saved and taken more lives than the entire graduating class combined, but that was all classified.

So why show up to a high school reunion to see people who had never been your friend, and had made your life a living hell just for being smarter than them, different from them.

All except Kane.

His best and only friend outside of Sherrie. Kane had been a senior in high school and had asked the younger Leroux to tutor him. He had, and they had become good friends, Kane the complete antithesis to Leroux's teenage loser. Kane was good looking and outgoing. A jock that every girl wanted to be with, and every guy wanted to be.

He was the personification of popularity.

And he had become Leroux's friend, because deep down, he had all the same insecurities. Kane had defended him from the bullies, essentially telling anyone that if they messed with Leroux, they messed with him.

It put an end to it.

At least until Kane graduated and left for college.

Then it had resumed, though never at the level it had been before.

High school had been horrible.

He looked at the gorgeous woman he loved, and who loved him, and wondered if it would be worth showing up with her on his arm. He smiled.

"Oh, if they could see me now."

"They'd be watching hidden camera porn."

He lowered her back down, sighing as his eyes rolled into the back of his head, the sensations he was feeling off the charts as they slowly enjoyed each other's bodies.

To hell with them. I have a new life now.

His phone vibrated nearby, indicating a text message.

He looked.

She grabbed his face, redirecting it to her breasts. "Ignore it. That's an order."

He buried his face in something more interesting as another message came in.

"Ignore it."

He tried.

Oh God did he try.

But it vibrated again.

"Ignore. It."

She was getting close, he was getting close.

No he wasn't.

Dammit!

"What's wrong?"

He sighed, dropping his hips back into the water. "It's distracting me."

She smiled. "I can tell." She nodded at the phone. "You better get it, droopy."

Leroux shot her a fake pained expression then grabbed the phone, his eyebrows popping up as Sherry continued to gently keep things alive. "It's from Dylan. Says he needs to speak to me, urgently."

Sherrie pushed off him, she knowing too well things were over. "I'm going to set up surveillance outside Fang's place next time he's visiting her then call every five minutes."

Leroux chuckled then climbed out of the hot tub. Sherrie reached forward, grabbing her favorite appendage of his. "No, you stay, I don't need him."

"Sorry babe, we're a packaged pair."

She lifted and looked. "Yup, there's a pair alright."

Leroux laughed as he grabbed a towel, Sherrie yanking it from him then quickly drying him off, mini-Chris taking interest once again when she dropped to her knees to dry his nether regions.

She smacked it. "You're off duty."

Leroux grinned, launching his secure messaging app to get the contact details for Kane. Done, he watched the greatest thing to have ever entered his life dry off, she teasing him with her slow movements, the towel barely visiting the front of her body.

He dialed.

"Hey, buddy, thanks for getting back to me so quickly. Hope I didn't interrupt anything."

Leroux's eyes hungrily drank in the sight before him. "Just a romantic night away from everything."

"Oh, shit, I'm sorry. Wait, no I'm not. I'm in burqa-town and haven't seen Fang in two weeks, let alone a woman. I spot a tablecloth and wonder if a chick is under it, then realize I can't do anything, even if there was."

Leroux laughed. "Ahh, the bachelor life, gone forever."

"Yeah. Wouldn't trade it for the world."

Leroux smiled at Sherrie. "Me neither."

She covered herself with a robe. "Shows over."

He frowned. "So, what's up? You said it was urgent?"

"Yeah, the professors have been kidnapped at gunpoint in Maryland, several dead. It looks like it might be the work of that Triarii offshoot he told me about. I've sent you a secure message with all the details. Fang is heading to Maryland now to rendezvous with Agent Hugh Reading. She'll be your contact on this one, I'm out of the loop."

"Got you. I'll check with the Director to see if it's okay to use Agency resources."

"Already done. He's approved your team looking into it. The Triarii are still of interest since our former President was killed by one of their people."

Leroux grunted. "Kind of keeps you on the radar."

"True. I've got to go, but keep me posted."

"Will do, talk to you soon."

The call ended and Sherrie's robe flew open. "I'm guessing you have to go?"

He nodded.

"Want to try and set a record?"

He grinned.

"Oh yeah!"

Maggie Harris Residence, Lake in the Pines Apartments, Fayetteville, North Carolina

"What are you looking at?"

Command Sergeant Major Burt "Big Dog" Dawson flushed, turning his phone slightly so his fiancée, Maggie Harris, couldn't see the screen. "Oh, umm, Niner sent me an email. Wanted to know what kind of tile was in some picture."

Maggie frowned, leaning over and turning the phone toward her, revealing a chesty woman standing in a hallway. "Uh huh. Tell him it's slate, and he's a pig." She tapped his chest. "And so are you."

"Hey, babe, just trying to help a fellow operator redecorate."

"With those two howitzers in the picture, I'm surprised you even noticed there was a floor."

Dawson glanced at the photo. "Huh, whadaya know. I never noticed her before."

Maggie shook her head. "Men! What is it about you guys and big breasts?"

Dawson shrugged, pocketing the phone. "I don't know." He squeezed his pecks. "We want what we can't have?"

"Uh huh. Would you want me to get implants like that?"

Dawson's eyebrows shot up, knowing enough about women that there was only one correct answer to a question like that. "Hell no! You're perfect just the way you are. I wouldn't want you looking like some freak show."

Maggie's eyes narrowed. "Uh huh. I wonder if the twins were bigger, if I would have had such a hard time landing you."

He grinned. "I guess we'll never know."

"Good answer."

"I thought so."

Her eyes smoldered and he knew he had done well. "Come here, you."

He leaned toward and she lay back on the couch, he lying atop her as she wrapped her arms around him, their lips meeting as he made a mental note to smack Niner later for almost getting him in trouble. He grabbed a breast and squeezed, eliciting a moan. "See, perfect."

She pushed up against the drill sergeant. "Ooh, is that for me, or the girl on the tile?"

"Oh, it's all for you, babe."

His phone vibrated, and she felt it.

"Are you on call?"

He sighed. "Yup. I better take it."

Maggie sighed, pushing him off her. "Tell the Colonel he has to work on his timing."

Dawson laughed as he fished his phone out of his pocket, his eyes narrowing at the number. "Hello?"

"Hey buddy, it's Dylan."

"Ah shit, what do *you* want?"

"Hey, is that any way to greet a friend?"

"Huh. The day you call just to say hi, is the day I know world peace has been declared and we're all out of jobs."

"Yeah, can't see that happening this week."

"Me neither. What's up?"

"I'll let you guess."

Dawson shook his head, immediately knowing who this was about. "What did they get themselves into this time?"

Kane laughed. "Our archeologist friends have been kidnapped at gunpoint from a mall in their hometown, several people are dead. Hugh says it's that offshoot of the Triarii you had to deal with in the West Bank."

140

Dawson was immediately alert, Maggie already picking up the signals and gathering his shoes and jacket. "Christ, those guys? I thought we killed most of them?"

"Nope, turns out Martin Chaney, the guy they handed the skull over to, might be one of the bad guys after all."

Dawson's eyes widened. "Holy shit! Didn't see that coming. So what do we know?"

"Not much. I've sent you a secure email with everything I have so far. I've sent Fang to coordinate in Maryland, and Hugh's apparently called in Laura's security team. I've got Leroux working intel as well."

"What do you need me for?"

"Muscle. See if you can get a few of the guys put on standby to deploy. I have a feeling this is going to require professional extraction."

Dawson chewed his cheek, his head slowly bobbing. "Okay, no promises, but I'll see what we can do. Might have to do it off the books."

"No problem, just talk to Hugh, he's got access to the funds."

"Copy that, I'll let you know as soon as I know."

"Thanks, buddy."

Dawson ended the call and turned to Maggie. "Sorry, hon, I'm going to have to head in to the Unit."

"Why? What's happened?"

"Jim and Laura were kidnapped at gunpoint. A few people are dead. Looks like some old friends from their past might be involved."

"Who?"

He shook his head. "Sorry, can't talk about that, classified, but let's just say you're never quite sure who you're dealing with, and whose side they're on."

Maggie frowned, shaking her head. "They're such nice people, it's horrible that things keep happening to them."

"I know. It's almost as if there's people out there who delight in their misery, some puppet master continually messing with their lives to keep his audience happy."

Maggie smiled, leaning in for a kiss. "Well, you go cut his strings but see if you can squeeze some time in back here before you head out. I want to make sure you forget Niner's remodeling project before you leave."

Dawson grinned. "Sounds like a *very* wise thing to do."

Northern Gaul, Roman Empire
October 22, 64 AD

"These hit and run tactics are taking their toll. If this keeps up, we won't have enough men left to fight if they come in strength."

Flavus nodded in agreement at his legate's assessment of the situation. They had lost a third of their men to dysentery, they having sent them back to safety with several hundred healthy men to protect them, the sick in no condition to fight should they come under attack. Thankfully, runners had confirmed they had reached safety, a relief to them all.

But there had been no relief from the Gauls.

"My men sick was bad enough, but we've lost another third to these attacks." Legate Catius spun, glaring at the box holding the crystal skull they had been tasked to transport. "It's all because of that damned thing. I have half a mind to bury it somewhere and return to Rome, telling them it was destroyed."

Flavus was surprised at the outburst, and knew it was simply frustration speaking, so many of their comrades lost over the past several weeks. Flavus had never fought a battle in his life, all his fighting in the training ring, his life never in real danger.

Yet all that had changed.

He had fought, hard, almost every day for weeks, surprising even himself with his skills, and earning the respect of the men he was now forced to command, so many of the senior officers dead or sick.

And he had his friend Lucius to thank for it, their constant training in their youth now paying off.

He looked at his legate. "Then why don't we do just that?"

The legate glanced at him then back at the box, saying nothing at first. "Do you wish that we do such a thing because you fear it may indeed be cursed, and destroying it will curse us all? If that is what your heart tells you, then how can you wish such a fate upon Rome herself? Could it be that it is indeed cursed as the emperor says, and that all this misfortune we have experienced is because of it? Perhaps when we reach our destination all will be well, but if not, better Britannia suffer than Rome."

Flavus bowed slightly, happy to hear his commander back to his old self. "You are right, of course, sir. I will do my duty to my emperor and to Rome. But if we are to succeed, we must think differently."

Catius turned toward him, his eyes narrowed slightly. "In what way?"

Flavus pulled in a quick breath, averting his eyes. "I hesitate to say this, as it may sound cowardly, and I assure you I am not—"

Catius stepped forward, putting a hand on Flavus' shoulder. "*You* definitely can't be accused of that."

Flavus made eye contact briefly, the feeling of pride he felt at that moment almost embarrassing. "Thank you, sir." Catius let go of his shoulder and took a seat, motioning for Flavus to do the same.

"What is it you wish to say?"

Flavus swallowed. "Well, sir, I've been thinking. We are constantly being attacked because we are too large a force not to draw attention. Perhaps it would be best if a small party were to break away and take the skull to Britannia, perhaps disguised as peasants."

Catius tilted his head back, his eyebrows rising as he contemplated Flavus' words. "It is an idea, that. Our policy of victory through strength hasn't served us. Perhaps a new way of thinking *is* needed."

Shouts erupted from outside the tent.

"The Gauls are attacking!"

They both leapt to their feet, Catius glaring once again at the box. "Curse their gods!" He pointed at Flavus. "Should it look like we are to fall, take the skull and what remains of the Triarii and make for Britannia. We will join you if we can."

Flavus felt his chest tighten as they emerged from the command tent. "But sir, those are your most experienced troops!"

Catius nodded. "The other lines will be sacrificed in order to ensure success." He grabbed Flavus by the shoulder, spinning him around so they were facing each other. "For Rome!"

Flavus placed his hand on his commander's shoulder. "For Rome!"

Milton Residence, St. Paul, Maryland
Present Day

Reading sat in silence on Milton's couch, his head falling forward, repeatedly waking him up, exhaustion taking over. In his haste to leave, he had forgotten his CPAP machine and his sleep apnea was taking its toll.

Tomorrow would be worse.

His sleep study had shown he was waking up over sixty times an hour, his body never actually getting any real rest, his brain never really sleeping. His first night with his machine had gone far better than he had expected, opting for a mask that covered his nose and mouth and wearing it for almost an hour while reading a book in bed, a suggestion the nurse had made to get him used to having it on.

He had slept like a log.

For eight hours.

The next day he had felt so refreshed he was tempted to kiss the bloody thing. When told he needed one—desperately—he had feared it would be loud, though with no spouse, he had dismissed that concern. It turned out the machine was nearly silent, though if the mask slipped, it did make a near comical farting sound.

Niner would probably be in hysterics.

"Why don't you go take a nap?"

Reading jerked awake, his eyes wide. He glanced over at Sandra Milton, her eReader set down on her knee as she looked at him.

"Pardon?"

"You're practically asleep. Go to bed, I've made up the spare room for you."

He sighed, closing his eyes. "I think that might be best." He dropped his gaze slightly. "You wouldn't happen to have a CPAP machine set to nine psi would you?"

She returned the look. "Umm, no. You travelled without your machine?"

He frowned. "Huh, so you know how bloody daft that is too."

She nodded as she rose. "Go to bed, I'm going to call my friend Theresa. She works at a medical supply store. I'll see if she can bring one over."

"It's prescription."

"She's a friend, we'll do this on the down low."

Reading smiled. "Don't do anything illegal, now."

"With a cop in the house? Who's daft now?"

Reading laughed as Gregory Milton entered the room, dropping into his very expensive looking massage chair. He activated the magic and sighed as the chair hummed and he gently vibrated, as if his entire being was slightly out of phase with the world around him.

"How's your back?"

Milton opened his eyes halfway. "Sore, but fine. Searching their car used muscles I'd forgotten about." He drew a breath. "Oh, yeah, that's the spot."

"Should I leave you two alone?"

Milton's eyes remained closed, though he chuckled as his hand gently patted the armrest. "Please. She and I haven't had much time together lately."

Reading smiled. "Don't let Sandra—"

The doorbell rang.

"Can you get that?" called Sandra from another room, her phone conversation with whom he hoped would be his savior, far more important than answering a door. Milton's chair shutoff.

Reading waved him off. "Sit. I'll get it."

"Yes, sir."

Reading pushed himself to his feet, his own muscles aching from his flight and the search. He opened the door to find an extremely attractive Asian woman standing there, a heavy looking duffel bag in her hand. "Yes?"

"Dylan Kane sent me to help."

Reading's eyebrows shot up and he stepped aside. "Come in."

The young woman entered, dropping the duffel bag against the wall as Reading closed the door. He held out his hand. "Agent Hugh Reading, Interpol."

The woman eyed his hand for a moment then shook it, the grip firm.

Very firm.

"Dylan says you can be trusted. My name must not be included in any reports or repeated to anyone."

Reading considered her, wondering just who this woman was. His eyes narrowed as recognition dawned. "Lee Fang."

She gasped, taking two steps back, her head whipping around as if searching for escape routes.

He held out his hand. "It's okay, you're safe here. I'm Interpol, so I recognize you from a report that came across my desk about a year ago. The Chinese government is after you."

She was still a bundle of tensed up muscles, but she nodded.

"Then you'll find no one in this house who wants to do you harm." He held his hand out, motioning toward the living room. "Come, sit down and meet the others."

She took several steps back, toward the living room, when Sandra poked her head out of the kitchen, the phone still pressed against her cheek. She smiled and gave Fang a little wave, pointing at the phone and mouthing a

148

"hello", Fang bowing slightly as she continued to warily back herself deeper into the house, Reading giving the nervous woman her space. He couldn't remember much of the file, not that it would matter, nothing that came from the Chinese ever the complete truth, and more often than not, a total fabrication. The Chinese mindset was like the old Soviet one. Their population believed their lies, so they assumed the outside world would as well.

It was almost laughable.

Just like the new Russia. Soviet Union 2.0 as Acton called them.

"Gregory Milton, I'd like you to meet Lee Fang."

Milton rose from his chair with a wince, shaking the young woman's hand then motioning toward the couch. "Please, have a seat." He dropped back into his own. "I'm sorry, but my back is a little sore."

"From the gunshot wounds you received." She sat down, bowing slightly in her seat at the surprised Milton. "Your recovery is remarkable."

"Umm, thanks." Milton's eyes narrowed. "Ahh, how did you know about that?"

She flushed slightly. "Dylan has briefed me thoroughly on his friends and contacts."

Reading sat in Sandra's chair, not wanting to intimidate the poor woman by sitting beside her on the couch. "Yes, about that. You said Dylan sent you to help us?"

She nodded.

"And just how exactly can you do that?"

She glanced about the room as if searching for the words. "I…let's say I'm *very* qualified."

"And just what are those qualifications?"

She shook her head. "None that I can discuss."

"Ahh," said Milton, smiling. "You're one of *those*."

She flushed again, dropping her head to her chest. "I used to be."

Milton waved his hand, ending the subject. "Enough said, I know you can't get into it."

Sandra entered the room, smiling, the phone gone. She stepped toward Fang who leapt to her feet, bowing. "Oh, dear, aren't you precious. I'm Sandra, Greg's wife."

"Lee Fang."

Sandra motioned toward the couch. "Please, sit. Can I get you anything?"

Fang shook her head, rapidly. "No, thank you."

"So Lee, what brings—"

Milton cut off his wife. "It's Fang, hon. Chinese surnames come first."

Sandra paused, her eyebrows rising slightly. "Oh, I'm sorry." Her eyes narrowed. "Huh, that makes a lot of sense, now that I think about it." She returned to Fang. "*Fang*, what brings you here?"

"Dylan Kane sent me to help."

"Dylan? And how do you know him?"

"We're, umm…" Fang flushed, clearly embarrassed. "Friends?"

Milton laughed. "It's good to hear he's finally settling down."

The poor girl practically turned crimson.

Sandra shot him a look. "Greg, leave the poor girl alone. So, Fang, you're here to help. In what way?"

Fang smiled slightly at Sandra, conveying with her eyes her thanks at being saved from further embarrassment. "I'm to be your liaison with the CIA and Delta teams, and to provide personal security should it become necessary."

"And you're trained for all that?"

She nodded. "Yes."

"Impressive." Sandra rose. "I'm going to make lemonade." She looked down at Fang. "When's the last time you ate?"

Fang shrugged. "I'm not sure. Breakfast?"

"Oh dear, you must be starving. I'll make you a sandwich. Any preferences?"

Fang shook her head, appearing almost too embarrassed to answer.

"BLT?"

Fang's eyes narrowed. "B. L. T?"

"Don't tell me you've never had a BLT before?"

She shook her head. "I-I don't *think* I have."

"Do you like bacon?"

Fang nodded, a little enthusiastically, Reading thought.

"Lettuce?"

"Yes."

"Tomato."

"Yes."

"Then you're going to love this."

Sandra disappeared and Reading turned things to business. "What can we expect?"

Fang sat upright, her posture perfect, all emotion wiped from her face. "Dylan has secured a team at Langley to provide intel. They are in the process of trying to track the professors. Dylan has also contacted Delta operatives he has worked with in the past. I have yet to hear if they will be made available to us, but he was optimistic. Have you made any progress here?"

Reading shook his head. "No. The FBI has essentially cut us completely out of the loop. They know I'm here unofficially and the asshole in charge—sorry, *agent* in charge—has said unless he's told otherwise, I'm to be treated as a witness and nothing more."

"So you aren't aware of the status of their investigation."

"No." Reading pointed to Laura's cellphone, sitting on the table. "I did manage to retrieve that from their vehicle, which was how I got Dylan's number. Other than that, all we know is that they were kidnapped and there have been no ransom demands. It's our belief it was an offshoot of the Triarii that took them."

Fang's head bobbed then she pointed at the phone. "Did you tell the FBI you found that?"

Reading shook his head.

Fang smiled. "In my country they would kill you for that."

Reading grunted. "Good thing we're not in your country, then."

A cloud seemed immediately to form around Fang, her mood noticeably changing.

He leaned forward, lowering his voice. "Hey, are you okay?"

She nodded, sucking in a deep breath. "We all have our problems, none of which will help the professors."

The doorbell rang as Sandra entered with a tray, carrying a pitcher of lemonade and four glasses. "I'll get it," she said, hurrying toward the table.

"Allow me." Fang leapt to her feet and drew a Glock from behind her back as Reading rose. She hurried to the door, her feet like cat's paws, not a sound heard. She peered through the side window, stepping back. "A young Caucasian male, one Asian female, probably Vietnamese."

"Oh, that's Tommy and Mai," called Sandra, "they're good."

Fang opened the door, the gun now hidden, Reading standing about ten feet back, watching the young woman at work.

She seems to know her stuff.

"Hi!" The word caught in Tommy's throat as he got his first look at the stunning Fang. "Umm, wh-who are you?"

Reading stepped forward, Sandra poking her head into the hallway. "Come in, kids, Greg is in the living room."

Mai Trinh eyed Fang then noticed her boyfriend staring. She stepped between them, the jealous girlfriend marking her territory. She extended her hand. "Mai Trinh."

"Lee Fang."

"T-Tommy Granger."

Mai grabbed Tommy by the hand and dragged him into the living room, Fang following, apparently oblivious to the affect she had on the poor young man afflicted with a serious case of Yellow Fever. Reading gave her the once over, discretely, a sudden stabbing pain in his chest causing him to almost gasp as he realized how much she reminded him of Kinti from behind.

He bit his cheek, the pain forcing the nightmare away.

Sandra emerged from the kitchen with two chairs and Reading took them from her. "Allow me."

"Ooh, such a gentleman. Keep it up and I might just trade Greg in for you."

"I heard that!"

"You were meant to!" said Sandra, giving Reading a wink as she disappeared back into the kitchen.

"I was shot in the back, chivalry went with my legs!"

"That excuse lost all meaning when you started walking again!" Sandra reemerged with two additional ice-filled glasses.

She placed them on the tray then gave her husband a peck. "It's okay, dear, when you're fully recovered I'm going to work you to the bone."

Milton reached forward and grabbed her butt, dragging her into the chair with him. "Looking forward to it!" He bit her gently on the shoulder as she giggled.

"Stop, you're terrible!"

He pushed her back to her feet and she fixed her hair. "Sorry you had to see that. My husband knows no bounds."

Reading was grinning, never tiring of seeing friends happy. He just wondered if he'd ever find happiness like that. He and his ex-wife had a few good years, though those memories were so far in the past they were basically gone, the emotions of the events lost to the textbook summary his mind now stored. And the much rawer memories of Kinti were too painful to think of, the joyful thoughts almost always stomped by the images of her painful death.

I'd rather be lonely all my life than experience that type of pain again.

"So you were mentioning the Triarii."

The room became silent at Tommy's words. Reading stared at him. "Excuse me? Where did you hear about them?"

Tommy's stunned expression at Reading's snapped question showed he knew he had overstepped some unknown line. "I'm sorry, I overheard your conversation when you were leaving the lab."

"You should forget that name."

Tommy flushed and Mai's eyes were suddenly wide with worry. She pressed herself against him. "I, umm, I looked them up."

"And I assume you found nothing."

Tommy nodded.

"Good."

"Until I poked around the dark web."

Reading dropped into his seat, closing his eyes. "Bloody hell." He sighed then looked at Tommy. "What did you find?"

"These guys are serious!" said an unleashed Tommy, eager to unburden himself with the knowledge he had apparently gleaned. "They're

154

headquartered in London. Did you know that the thing the professors were caught up in a few years ago was related to them?"

Everyone in the room nodded, much to Tommy and Mai's surprise.

"Oh." The wind in Tommy's sails died. "Umm, what else don't we know?"

Reading's eyes bored into Tommy's. "A lot, and it's going to stay that way for your own protection."

"Okay, umm, well, it might be too late for that. I decided to put some bots out there to watch for anything involving the UK that was unusual, and I found something."

Reading wasn't sure whether he should be angry with the boy or not. "What?"

Tommy fished a tablet from his backpack, tapping it several times before handing it to Reading. It showed a large number of links. "What am I looking at?"

"A bunch of reports coming out of Surrey, just outside of London, about a massive gun fight at an old estate."

Reading felt his chest tighten and he exchanged glances with Milton and his wife before peering back at the screen, Tommy continuing.

"When the police arrived everyone was gone, just the bodies left behind."

"Odd for the UK." Reading turned to Tommy. "What makes you think this has anything to do with Jim and Laura?"

Tommy took the tablet and brought up a photo. "Look at this. It just hit LiveLeak, that's why we came here."

Reading looked at the photo of a dead body then back at Tommy. "So, hardly remarkable."

"No, man, you're missing it. Somebody got shots of things before they cordoned off the area."

"So what?"

"So what? So that means these are photos you're never going to see. The state controls the message, and if the state doesn't want the message to be heard, you're never going to hear it. This"—he jabbed a finger at the tablet—"is the great equalizer. Unfiltered news, available to the masses, uncontrolled by the government and their corporate overlords."

Reading rolled his eyes. "This better be leading somewhere."

Tommy grabbed the tablet, using his fingers to zoom in on the photograph, then jammed it back into Reading's hand. "What do you see?"

Reading glared at him then stared at the photo, now zoomed in on the dead man's wrist.

And gasped.

It was the Triarii tattoo.

1st Special Forces Operational Detachment - Delta HQ, Fort Bragg, North Carolina
A.k.a. "The Unit"

Command Sergeant Major Burt "Big Dog" Dawson stepped into the gym, the sound of the country's best working out hard, music to his ears. He loved training, lived for it, and on most days while on duty and not deployed, his team, Bravo Team, could be found either exercising, training or studying. Not a man in the unit didn't speak multiple languages, were masters at hacking, could shoot, toss, throw or hurl every manner of weapon imaginable, and operate any vehicle, whether car, boat, plane or transport vehicle, that they might encounter in the field.

They were Delta Force, officially 1st Special Forces Operational Detachment—Delta, America's best and most secretive Special Operations force, and the only military unit that could legally operate on American soil should the President deem it necessary, he having the power to suspend Posse Comitatus for this unit only.

They were lethal, they were dangerous, and they were dancing.

Dawson shook his head, a smile on his face as Jimmy and Niner danced in synch in the square circle, Atlas standing in one corner looking on in disbelief, Spock in the other, both with gloves on, there apparently a bout underway.

Dawson walked toward them, the rest of his team surrounding the ring. "What is this?"

Sergeant Carl "Niner" Sung waved. "We're the half-time entertainment." Sergeant Gerry "Jimmy Olsen" Hudson spun, pushed his ass out toward Dawson, then smacked it with an "Oooh", repeated

157

immediately by Niner, who added a smack to Jimmy's ass. "We've been practicing."

"I can tell. Let's see how that goes over in Raqqa. The ISIS boys will probably toss you off a building."

Niner blew kisses to the clapping onlookers then daintily held the ropes for Jimmy to exit the ring. "A good USO show is what those boys need. They need to loosen up. All that killin' and goat humpin' has got to make a man tense."

Dawson chuckled as the others gathered around him, Atlas and Spock leaning on the ropes. "I've got something, off the books, if anyone's interested."

Sergeant Leon "Atlas" James swept Spock's feet from under him, the operator smacking the floor, hard. "I'm in. Not sure about him."

Sergeant Will "Spock" Lightman rolled onto his back, cocking an eyebrow as he stared up at Atlas. "Not exactly fair."

"Life isn't fair. You think just because BD starts to talk, the enemy won't attack? I don't think so."

Niner leapt up onto the ring, grabbing the top rope and swinging over it, launching two feet squarely into the massive Atlas' chest.

The man didn't budge, Niner merely dropping unceremoniously onto the canvas.

And Spock.

Atlas feigned a shot at Niner's face.

"Hey, not the face. I'm too pretty and besides, I plan on being a male model when this career is over."

"Now that I'd pay to see." Atlas reached down and hauled Spock to his feet, his massive muscles rippling, his nickname assigned in his early days when someone spotted him working out on one knee, a large medicine ball on his shoulder, Atlas Shrugged immediately coming to someone's mind. It was a nickname Atlas bore with pride.

Niner helped himself to his feet, Atlas not offering a hand. "Huh, I didn't know you swung on that side of the vine." Niner bent over and smacked his ass, replaying the end of his dance. "How's that? Feelin' something?"

Atlas turned to Dawson. "Please, BD, if we go on an op, can we leave him behind?"

Dawson shook his head, the smile gone. "Fun's over. Yesterday Professor Acton and his wife were kidnapped at gunpoint at the Home Depot in Annapolis. Several people were killed. Eye witnesses say those killed were the first to attempt the abduction, then a second group arrived, killed the first group, then took the professors."

Niner whistled. "Christ, these two are just magnets for trouble. Who's so hated that *two* groups try to kidnap them at once?"

Dawson continued. "Acton's phone was destroyed and tossed out of the van, Professor Palmer's was left at the scene."

Jimmy, his nickname earned after someone learned he had been editor of his high school paper, sat perched on the edge of the ring. "Any contact since?"

"None, however Agent Hugh Reading—you all remember him"—nods from all around—"had a meeting with the Triarii—"

Niner groaned. "Shit, not them again?"

"Yup, one and the same. They are claiming that Martin Chaney has betrayed the organization and is behind their abduction. At this point we don't know who the good guys are and who the bad guys are, but your mission, should you choose to accept it—"

Niner pointed at Dawson, looking at the others. "I like that."

"—is to accompany me and try to effect a rescue."

Atlas' hand darted out, shoving Niner off his feet. "Do we know where they are?"

Dawson shook his head as Niner mooned Atlas. "No clue at this point, but CIA is going to start feeding us intel shortly." Dawson paused, everyone becoming serious again. "This is off the books with the Colonel's nod, so this is voluntary."

Atlas stood up straight, his eyes squarely on Dawson. "That pretty lady has had too many bad things happen to her. I'm in."

Spock stepped forward, joining Atlas. "Me too. Those two saved our asses getting us out of Saudi Arabia. I owe them one."

Niner dusted himself off, standing beside Atlas. "Same here. If it wasn't for them, I'd probably be in some Vietnamese prison."

Jimmy opened his mouth, but Dawson waved him off. "Sorry, buddy, I can only take three. Red needs you and the others for an op."

Jimmy frowned, clearly not pleased. "Any idea what?"

"You're headed to Columbia to do some training."

Niner punched Jimmy. "Shoulda spoke up sooner."

"I was being polite."

"What are you, Canadian?"

Dawson smacked his hands together. "Okay, say your goodbyes, get yourselves squared away, and be ready to leave on a moment's notice. Hopefully we'll get a phone call that they turned up at a romantic retreat, but with the Triarii involved, I think we're not going to get that lucky."

Northern Gaul, Roman Empire

November 1, 64 AD

Flavus swung his sword, slicing open the stomach of a filthy Gaul, stopping him in his tracks as he gripped at his innards spilling over his hands. But Flavus had already moved on, the battle continuing to rage, the Legion attacked in strength from all sides. The screams of the dying from both parties surrounded him, the pounding of hooves, the clanging of metal on metal, of fist on flesh, was overwhelming, and though his fellow Romans were holding their own, they were losing too many.

They would prevail tonight, hopefully, yet it wouldn't matter.

They were too few to make it to Britannia.

It was time.

He glanced over at his legate, directing the battle from his command tent, the man calm through it all.

He would miss him.

"Triarii, with me!" he shouted, his sword raised high.

A roar rose from the teeming masses and a wedge of men formed around him, they already informed of what would happen should things look dire. They charged through the hordes of attackers, slicing through the lines like an arrow through a buck's hide.

Something leapt through the air to his left. He spun to see a Gaul clear the line of men guarding him, swinging an axe. It grazed Flavus' shoulder and he cried out as he swung his sword, cleaving the man's head in two. As he continued forward he reached behind him, feeling for the cloth bag carrying the skull, sighing in relief that it was still intact.

The brave warriors of the Triarii, the third and final line of defense of the Thirteenth Legion, carved through the enemy and reached the tree line, a rear guard forming to block any pursuers, Flavus and the rest charging forward through the trees, encountering fewer and fewer of the enemy. They pressed onward, the din of the battle behind them growing faint until soon there was nothing.

Flavus signaled a halt in a clearing and they stopped, the Triarii that remained, less than thirty, forming a circle around him, though all eyes were on the distance, the battle casting an orange, flickering glow on the thick clouds overhead.

"I can't believe we left them," said one of the men.

Flavus felt the same, and though he was young, he knew this type of talk would do no good. "We have our orders. They sacrificed themselves for the good of Rome. Our mission is to get this skull to Britannia and to end the curse it has inflicted upon our home and her people."

He began to strip off his armor and other accoutrements of the trade, leaving it in a pile, the others reluctantly doing the same. Within minutes, they appeared not as the most elite of Roman soldiers, but mere weary peasants.

Not worthy of attention.

Flavus turned to the men. "I know I am young and inexperienced, but by rank I am the senior officer."

The most senior of the remaining Triarii snapped to attention. "Your orders shall not be questioned!"

The others all turned to face Flavus, snapping to attention, their shoulders square, their heads held high with pride.

Flavus smiled. "Good, I had no doubt. You are all the best Rome has to offer, and together we shall protect her from the cursed evil that this statue represents." He raised his sword, pointing it toward the sky over the distant battle, the others joining him as they faced their comrades still being slaughtered. "We the Triarii salute our fallen brothers! May the gods protect the souls of the Thirteenth Legion and grant the fallen their much deserved peace in Elysium!"

The Triarii roared in unison, three times, then dropped to a knee, burying their swords into the ground as they bowed their heads.

"May I join you?"

The men leapt to their feet, all swords pointed toward the voice emerging from the darkness.

"Halt, who goes there?"

"A friend, I assure you."

A little old man was quickly surrounded as he approached Flavus.

"And who are you, old man?" asked Flavus, the man appearing vaguely familiar.

"I am Ananias, the keeper of the skull you now possess."

Operations Center 2, CIA Headquarters, Langley, Virginia
Present Day

"What have you got?"

Leroux entered the operations center, swiftly taking his spot at the hub of activity, his team manning the various terminals surrounding him as his eyes came to rest on the massive displays arcing around the front of the room.

One of his techs, Randy Child, pointed at the center screen. "Homeland reports that Professor Acton's and Palmer's passports were used yesterday for a charter flight to England."

Leroux's eyebrows shot up. "Really? Do we have footage showing it was actually them?"

Child nodded, hitting a few keys, footage immediately playing that showed the two missing professors exiting the private terminal, unaccompanied.

What the hell is going on here? Are we on a wild goose chase?

An ember of anger formed at the thought of what he was missing back at the hotel thanks to these two people, who looked for all intents and purposes to be heading on a rather well-heeled vacation, something he could never dream of affording.

"They arrived in England seven hours later at a private terminal at Easton Airport, and were met by these people."

Leroux's eyes narrowed, the anger subsiding slightly.

These guys don't look like valets.

"Any IDs yet?"

Child nodded. "Yup." The image zoomed in on the man who seemed to be the center of attention. "This is Rodney Underwood."

The name sounded vaguely familiar. "Why do I know that name?"

"He was an employee at the British Museum, a security guard at the time of the incident in London with Delta. All the files on that op are classified way beyond my clearance, so there's not much more I can tell you, but since Professor Palmer used to be head of archeology there, I think there's a good chance she knows him, and since his employment terminated right after those events, I'm guessing he was involved somehow."

Leroux nodded, the file now recalled, and it was indeed way above Child's security clearance. "Logical assumption." Leroux frowned. "So, we've got two wealthy professors, boarding a private jet alone, landing in England, and being met by someone one of them used to work with." He shook his head. "Could this just be an innocent trip? They didn't tell people their plans?"

Sonya Tong, another analyst who happened to carry a torch for her boss, spoke up. "That wouldn't explain the shooting at the mall, nor this." She tapped some keys and another image appeared of Rodney Underwood. She zoomed in on his left side, a shoulder holster clearly visible. "That's something you don't see often in the UK."

Leroux agreed. "True."

"And also, Professor Palmer didn't pay for the flight."

Leroux's eyebrows rose slightly as he turned to Tong. "She has a private jet, doesn't she?"

Sonya nodded as she tapped the keyboard, a flurry of scanned receipts and bookings flashing on one of the displays. "She's part of a sharing network. That's basically how they've been travelling the past couple of years, exclusively. If this were some planned getaway, wouldn't they have flown on one of the jets available to her? And even if it wasn't, from her records, she seems to be able to get one at a moment's notice."

Leroux pursed his lips, processing the intel. Two rich professors with a penchant for getting into trouble, definitely kidnapped—or perhaps rescued—now apparently voluntarily boarding a private jet paid for by someone else, then landing in London and meeting a former security guard, possibly tied up with the Triarii affair from several years ago.

Something didn't add up.

"They're being coerced."

Everyone turned around to face him. "What are you thinking?" asked Child.

"I'm thinking that someone tried to kidnap them. Someone else intervened, saving them. But if their saviors did it for purely altruistic reasons, then the professors would have been released by now. Instead, they board a plane for London. They wouldn't do that, not with what had happened in the parking lot. They would know the authorities and their friends and families would be looking for them, worried." He shook his head. "They got on that plane, but it wasn't by choice." He turned to Child. "Do we know where they went after they landed?"

Child shook his head. "Not yet. We're having CCTV footage pulled, but it's going to take some time. But"—he held up a finger—"I may have a lead on that."

"What?"

His fingers flew over the keyboard then Child pointed at the screen, LiveLeak videos appearing. "We've been pulling anything unusual in the UK after their arrival, and found this."

Leroux watched several different videos displaying simultaneously of what appeared to be a busy crime scene, dozens of emergency vehicles involved, along with reporters and onlookers. "What am I looking at?"

"The aftermath of a shootout. A *very* bloody, *very* violent shootout. Lots of bodies. But look at this." A video appeared on the main screen of a body on a gurney, a gust of wind catching the sheet covering it, revealing the face. A tap of a key and the image froze. "Now look." Another image appeared beside the dead man's face, a file photo of one Rodney Underwood.

Leroux whistled. "Christ, that's him!" He looked around at his team. "Excellent work, people. Soon you won't need me to bother coming in."

Smiles were exchanged, Sonya's longing eyes suggesting that wasn't the outcome she had been hoping for.

"Okay, so I think we can safely say the professors may have ended up here." He paused as he realized what that meant, the footage showing body after body wheeled past. "We need to find out if any of the bodies match their description."

"I'm on it," said Child.

"And see if we had a bird over the area. I want to see if we have anything showing this going down."

Milton Residence, St. Paul, Maryland

Reading woke to the sound of his phone ringing on the nightstand. He sat up, removing the CPAP that had arrived within less than an hour of Sandra's call, all properly set and ready for him.

It's who you know.

He glanced at the phone, it an unknown caller. He hit the button turning off the machine and pulled the mask from his face.

"Hello?"

"Agent Reading, this is the Proconsul of the Triarii."

Reading was immediately alert, the clock on the wall suggesting he had been asleep for a little over an hour, though with the miracle of the CPAP, that one hour would last him for another eight. "You have news?"

"Yes. Mr. Chaney's people have taken the professors to an unknown location."

Reading frowned. "How do you know this?"

"A lot has happened, Agent. It would appear that the professors were working for Mr. Chaney, apparently willingly."

"Why wouldn't they? They know him, he's a good man."

"He's not the man you once knew, Agent."

"I'll be the judge of that."

"Well, have you heard what happened in England tonight?"

Reading frowned. "You mean the mass shooting?"

"Yes."

"What of it?"

"That was a result of Mr. Chaney and his Deniers attacking our compound."

Reading felt his chest tighten. "Are Jim and Laura okay?"

"They survived the attack, if that's what you mean."

"What the bloody hell does that mean? They're either okay or they're not!"

"I mean, Agent, that they survived the attack then left with Mr. Chaney and his men for a location known only to them."

Reading's hand shot up and grasped his temples, massaging them. "I don't understand."

"The Deniers now have all thirteen skulls and they plan on uniting them."

"Frankly, sir, I don't give a shit about the skulls. I want Jim and Laura back."

"I don't think you understand, Agent. Professor Acton and Professor Palmer left with Mr. Chaney, voluntarily."

Reading froze. "Excuse me?"

"They left with him quite willingly."

Reading shook his head, knowing his friend well enough that the ridiculous notion could indeed be true. "Why the hell would they do that?"

"Part curiosity, part, I think, hoping they could stop them if anything went wrong."

Reading pursed his lips. "They're not buying into this garbage, are they?"

"Perhaps, perhaps not, but I will ask you one thing, Agent Reading. What was your reaction when you first saw the skull from the British Museum. The genuine one, not the fake."

Reading shrugged. "I don't know. It was impressive. Beautiful, I guess."

"Any physical reaction?"

Reading thought back to that moment in Laura Palmer's flat when the skull had been first revealed to him. He remembered cradling it in his hands, of the uneasy feeling that had spread over him. "I don't know. Butterflies maybe. Wait, I think I shivered. Is that what you mean? Come to think of it, I shivered when I saw the skull in Venice."

"As most people do. Do you know why?"

"Because it's goddamned creepy looking?"

The Proconsul chuckled. "To some, yes, but even we who are so used to them have the same reaction."

Reading rolled his eyes. "Listen, if you're trying to suggest that it's some sort of magical power, I'm not buying it, and I can't see Jim buying it either."

"Yet he did go with them."

Reading sighed. He couldn't explain away that one fact. "Where did they go?"

"I don't know, but I will."

Reading sat up a little straighter. "How?"

"We planted trackers on the professors, unbeknownst to them, and they are still transmitting. We have what little remains of our people trying to get to them, but I'm afraid our situation isn't what it once was."

"What do you mean?"

"Many of our people are dead. The Triarii is fractured down the middle, and most of our funds have been stolen or frozen, each council member having a substantial portion of our money under their direct control. When the council split, they took their funds with them. And after the events of London a few years ago, it had taken many millions to cover that up, draining a significant portion of our reserves."

"So you're broke."

"Compared to before, yes, but we do have funds. Our problem at the moment is manpower. It is spread across the world, with half of it out of touch with their primary contact now on the wrong side."

"So you need help."

"Frankly, yes."

Reading rose. "I may be able to get you it, but you'll probably want to stay out of their way."

"Why?"

"They'll be the same people who killed most of your staff in London."

"I see. Can they be trusted?"

Reading grunted. "I trust them more than you."

The Proconsul chuckled. "I can understand that. All I ask is that they do nothing to harm the skulls."

Reading strode out of the room, heading for the stairs. "Their priority will be Jim and Laura, anything beyond that is of no concern to me."

"Very well. When they are done, please let us know so we can send people in to recover the skulls."

"I'll see what I can do."

"That's all I can ask."

"Do you have any idea where they might be heading?"

"Our best guess at the moment is Iceland."

Reading's eyebrows shot up as he entered the living room, everyone turning expectantly. "Really?"

"It makes sense. It's close, yet remote. If something goes wrong, I assume they are hoping to minimize civilian casualties."

"How thoughtful of them. Let me know when you know for certain."

"I will."

Reading ended the call, turning to Fang. "Tell Delta to head for Iceland immediately."

The Unit, Fort Bragg, North Carolina

"It looks like they might be heading for Iceland."

Dawson's eyes widened slightly at the news from Lee Fang. He had been to Iceland before for some survival training, though that was it. He had never fired a shot there, and in his wildest dreams—save Red Storm Rising fantasies—had never thought he would.

Looks like you might get your chance.

"Do we have any idea how many hostiles?"

"Negative, and the destination is just a best guess from the Triarii."

"What makes them think they're heading there?"

"They've apparently placed trackers on the professors."

"Huh. Let's hope these Deniers don't figure that out."

"Yes."

Dawson sensed Fang hesitate. "What is it?"

"Well, with the little I know about the Triarii, I don't trust them."

Dawson grunted. "Neither do I, but from what I know, they are standup people, though misguided and singular in their beliefs. When will we know?"

"If they are indeed heading for Iceland, then shortly."

Dawson nodded. "Okay, we've got a jet on standby here. We'll head for Iceland now and change course if need be. Have Leather's team head there as well."

"I will."

"Good, I'll make some calls and make sure some transport and equipment is ready for us when we arrive."

"Good luck."

HM Coroner's Court, Woking, United Kingdom

"Agent Reading sends his regards, and appreciates you taking the time to help us out."

The coroner, Alicia Malone, nodded, pulling out the final drawer holding the victims from the recent slaughter outside London. "How is Hugh doing? I haven't seen him since he went to work for Interpol."

"I haven't seen him in a while, but my understanding is he is doing well. Getting to see more of the world than I think he anticipated."

Malone laughed. "I can't picture him the world traveler, he's so stuck in his old ways."

Leather smiled as he checked wrist after wrist while Malone wasn't looking, each one branded with the Triarii tattoo. He stopped bothering after the fourth, it clear this was indeed a Triarii incident. "This is all of them?"

"Yes."

"Any wounded?"

"Yes, but we've confirmed none of them are Professor Palmer or Acton."

"Good." Leather finished checking the faces of the deceased, relieved to find neither of his charges lying on slabs. "Any leads on who did this?"

Malone shook her head. "No, not yet. We've had some reports of helicopter activity in the area so we're trying to track that down, but the type of people who do this don't file flight plans."

"True." Leather handed her his card. "This is my personal cellphone. Please call me if you come up with anything. Professor Palmer has been good to me and my men. I'd hate to let her down."

Malone began pushing the bodies back into their drawers. "Reading tells me you're ex-SAS."

Leather smiled, but said nothing.

Malone chuckled. "Okay, I get it. If I hear anything, I'll let you know."

Leather bowed slightly then left the chilly room, his phone vibrating in his pocket. "Hello?"

"Hello, sir, this is Lee Fang. Our Triarii contacts indicate they have tagged the professors and are tracking them. Best guess on their destination is Iceland. Delta is heading there now."

"How many?"

"Only four."

"Any intel on how many we're facing?"

"None, but I'm guessing much more than four."

Leather grunted. "Me too. Okay, I've got six here. We'll be wheels up in less than an hour."

"I'll inform the others and send you updates as we receive them. Good luck."

Leather shoved his phone in his pocket as his body continued to warm up.

Only four Delta.

With him and his six, they were eleven against God only knew how many.

This could turn bad, fast.

Off the coast of Britannia
December 25, 64 AD

Flavus coiled the rope around his forearm, gripping the side of the boat with all his might, and only one arm, the other clenching the bag containing the skull. He wasn't about to lose it now, not after all they had been through, not after so many had died.

But the storm they were battling had other intentions.

The winds howled, the waves crashed, the rain stung, yet they hung on. He wiped the water from his eyes, trying to spot the others. Dark shadows of those closest were barely visible, the other side of their boat nothing but a gray blur.

He heard someone cry out, a dark form sliding down the deck toward him. As he neared, Flavus caught sight of a face, it the old man from the forest, the old man he had recognized from Rome, lurking in the background near the skull. His face was filled with terror as their eyes met. Flavus began to move the bag to free up a hand when the old man held out his hands, shaking his head as he continued to slide, the prow high now.

"No, you mustn't! Save the skull! Forget me!"

One of the surviving Triarii reached out of the darkness, grabbing him and pulling him to safety as the prow slammed back down, another wave crashing over the deck. Flavus saw the old man secured with a rope, he now safe. He gripped the bag containing the crystal skull tighter. The old man had been willing to die for it, had tracked them all the way from Rome, and had somehow known the deception perpetrated, finding them in the woods, away from the battle they were meant to die in.

175

Yet he had given no explanation, other than that he was an old man—a *very* old man—and was meant to be with the skull.

Flavus had ordered him away, and he had complied, yet he had kept trailing them in the distance.

It had been an annoyance at first, but annoyance had turned to admiration that a man so old could keep up with the finest Rome had to offer.

He had invited him to their fire after the third night.

He hadn't left their side since.

The prow rose once again, someone else crying out, the shriek fading into the distance, another of their dwindling number lost to the gods.

We truly are *cursed.*

He wanted to throw it overboard, to rid them of what he now believed was the cause of their misery. It had nearly destroyed Rome, had led to the slaughter of the Thirteenth, and now was doing its utmost to remove the Triarii from the gods' creation.

Something flew toward him from the darkness, smacking him on the head. He cried out in pain, the world flashing between black and gray as he stumbled to his knees then collapsed, his left arm still tied to the boat, the skull underneath him, the storm fading in the distance.

"Flavus!"

Flavus moaned.

"Sir, are you okay?"

He moaned again, the voice closer now, the fog in his ears slowly clearing.

Seagulls?

His eyes fluttered open then shut again, the sun bright. He opened them a slit.

"Sir, are you okay?"

He looked toward the voice, recognizing one of his men. "Yes." He held his arm out. "Help me up."

Hauled to his feet, he stared back at the now calm seas. It was as if it were an entirely different body of water than the one that had tried to kill them earlier. "Where are we? Elysium?"

The man chuckled. "I doubt that, there's no way they'd let me in." He pointed at stark white cliffs nearby. "I believe we're in Britannia."

Flavus smiled, suddenly noticing the bag the skull was in, still gripped tightly in his arm. He looked about. "How many?"

"Only six from our boat, sir, but look." He pointed farther ashore, at least a dozen more of his men rushing toward them, waving.

"Thank the gods!" Flavus dropped to his knees and kissed the sands of his new home, knowing those of his beloved Rome were forever lost to him.

The landscape was barren, grays rather than greens dominating nature's palette here. And it was cold. They had been travelling for hours on the highway that ringed the island nation of Iceland, and Acton wondered what would happen should someone's vehicle actually break down here.

It was as barren as the moon.

Which might be why Apollo astronauts trained here in the sixties.

Fortunately being stranded wasn't a possibility for them, there several vehicles in their convoy. He sat in the back of one of the SUVs, Laura beside him, Chaney in the passenger seat with an unnamed driver. Laura's head rested on his shoulder, she having passed out from exhaustion over an hour ago.

He was still running on adrenaline, though he'd be crashing soon. He just hoped he'd last long enough in case he had to take some sort of action. Escape wasn't his endgame. In fact, he couldn't quite believe he was here. The entire notion that there was some sort of power inside these sculptures was ridiculous, yet he couldn't deny some things. Laura had convinced him that no known method—modern or ancient—could manufacture them, unless some forgotten technique had been used. They had been found spread out across the world over millennia, all manner of cultures possessing them.

They were an enigma.

And he couldn't explain the physical reaction he had almost every time he was near one.

The shiver.

A tingling sensation racing up his spine then spreading out over his body. He was certain it was just a physiological response to an emotional reaction. It was hardly the first time he had shivered. Lots of eerie moments in his life, whether it was out on a dark night, deep in a damp cave, crawling through a narrow passage leading to an ancient chamber not seen in thousands of years, or just watching a great horror movie, all had led to a shiver exactly like it.

The skulls were creepy looking, and the way light would gather in the eye sockets gave it the appearance it was glaring at you.

Definitely enough to trigger a psychological reaction.

No magic involved.

So why was he here?

He looked at his sleeping wife and knew she was part of it. She believed there was something special about the skulls, beyond their unknown method of manufacture. She had told him once she believed that when man was ready to understand them, then their secrets would be revealed.

Definitely not very scientific.

Yet that was only part of it.

He was here for his own reasons. Perhaps it was his penchant for sticking his nose where it didn't belong, or his sometimes nearly fatal curiosity. Whatever it was, something had compelled him to come along. Though he was positive nothing would come of this, he couldn't deny himself the opportunity, no matter how slim, to see what could be a discovery that would change mankind forever.

And tonight, what was sure to be the biggest disappointment in the Triarii's two thousand year history, would soon be over, and his involvement with these people would be too. He and Laura would head home, and the skulls would be done with.

A disappointment for Laura, for certain, though the mystery of how they had been made would remain.

And he was sure the true believers would claim they just hadn't been ready to receive the power, and the mystery would continue, left for a future generation of Triarii to challenge.

A generation he hoped would come long after he was dead and buried.

They crested a rise and Chaney pointed. "Do you see it?"

Acton leaned forward, disturbing Laura who woke, rubbing her eyes.

"Are we there?" she asked.

"Apparently."

Acton searched the area Chaney was pointing at yet saw nothing, just rock. Nothing but rock. Laura poked her head between the seats beside him. His eyes suddenly narrowed, spotting something then losing it as the car dipped slightly. He caught it again, still not sure what he was looking at. It still appeared to be rock, but there was something wrong, something out of place.

"Do you see it?"

Acton shook his head. "No, but yes. I don't see it, but I know there's something there, something wrong."

Chaney chuckled. "Then the designers got it right." He pointed slightly to the left. "Look at the dark spots."

Acton leaned further forward, still seeing nothing, when suddenly it all snapped into focus. He gasped. "I see it!" The dark spots were too symmetrical, too smooth, whatever they were apparently not lending themselves to the camouflage the rest of the facility utilized. Laura gasped beside him as she too finally spotted it.

"What is it?"

Chaney turned in his seat. "A location we've been preparing for over a decade for just this occasion."

Acton looked at him then back at the rapidly approaching installation. "What, some sort of Dr. No lab?"

Chaney chuckled. "Exactly, just a lot less evil."

Multiple Austin Powers lines leapt to mind, but Acton bit his tongue as the driver reached up and pressed a button, a large chunk of rock just down the road and to their left sinking into the ground. The driver slowed, making the turn quickly. Acton leaned back in his seat, Laura beside him, gripping his arm as they sped through a narrow road cut into the volcanic rock. Acton glanced back to see the other two vehicles behind them, the large rock rising as they passed, hiding their path from the road. Looking to the sides his eyes narrowed. He leaned toward the window and stared up, suddenly realizing the road had been cut so deep, that the stone arced over their heads, leaving only a sliver of sky visible.

It was probably completely hidden from aerial view unless you knew to look for it.

And why would anyone?

"Very impressive."

Chaney smiled. "This is nothing. Just wait." He pointed at a looming stone outcropping, the driver not slowing down. Suddenly the wall parted like a massive set of French doors and they plunged into the darkness, the vehicle immediately tipping forward as they descended what Acton had to hope was a ramp. He glanced back at the other vehicles, the doors already closing behind them, the sliver of light from outside suddenly gone.

Lights flooded the entire area, forcing Acton to blink a few times to adjust. He turned toward the front and gasped as Laura gripped his arm.

"Unbelievable!"

Hilton Reykjavik Nordica, Reykjavik, Iceland

Someone knocked at the door of the hotel room, killing the conversation. Dawson motioned toward Niner and Spock to check it out. Both drew their weapons and made for the door in silence. Niner peered through the peephole and waved Spock off.

"It's Leather." He opened the door and Leather's team entered without saying anything, the last man closing the door.

Dawson rose, shaking Leather's hand as everyone introduced themselves. "This room is too tight for everyone. I've got two rooms next door for your team plus equipment. Get a quick bite and get your equipment squared away. We're leaving in one hour." Dawson pointed to a table near the door, two cardkeys sitting on it. "Six-twelve and Six-fourteen."

Leather nodded to his team and the room quickly thinned out, Leather remaining. "Sitrep?"

Dawson motioned to an empty chair then spun a laptop toward him with a map of the island. "They took a vehicle around the island, so we've gained a lot of time."

"Nice of them. I thought these guys were well funded. Why not take a chopper?"

"I'm guessing they don't want ATC wondering where they're going. If they've got an installation here, chances are the government doesn't know about it, and frequent air traffic might demand an investigation." Dawson smiled. "Luckily, *we* have no such concerns, so I've arranged two choppers that will carry us to their last known location, which is here." He pointed to a glowing red dot along the northern coast. "This is where their signals were cut off. We're assuming they're inside some sort of shielded structure, but satellite images from Langley are showing nothing."

"New images arriving now," said Niner, clicking a few keys. "Sending them to your laptop."

Dawson opened up the new images. "These are better."

"Much," agreed Niner as he zoomed in, Dawson doing the same. He and Leather leaned in closer, examining the area, two red dots indicating the last known location of the professors, the entire area rock with little else, the ring road in the bottom of the frame. "I'm not seeing anything, are you?"

Leather shook his head then pointed at a sliver in the photo, leading from the ring road to the dots. "Is that a road?"

Dawson zoomed in the photo some more. "Can't be. It's way too narrow to fit a vehicle."

Atlas peered at their screen. "Some sort of lava tube or whatever they're called, the top of it eroded away maybe?"

Spock nodded. "Or a channel cut by glacier runoff. That could mean it's hollow inside, big enough to hold a vehicle."

Niner opened his mouth to say something when he stopped, pressing a finger to his headset. "I've got that call from Langley."

Dawson motioned to the speaker at the center of the table and Niner activated it. Dawson leaned in. "This is Zero-One, you're on speaker, all trusted personnel."

"Hello Zero-One, Control Actual." Dawson smiled slightly, recognizing the voice of the analyst he had dealt with on several previous occasions, Chris Leroux. He was young, though good at his job—in fact, excellent at his job. He had the added bonus of being a good friend of Dylan Kane's, and if Kane trusted him, Dawson did too. "I'm calling about your request to retask a bird on that area. As this is a semi-unauthorized mission, I wasn't able to get that for you, but the regularly scheduled bird just flew past. I've got footage streaming to you now."

Dawson pointed at the laptops and Niner nodded, pulling up the stream and spinning it around so everyone could see. "I've got that footage now, Control."

"Good. As you can see, there's nothing obvious there. Just a bunch of volcanic rock. But watch what happens when you switch to thermal." The stream suddenly switched, everything a dull blue or black, with several large red and yellow hotspots. "You see the hotspots?"

Dawson nodded. "Yes."

"Obviously those shouldn't be there. They've done an excellent job at heat dispersion, and if you weren't looking for something, you'd just dismiss it as either volcanic activity of heat retention from the sun."

Dawson pursed his lips, glancing at the others. "But we're sure it's neither."

"Yes. No matter how much you want to hide things, you need some sort of exhaust for your ventilation system. In cases like this, you try to pipe it away from your location so if it's discovered, at least your main site is still secure."

"But how do we know these heat sources are from exhaust ports?"

"From this image, you can't. But as the satellite continued, we got an angle shot." The screen changed and a new image appeared. "Do you see it?"

Dawson leaned in then smiled, his head bobbing as he leaned back so the others could look. It was clearly a rectangle, clearly manmade.

"Looks like a grate," observed Atlas, his booming voice excited. "I think he's found it."

"That's our assessment as well," said Leroux. "This appears to be their final destination, and the facility appears to be underground, which would explain why their tracking devices stopped transmitting."

"We'll be heading there in less than an hour."

"Understood."

"Any signs of sentry guns? After what happened in London, I don't want to be walking into a wall of lead."

"We've been going over the images and we haven't been able to find anything, however that doesn't mean they're not there. The ones they used in London were designed to be completely hidden until it's too late."

Dawson frowned, everyone exchanging glances. He hated automated defenses, which was one of the reasons air support was so important. Bomb the shit out of an area, and you had a good chance of taking out any sentry guns.

That wasn't an option in Iceland.

"Any signs of a way in?"

"Nothing beyond the vent."

Dawson leaned in, examining the image. "What's the scale on that? Can we fit?"

"You can definitely fit through the opening. No promises as to the rest of the way, or where it goes. They'll probably be monitoring it so you'll need to bypass any security."

Niner leaned toward the speaker. "Any idea where they're getting their power?"

"Good question."

"Of course."

Leroux chuckled, Atlas punching Niner in the shoulder. "Respect, dude!"

"There's no evidence of any wind or solar, and not enough heat is being vented for diesel or some other type of fossil fuel generator."

"Batteries?" suggested Spock.

"They'd still need to be vented, and to be charged. But, we did find this." A new photo appeared showing the waterline and some sort of manmade structure extending into the water."

"What the hell is that?" asked Niner.

"Our guess is they have some sort of tidal generator, and the electricity is fed into the facility through wires underneath this covering."

Dawson nodded. "So if we cut those, they go dark."

"They'll probably have some sort of battery capacity that will kick in, but someone will definitely poke their head outside to take a look."

Dawson smiled. "And that will tell us where the damned door is." He checked his watch. "Okay, anything else?"

"Not at this time, but we're still going over the data. If we find out anything, we'll contact you."

"Good. We leave in thirty mikes."

Denier Installation, Iceland

"My God, I feel like I'm on the set of a James Bond movie!"

"Thanks," replied Chaney, he leading Acton and Laura deeper into the buried facility. "I have to admit that every time I come here, I get goosebumps."

It was everything Acton could do to keep his jaw shut, each new glimpse causing it to drop, Chaney freely answering all their questions as they walked through massive open areas with vehicles, piping, ducts, cable bundles and more, along with dozens upon dozens of personnel in color coded jumpsuits. It was a marvel of modern engineering, built inside what appeared to be long dormant magma chambers.

"This must have cost a fortune," said Laura, her head on a swivel just like his.

"It did."

"Where did you get the money?"

"The Triarii is very wealthy."

"Yes, but you're not the Triarii."

Chaney tossed a smile over his shoulder at her. "Noo, but many who controlled the purse strings joined us." He extended his hands to either side, encompassing the sight before them. "It's the dawn of a new age, Professor, and many of our people wanted to join us in our quest. This entire facility is a dream taken form, a means to an end we've been seeking for two thousand years."

Acton stared at what appeared to be massive capacitors. "And when it's all over, and you've either proven or disproven your theory, what then?"

Chaney paused, turning to face them. "I would hope we could find peace among ourselves and reunite, stronger than ever, knowing once and for all the answers to the questions we have been asking for so long."

Laura looked at him. "You truly are convinced this will work."

"Absolutely." He smiled, leaning slightly toward her. "And Professor, I think you are too, otherwise you wouldn't be here." He tilted his head toward Acton. "And you as well."

Acton smiled slightly, wagging a finger. "Don't mistake my being here for anything other than self-preservation. Scientists were afraid that if they detonated the first atomic bomb, it might start a chain reaction that would destroy the entire planet."

"Yet it didn't."

"No, after a bunch of mathematics, they were *pretty sure* it wouldn't. Yet they weren't a hundred percent, and they went ahead anyway."

Laura nodded. "And many feared turning on the Large Hadron Collider would create a wormhole that would consume the planet."

Chaney chuckled. "And again, it didn't."

Acton shook his head. "I'm not sure if that thing's at full power yet, so the jury might still be out on that one."

Chaney laughed. "Sceptics. Think of it this way, Professors, if a wormhole *is* created, none of us will care, will we?"

Acton grunted. "We will for a few seconds."

Chaney snorted. "And I'm sure they've got someone on a kill switch, just in case they spot something odd."

Acton pulled in a slow breath, any levity gone. "And that's why I'm here. I kill this if anything strange happens. Agreed?"

Chaney bowed. "Absolutely. We're here to learn, not destroy. Tonight is the beginning of what will be a fascinating chapter in humanity's history."

Laura's eyes narrowed as they resumed walking. "Haven't you already had time for experiments? You've had nine skulls now for days."

"Our scientists have been working hard on getting things ready for today's final experiment. The machine is only now ready to go online, which was why we triggered the endgame when we did. We now have all thirteen skulls, and the machine that we've been working on for a decade is ready."

"What machine?" asked Acton.

"One designed to safely harness the energy released by the skulls."

Acton shook his head, giving Laura a look behind Chaney's back. "Energy you've never actually witnessed."

"Personally, no, but we know what happened in London in 1212. That disaster won't be repeated."

"If only *three* skulls destroyed half of London, how could you possible hope to handle *thirteen*?"

Chaney stopped in front of a set of doors, flanked by two guards with very serious looking FN P90s. "With this." The guards pulled open the doors and they stepped inside.

Acton gasped, his jaw forgotten, his mouth agape. They were standing in a large control center, ringed with monitors and workstations, the only gap the door they had just entered through. It was stark white, the only color from the displays, all showing various readings, of what, Acton had no clue. The floor was translucent and below them was bare rock, the chamber they were in mounted on pylons driven into the ground below, large springs coiled at the midpoints suggesting the entire structure was designed to handle any type of seismic event that might be thrown at it.

Laura gasped. "Oh my God!"

He turned toward her to see her head tilted back as she stared above. He looked and his eyes shot wide open, his chest tightening at the sight.

Thirteen telescoping arms surrounded the structure in a circle, all equally spaced, all but four with a crystal skull mounted to the end. Each of the empty arms had teams in cleanroom suits working to mount the newly arrived skulls.

He hugged himself, cold, noticing Laura doing the same.

Chaney smiled. "See, even I'm shivering, and it's worse now that all thirteen are here."

Acton willed himself to stop shivering. "It's cold in here, that's all."

Chaney laughed. "There's no convincing you, is there? But yes, it is cold. The scientists say electricity conducts better in the cold. Outside this chamber, where the skulls are, will be lowered to near absolute zero when they're ready." He held out his hand. "Please, feel free to look around and ask questions. We're all friends here."

Acton nodded, beginning to stroll around the perimeter, peering at the displays and listening to the scientists' conversations as he passed by. He glanced over at Chaney, who stood in the center of the room. "I can't believe you haven't tried to unite at least a few already."

Chaney handed a tablet back to one of the scientists. "Trust me, the temptation was there, but we knew without the proper equipment in place, we'd just end up destroying the facility. It's only now that things are ready."

Acton motioned at the skulls above. "And just how will all this protect us?"

"We're expecting a massive energy surge that this chamber has been designed to absorb then project away harmlessly. As soon as we see any reaction, we'll pause, analyze the data, then continue. Your job will be to hit the kill switch if you see anything that concerns you that we don't see, or if you hear someone ordering things killed." Acton felt his chest tighten at the responsibility, Chaney picking up on his unease. "Don't worry, Professor, anyone here can halt the experiment, it's not all on your shoulders. You just have an additional switch that can kill things. A safety valve for our enthusiasm, shall we say."

Laura came up from behind, taking Acton's hand and squeezing it tightly. She was nervous. He was nervous. Hell, he was terrified. His entire body was shaking with adrenaline, it having nothing to do with the skulls overhead, of that he was quite certain.

Chaney, the highly trained Scotland Yard detective, again noticed. "Professors, if you want to leave, you can. We'll take you to a safe distance. We'll need to hold you until we're done, of course, since you know where we are, but after we've finished our work, you are free to go with our thanks." He smiled. "No one is a prisoner here."

Acton looked at Laura and noticed her shaking her head almost imperceptibly, her eyes imploring him to stay.

She's almost as obsessed with this as they are!

He sighed. "We'll stay."

I just hope it doesn't get us all killed.

Off the coast of Iceland

The Triarii Proconsul, Derrick Kennedy, gripped the railing as their boat skipped across the waves, racing toward the last known location of the two professors. They would hold twenty kilometers offshore, it hopefully enough distance should anything go wrong. He knew from their own history that three skulls brought together had resulted in a massive explosion, or energy release, that had wiped out everything around them, almost destroying medieval London in the process.

And the skulls had been unscathed, simply sitting in the center of the blast wave. If the same were to happen tonight, Chaney and his people would be killed, and it would be his team's responsibility to get in there first and retrieve the skulls before authorities arrived.

He just hoped twenty kilometers was enough.

Though if it weren't, most likely no distance would be enough.

Life as they knew it would probably be over.

The motor began to throttle down and he glanced back at the pilot, who pointed at the shore.

They were here.

And either nothing was going to happen, or history was going to be made. He genuinely did hope for the latter, though the thought terrified him.

For if things went wrong, there may be no one left to write that history.

Approaching Denier Installation, Iceland

Dawson tossed the rope aside and waved up at the chartered AS365N Dauphin chopper overhead, the rope quickly retracting, the pilot banking toward Reykjavik. He looked about to see his team and Leather's taking knees, all directions covered. He checked his tactical computer and motioned toward a nearby hill.

"The target is just over that rise. Niner, you've got point, let's move."

Niner took the lead, the team of eleven quickly advancing toward the rise. It was night, the light of the moon fading in and out as a partially cloudy sky blocked the light. Between scanning his path ahead for anything that might twist an ankle or worse, he had to admit he was enjoying the landscape. It was so completely alien to anything he was used to, its barren nature was intriguing. If he shut out what was happening around him, he could almost imagine he was on the moon.

And messing up his line, if you believed some of the conspiracy theorists.

That's one small step for a man, one giant leap for mankind.

He didn't believe for a second the "a" had been said or intended. It just messed up the flow of the sentence. Sure, it was probably more grammatically correct, but historic lines like that were meant to sound good to the masses, not the literati.

His comm squawked. "Zero-One, Control Actual. Do you read, over?"

"Go ahead, Control."

"Zero-One, something's happening."

Dawson held up a fist and took a knee, everyone else doing the same, weapons aimed to cover all approaches. "Control, can you be more specific?"

There was a pause. "It's hard to describe, but, umm, have you ever seen You Only Live Twice?"

Niner's head spun toward him with a grin and a thumbs up, Spock cocking an eyebrow as high as Dawson could remember. "Ahh, you mean the volcano lair of Blofeld?"

"We're sending you images now."

Niner quickly joined him at a crouch, Atlas taking his place at point. He removed his laptop and within moments they were examining new satellite images.

"Jesus Christ!" hissed Niner. "Man, I didn't know what to expect, but it wasn't that."

Spock glanced over his shoulder at the image. "Holy shit, is this for real?"

Niner looked at Dawson. "BD, these guys look serious."

"Seriously deranged," said Spock, already watching the landscape surrounding them.

Dawson's head bobbed, a deep frown creasing his face. "Deranged people with deep pockets are dangerous. There's no way they don't have some significant firepower defending that place. Control, have you had any luck locating any automated defenses?"

"Negative, Zero-One. And now that we've seen these latest shots, I'm guessing they'll be *very* well hidden."

Dawson pursed his lips, pulling in a deep breath through his nose then blasting it out. "Okay, we have a mission to complete. Let's get in there, get our people, and get the hell out."

Niner raised a finger. "Umm, one question."

"What?"

"Well, are we stopping them from doing whatever it is they're doing, or just getting our people?" He waved the laptop. "I mean, look at this thing! This is some serious sci-fi, James Bondish shit. I've got a really bad feeling about this."

Spock glanced back over his shoulder. "Yeah, BD, maybe we should be taking this thing out. Didn't you say the Triarii thinks doing what these guys are doing could destroy the world or something?"

Leather was now at his side. He watched the images flashing on the screen, shaking his head. "That's like some space agency looking stuff. What do you want to do?"

Dawson shook his head. "This is where having someone else on the other end of the earpiece making these kinds of decisions is worth it." He activated his comm. "Control, unless we hear otherwise, we're leaving the facility untouched. It's not our mission. However, if the professors indicate there is a legitimate danger, we'll take it out."

"Copy that, Zero-One. I'm going to try and get a decision on this end on what to do. But as soon as I do, this might go official, and Iceland may object to you being there."

Dawson shrugged. "By the time they get here, we'll be dead or done. Zero-One, out."

Londinium, Britannia, Roman Empire
June 3rd, 72 AD

"I need a woman."

Roars of laughter met Atticus' proclamation, the two dozen that remained of the Thirteenth Legion gathered in Flavus' recently completed home. He smiled, taking a drink of wine, everyone feeling pretty good at this point.

"I'm sure there's plenty willing to service you for the right price!" shouted Livius, more laughter following.

Atticus shook his head. "That's not what I mean. I had a girl back home, we were to be married. It's been eight years. I want to have sons who will carry on my name, a wife to share my bed with, not some serving wench looking for extra coins to fill her purse."

There was no laughter this time, Atticus' words clearly echoing the deeply repressed ones of the gathered men. Even Flavus felt it, though he had never known love, he too young when he joined the army to experience the joys a woman could bring beyond the bedchambers.

As he looked about the room, he could feel the weight of leadership, leadership he hadn't been ready for, though had grown into, these men now accepting him as their undisputed legate, this still a Roman military unit, despite its size.

Thousands of men.

Dead.

It was a shame.

No one had followed them, Legate Catius and what remained apparently slaughtered. Word had it only a few hundred had survived beyond those

196

who had been sick, retreating to Lugdunum, most of the officers dead. After Flavus and the Triarii had left on their secret mission, the Gauls had apparently let the few that remained leave unharmed.

The curse of the skull?

Over the years of exile in Britannia, he and his men had come up with many theories, and most agreed that their misfortune indeed related to the skull they continued to guard, though since they had arrived at their destination, nothing untoward had happened to them. Their lives were normal. Uneventful. Boring.

Perhaps it's content with its new home.

There had been questions about why they remained, especially now that Nero was dead, however those were mostly settled when he described the meeting between their legate and Nero himself, a meeting they were all impressed he had attended. The emperor's belief that the skull had caused the great fire that had consumed much of Rome, and their own misfortunes on their travels, from dysentery to unusually restless Gauls, had convinced them all the skull truly was cursed.

At least at first.

But now with years of no untoward happenings, even he questioned this wisdom.

And the little old man who sat in the corner wasn't helping.

He was a curious creature. Clearly aged, yet unusually spry. He had followed them from Rome, pressed himself upon them in Gaul, and survived the voyage across Oceanus Britannicus. Things had gone their way since he had shown up, and the men had started to think of him as a good luck charm. At the moment, he and Atticus shared lodgings in this bastion of Rome that had sprung out of the barbary of this desolate island, its constant gloomy skies enough to drive mad anyone used to the sunny skies of Rome.

The old man though seemed to take their situation in stride, he happiest when he was within the presence of the skull, it still in its case, locked in a large chest in the corner of the room. The skull was never spoken of in public, their true identities never revealed to the masses that surged around them.

They all had jobs, he himself following in his father's footsteps as a blacksmith, a trade he had learned as a youth and had been determined never to follow.

Life sometimes has a funny way of working out.

As a brotherhood, they pooled their resources, all living as equals, helping, sharing, slowly establishing themselves to better not only their own lives, but those of their comrades as well.

But the problem put to him by Atticus' frustrated utterance was one he had been giving much thought to lately, Atticus not the only one feeling the emptiness. They were soldiers, soldiers who would normally know no family until they retired or left the service for some other reason. Yet here, now, they were in permanent service until the day they died, in a land foreign to them. No families, no lovers, nothing but their duty.

And duty should be enough.

Though it wouldn't be if their future were to unfold as he expected it would.

"Old man!"

The room became silent as everyone looked at him then Ananias, sitting in the corner, rocking back and forth in his chair, a smile on his face, his hands clasped around a heavy cane fashioned for him by one of the men two years before.

"Yes, my son?"

"You claim to know the truth behind the skull, yet you refuse to tell us what that truth is. A decision needs to be made. Here. Tonight. I need more information in order to make the correct one. Will you finally reveal what you know?"

The smile grew. "And what decision is that?"

"Our future. What is to become of us."

The old man's head bobbed. "It is an important one, that is. But you already know in your heart what the right decision is. You need nothing from me. You merely need the courage to commit, and all will be well."

Flavus felt his chest tighten slightly in frustration as his jaw clenched. He jabbed a thumb over his shoulder at the chest. "If we return to Rome, what will happen?"

The old man shook his head vigorously. "You mustn't, as you already know."

"But why? Is it cursed?"

"Whether it is cursed or not is irrelevant. Your emperor gave you an order and you must obey."

"He is no longer the emperor. He is dead."

"When one ruler dies, do you ignore all his decrees automatically? If that were the case, there would be chaos, each new emperor having to reissue all previous decrees from centuries before." He shook his head. "No, you know as a soldier that the decree stands." He nodded toward the chest. "The skull must never again be taken to Rome."

"Then let's just bury it and be done with it!"

Tepid agreement from the room at Atticus' outburst suggested to Flavus they knew why they couldn't do that.

For the same reason they couldn't take the skull back to Rome.

The emperor had decreed the Thirteenth Legion not only take the skull to Britannia, but also assure it never return.

For all time.

Flavus sighed then murmured the three words that had been haunting him. "For all time."

"Sir?"

Flavus turned to Atticus. "For all time," he repeated, louder. "Our orders, from the mouth of the emperor himself, were for the Thirteenth to take the skull to Britannia, and ensure it never returned to Rome *for all time*."

"But what does that mean?" asked Atticus, slamming his cup onto the table, wine spilling over the edges. "For all time? What is that? Eternity? After we're dead? Are we to forgo Elysium and instead remain here, our spirits forever condemned to guard this damned thing!"

"He really needs to get laid," muttered Livius, the room roaring in laughter, Atticus joining in before Flavus held up his hand, ending the frivolity.

"You are right, my friend. It is an impossible order for *us* to keep."

Atticus leaned forward, his eyes narrowing. "You say *us* as if there are others who can fulfill *our* duty. We are sworn to secrecy of who we are and what we guard. How can we possibly bring in others, for that *is* what you are talking about, isn't it? Others to replace us after we are gone?"

Flavus nodded, slowly looking about the room at the men gathered. He was the youngest there by almost a decade, some of the men in their forties. His eyes came to rest on the old man who had a smile on his face that suggested he knew exactly what Flavus was considering.

Ananias nodded slightly, as if giving his blessing.

Flavus sucked in a quick breath then looked at his men. "*We* are the Triarii, the last of the Thirteenth, the greatest legion Rome ever fielded." Cheers and raised glasses interrupted him, an interruption Flavus allowed. "But *we* cannot possibly guard Rome from the dangers of this sculpture, this skull, this oracle of the gods"—he raised his eyebrows slightly and tilted his head back as he found the words he was searching for that would have some spiritual meaning to his men—"this Oracle of Jupiter. If our duty is indeed eternal, then it will be future generations that must continue our duty after we are gone."

The room was subdued now, the wine forgotten, their desire for female companionship pushed aside as they all listened to their leader. "What is it you are saying, Legate?" asked Atticus.

Flavus smiled, his decision made. "No matter how much we may hate this miserable patch of rock, no matter how much we miss the warm sun on our faces, the beautiful women of Rome, the greatness that is the Empire, we will never see it again." He spread his arms out. "*This* is our home now. And our duty hasn't changed. *We* are the Triarii. *We* are the Thirteenth Legion. Rome is where our hearts lie, but *here* is where our duty has taken us. We have known it for years. We will never leave this land, and our duty cannot be passed on to just anyone. We need people we can trust to carry on our legacy, to carry on our duty."

He leaned forward, the rest of the room joining. "We need families. Families that can continue the duty handed to us. Families we can *trust* to not betray the *honor* bestowed upon us, the honor of protecting the greatest empire to have ever ruled the world." He rose, kicking his chair back and lifting his glass high. "Brothers! Romans! Let *this* be our home, let us embrace it with all our hearts and bring joy into our lives by doing so! The past is done. It is time to look to our future! What say you, men? Shall we get Atticus a woman so she can bear him many sons, sons who will continue our duty for all time?"

The men burst to their feet, glasses raised, a roar of approval shaking the walls.

And the little old man watched on, apparently pleased, though hunched over a little more than Flavus had seen before.

As if he had aged decades.

Outside the Denier Installation, Iceland
Present Day

This is unbelievable!

Dawson lay prone, the hard rock-strewn surface jabbing into him, making him wish he had a ghillie suit on, its thick burlap at least providing some cushioning. As he and the others peered through their binoculars, the silence after the initial gasps suggested they were all as amazed as he was.

What had been barren landscape in the satellite photos was now awash in bright lights, large camouflaged doors having slid open, revealing an intensely white circle at least a hundred feet across. After his eyes had adjusted, he was able to make out what appeared to be a state of the art laboratory with men and women in jumpsuits, rushing around as if something big were about to happen.

He didn't know what he was expecting, but it wasn't this.

Leather grunted. "Are those what I think they are?"

Dawson nodded, shifting his focus to the thirteen arms projected above the lab in a circle. "If you mean a whole whack of crystal skulls, then yes, it would appear so."

"I've heard about them but I've never actually seen one."

"Wait 'til you see one up close," muttered Dawson. "It's a whole different experience."

"In what way?"

"It's creepy, for lack of a better word. When I saw it the first time, it sent chills up and down my spine. It was weird. It takes a lot to weird me out, but this did."

202

Leather pulled away from his binoculars, glancing over at Dawson, saying nothing.

Dawson looked at him. "I've seen a lot of weird shit in my life, but I still think about it to this day."

Leather returned to peering through his binoculars. "Sounds like I need to see one up close."

"You enjoy nightmares?" asked Niner.

"Nope, but I've been doolally since I was a kid when my parents let me watch The Time Machine."

Niner rolled to his side, staring at Leather with a grin. "Me too! When the Morlocks came out that first time? Man, I've had nightmares about that going on twenty years. That and pink elephants. And now the word doolally."

Atlas' voice rumbled. "Pink elephants? I'm not even going to ask."

"I think you just did."

"Save it for your shrink's couch."

Dawson surveyed the area around the large opening. "With those bright lights we should be able to get into position undetected."

"Agreed," said Leather.

"Colonel, have two of your men get down to the shore and set the charges on those power lines then get the hell out of there. I'm guessing the place will be swarming with guards as soon as they go off. I want to try and keep the killing to a minimum if we can."

"Do you think that's possible?"

Dawson grunted. "I'm not optimistic. If they start firing, I want sniper teams here, here and here," he said, indicating the three positions. "Take out anything in sight, but watch out for our professors." He lowered his binoculars, looking to his left and right at the men on the ridge. "You all know what they look like?" he asked, his question for the benefit of Leather's team.

Leather was the only one to reply. "We've been guarding them for several years now, so don't worry."

Dawson grinned at him. "Forgot about that." He raised his binoculars, searching for the air vent Langley had found. "We're going to have to try and get in through that air vent. If we can effect entry, we'll signal you to detonate the charges."

"Something's happening," said Spock.

Dawson adjusted his view, the lab coming back into sight. His eyes narrowed, those in the lab clearly focusing on their panels, others staring up at the skulls overhead. "Okay, I think their experiment is about to start."

"Which means this entire area could be about to blow," said Niner.

"Then let's boogey. I don't care what they're doing, but they do, which means they're probably distracted."

He rose.

"Let's move!"

Control Center, Denier Installation, Iceland

Acton's heart slammed against his ribcage as his head pivoted between staring at the needle in front of him and up at the skulls moving almost imperceptibly overhead. His right hand hovered over a large red button, his other gripped the edge of the panel.

He was sweating and shaking all over.

Laura put a hand on his shoulder and he flinched, almost hitting the button.

"Relax, dear."

He nodded, taking a deep, slow breath, then holding it before exhaling slowly out his mouth, the tactical breathing exercise calming his adrenaline-fueled excitement.

"Sit." Chaney pointed at the chair bolted to the floor in front of Acton's terminal. "You'll be able to see better and perhaps not hit that button prematurely." He gave Acton a wink then turned back toward the center of the room.

Acton frowned, knowing he had been caught. He sat, Laura standing behind him, massaging his shoulders as the activity continued around them, the voice of the woman controlling the proceedings echoing overhead through speakers, apparently the entire complex listening in. It made sense. The installation wasn't manned by just anybody—it was manned by believers. They were not just Deniers, but Triarii, all men and women who had dedicated their lives to the crystal skulls and what they represented.

All eager to discover the truth.

From the scientist who manned one of the terminals, to the man who pushed the broom in a lonely corridor.

Today they were all equals.

And Acton had no damned clue why he was here.

He was terrified, why, he didn't know, though as he continued his breathing exercise, he began to calm, his racing pulse easing, the roar in his ears, the hammering in his chest, subsiding, his wife's ministrations helping. He looked up at her. "Thanks."

She smiled down at him. "Better?"

He nodded. "Much."

She wiped the sweat off his brow with her fingers, her eyes wide in excitement. "I can't believe this is happening!"

He stared back at his gauge, it not having budged from the zero reading since the process had begun moments before. The screen in front of him showed images cycling between various cameras documenting this important moment in Triarii history, all the data apparently live streaming to secure servers on the other side of the planet, just in case something were to go wrong.

He had questioned the choice of locations when he had heard it. "Why are you going through with this if you think there's the chance you might blow up half the planet?"

Chaney had smiled at him as if humoring a child. "It's merely a precaution. If we truly thought that might happen, we wouldn't proceed. We're not insane, simply abundantly cautious."

But the zeal in the eyes of those manning the control room suggested otherwise, and even his wife's had him realizing that those who had spent their lives dedicated to the skulls, even outside of the Triarii, had been affected by them.

And so had he.

He *wanted* something to happen. Anything. Not a disaster of course, but he found himself praying for something to happen, for the needle to move, for the skulls to actually release energy of some sort. He wasn't sure why. Perhaps it would give some meaning to all the death that had surrounded them over the years. His students in Peru, the Triarii in London and around the world, the Delta Force members that had died before he had become friends with their surviving comrades.

For young Robbie Andrews who had sacrificed his life trying to save his professor.

Years of fear, of nightmares, of death, of guilt, wouldn't come to an end tonight, though they might at least be given some meaning. Did they all die, did they all suffer for some curious sculptures with no meaning, or did they die because these skulls *were* actually special?

There has *to be something. It can't have all been for nothing!*

"Advance another ten millimeters."

Acton tore his eyes from the skulls and focused on the gauge in front of him.

"Movement complete. Report on readings."

His needle hadn't budged.

"Negative indications," reported another voice over the speaker.

He eyed the right hand side of the gauge, the large red swath indicating the danger zone. If the needle entered that area, even for a moment, he was to hit the button and abort the operation, the skulls immediately retracting away from each other and into nonconductive holding chambers.

They all had such a button.

But he was the control. The only one here not motivated by a near religious fervor to discover the truth.

Though he was definitely caught up in the moment.

"Advance another ten millimeters."

Again, his gauge showed nothing. He looked up at the skulls and wondered if indeed something were to go wrong, would the precautions the

Triarii had taken be enough. They were operating under the assumption that they would be dealing with some sort of power that could be harnessed like electricity. What if it were some sort of explosive force, or worse, radiation?

Get a grip, Jim!

He shook his head, watching his gauge as the skulls advanced again. His mind was running wild with scenarios as the excitement of the others pulled him in, and if he weren't careful, he'd forget his true purpose here.

To make sure things didn't go too far.

"Advance another ten millimeters."

And still nothing.

Exactly as he had expected.

It *was* disappointing. He had been hoping for an Indiana Jones moment, where a little bit of the mystical might prove to be real, returning wonder to the world if only in a small way.

But he was a scientist.

Even if something were to happen here tonight, it would be for a scientific reason, not supernatural. *If* something were to happen, then it would have something to do with the composition of the skulls, their refractory properties, or something else scientists who specialized in these things would be able to explain.

But the supernatural?

Never.

He closed his eyes for a moment, they burning with fatigue.

But it would be nice.

"Advance another ten millimeters."

The needle jumped as did he, before it settled back down to zero. He spun toward Laura.

"Did you see that!"

Off the coast from the Denier Installation, Iceland

Proconsul Kennedy stood at the prow of the ship, watching through binoculars the events unfolding in the distance. He could make out little beyond the bright lights now coming from the installation, their position intentionally far enough that they would be protected from any potential blast.

Any blast worth surviving.

"The drone is in position now, sir."

Kennedy nodded, returning to the bridge, a display showing the footage from their drone launched a few minutes ago.

"I never thought I'd see the day," muttered Terry Simmons, one of the crew, as they all stared, Kennedy counting the skulls.

Thirteen.

All of them.

"They're really going to do it!" cried another. "They're insane!"

Kennedy nodded then closed his eyes, tilting his head toward the heavens.

May the gods protect us all.

Outside the Denier Installation, Iceland

Leather held position behind a large rock, listening. All he could hear was his own breathing and the sound of the ocean, it loud enough unfortunately to obscure anything that might be approaching. He scanned the area with his night vision goggles.

All clear.

He motioned for Jeffrey Moore, one of his trusted men, to advance, he rushing forward toward the cables Langley had spotted, Leather holding his position as he continued to scan the area for any hostiles. He flipped his goggles up, the bright light from the complex a couple of hundred meters away simply too much for them to work effectively across the entire area. It was causing deep shadows everywhere, shadows that could hide the enemy, though if he was right, it was an enemy so distracted by what was happening, they could probably park a tank on their front door and no one would notice.

If they knew where the damned front door was.

Moore rushed back, giving a thumbs up. "I was able to remove the cover. They were definitely cable bundles, but some pipes as well. Hard to say what's inside. Could be more cables or some sort of drainage."

Leather nodded. "Good. Let's hope they lead to their primary power source and not just some damned sewage disposal."

Moore grinned. "If it is, then I guess we're really blowing the shit out of the place."

Leather didn't bite. "Your charges are set?"

Moore held up the detonator. "Ready to blow the shit—"

Leather held out his hand. "I'll take that."

Moore placed the detonator in Leather's palm. "Don't trust me?"

"Once I knock you out you won't be able to operate this."

"So, no more jokes?"

"No more jokes."

Dawson knelt behind Niner as the operator examined the vent Langley had discovered. They had managed to reach the position without encountering any opposition, and to this point, none of the teams had seen any hostiles, nor encountered any of the sentry guns that had him so concerned. If they could actually gain entry here, they might be able to avoid them all together, if they did exist.

But things never seemed to go according to plan.

Not when the Triarii were involved.

Niner turned. "Definitely leads somewhere."

"Sensors?"

"Yup, but I've bypassed them, no problem." Niner leaned over slightly, nodding toward Atlas. "But we do have another problem."

Dawson's eyes narrowed. "What's that?"

"Well, my sexy ass is going to fit in this no problem, but there's no way my brotha's big boned figure is getting in here."

Atlas crawled over from his covering position and peered at the narrow opening. "Umm, as much as I *hate* to agree with this scrawny excuse for a man, I think he's right."

Dawson frowned. "Okay, we're a man short."

"Greenhorn!"

Atlas turned toward the challenge, Dawson ignoring it, he recognizing Leather's voice. "Tenderfoot!" responded the big man as he resumed his covering position.

Leather and one of his men joined them. "Charges set."

Dawson nodded. "Were they cables like Langley suspected?"

"Affirmative. Plus some piping. Hopefully they're powerlines otherwise your diversion is just going to be a loud bang."

Dawson pointed toward the opening as Niner removed the grate with a cringe, no alarms sounding anywhere, though a silent one could still be flashing on someone's panel inside. "We're a man short." He jerked his thumb at Atlas. "My friend here is carrying some winter weight."

"Hey, four percent body fat," rumbled Atlas in protest.

"And my Uncle Charlie is the other ninety-six," interjected Niner.

Dawson chuckled. "Care to join our act?"

Leather smiled. "Absolutely."

Dawson turned to Atlas. "Okay, you take the Colonel's position in Sniper Team Two. Keep your eyes and ears open, this could turn into a Charlie-Foxtrot quickly."

"Roger that."

Leather handed the detonator over to Atlas. "You best hang onto this." Atlas took the small device and tucked it into a pocket, Velcroing it shut.

Dawson activated his comm. "Control, Zero-One, anything on our mission parameters, over?"

"Zero-One, Control. Negative. It's going up the chain quietly. Nobody wants to admit this is going on. For right now we've designated this as a CIA op with classified operators. No one knows who you are. That should protect you, but right now I can't give you the all clear to use deadly force unless it's absolutely necessary. Remember, you're on a foreign ally's soil."

"Understood, Control." Dawson and Leather exchanged knowing glances, both having been in positions like this before, he was sure. Somebody was covering their ass back home, which he had to admit he understood. After all, they *were* off the books, and they *were* dealing with a cult of skull worshippers that were so secret, even among the intel community, that few knew they existed, and fewer still knew that the late president had not only been killed by one of the Triarii, but had been a member of this breakaway sect known as the Deniers.

In fact, it was a miracle they were getting the support they were, considering the situation. If it were him making the decisions, without a personal connection to the professors, he would have probably washed his hands of the entire matter.

But it wasn't him making the big picture decisions, he was making the more important ones on the ground.

"And the experiment?"

"No word on that. Exercise your discretion. Bottom line, Zero-One, is that you and your team aren't there, we don't know who you are, and you're free to do whatever you feel is necessary as this isn't a sanctioned op, and if something goes wrong, your government will deny any and all knowledge of you."

"What else is new?" muttered Niner.

"My completely off the record advice is to do whatever is necessary to complete your mission without risking your own lives. These are *not* the Triarii you dealt with in the past. We've confirmed the reports we received from Agent Reading. There were nine attacks across the globe in the past week, most with deaths, not including the kidnapping of the professors. Nobody put them together before, but once we knew what to look for, we did. If this is indeed the Deniers, they won't hesitate to kill you."

Dawson let a burst of air out. "Copy that, Control. I'm making a command decision. Enjoy the show. Zero-One, out."

Their mission was the professors, not the experiment, not world politics, not treaties between nations. Langley had confirmed what he already knew. Their opponent was determined and willing to use deadly force, and he wasn't about to tiptoe around them, putting the men under his command at risk.

He activated his comm, broadcasting to the entire team.

"Bravo Team, Zero-One. Use of deadly force is authorized."

Control Center, Denier Installation, Iceland

"Advance another ten millimeters."

Acton's heart pounded hard, the sweat beading on his forehead ignored, the back of his shirt damp. The excitement in the room was electric, even the once monotone drone of the announcements over the PA now laced with adrenaline.

The needle had moved.

Something had happened.

They had paused for nearly five minutes to review the readings, to see if anything else would happen, but nothing had. The needle had jumped slightly as the skulls moved toward each other then settled back at zero.

Laura's nails dug into his shoulders, the pain finally making itself felt. He patted her hand and she immediately eased up.

"Sorry."

He shook his head, dismissing the unnecessary apology, instead his eyes shifting from the monitor showing the skulls moving almost imperceptibly forward, to the readout in front of him, his hand hovering near, though not over, the kill switch.

The needle jumped.

Gasps and aborted cheers erupted before it immediately settled back down to zero.

But it was enough.

Acton was convinced.

There was something to this.

Could the Triarii history be accurate, and not just a misinterpretation of past events, or worse, a boldfaced lie? Could London indeed have been nearly destroyed in 1212 because three of these had been placed next to each other? The story told to him by Rodney Underwood had been that there was a humming sound that was ignored, then eventually a massive explosion. Could this delayed reaction be what they were seeing?

His chest tightened and his mouth went dry as a thought occurred to him.

"Umm, Martin."

Chaney held up a hand, cutting Acton off as he discussed the latest results in a huddle with several scientists. They broke, Chaney striding quickly over to Acton's station. "Yes?"

He sounded impatient.

And excited.

His eyes were filled with a fervor that Acton had only seen in fanatics.

And it was perfectly understandable.

He felt it himself.

"I assume you've confirmed these aren't instrument malfunctions."

Chaney nodded. "Of course."

"Then shouldn't we be mindful of what happened in London?"

"Excuse me?"

"In 1212."

Chaney's eyes narrowed. "I'm afraid I don't follow you."

"If I remember Rodney's explanation"—a momentary flash of shame and anguish clouded Chaney's face at the mention of his old friend's name—"he said there was a humming sound before the explosion, and I believe there was some time between the explosion and the skulls being placed together."

Chaney pursed his lips, taking a slow breath as he considered Acton's words. "Yes, actually, that's right. Why?"

"Well, these spikes that are happening, could it be a delayed reaction of some sort? I mean, could things be building up that we don't realize, and before we know it, there'll be a sudden release that we can't control?"

One of the scientists stepped over, apparently having listened in. "We're showing no indication of any buildup within the skulls, and the system is designed to handle a surge."

"How much energy has been produced so far?" asked Laura.

"Very little." The scientist motioned with her tablet at the lights overhead. "Not even enough to power these lights for a few seconds."

Acton felt his tension ease somewhat. If they were dealing with such a small release each time, then it would suggest any buildup to this point—if there was any at all—would be equally insignificant. "Where's the power going?"

"Into a set of large capacitors that then drain."

"How much power can these capacitors hold?"

"A lot, but if they're overloaded, these large dishes"—she pointed overhead to an array of what Acton had mistakenly assumed were satellite dishes—"can transmit the energy harmlessly as microwaves."

Acton nodded. "And their capacity?"

The scientist smiled. "Massive. Don't worry, Professor Acton, we've been planning this for a long time." She turned to Chaney, placing a hand on his shoulder. "And it looks like it's about to pay off." She returned to her station, Chaney's eyes following her, Acton getting a sense there might be some budding romance between the two. Chaney's eyes returned to his guests.

"Satisfied?"

"As much as I can be, I guess." Acton looked at the man, feeling his excitement building within himself. "I guess you were right."

Chaney grinned like a child. "It would appear so." The grin faded. "I just wish the Proconsul were here to see it." He sighed. "And all the others who had to die to make this happen."

Main Venting Port, Denier Installation, Iceland

"Come out to the coast, we'll get together, have a few laughs," muttered Niner, channeling his best Bruce Willis imitation as he crawled through the narrow ductwork, a steady hot breeze pushing against him, though nothing serious. He activated his comm. "Zero-Seven, One-One. Just wanted to report that there's no way your ample hips would have fit in here, over."

"One-One, I'll have you know big hips run in my family so I feel no shame."

"So, what you're saying is"—Niner channeled his inner Kat Graham— "I got it from my mama, I got it, got it, g-got it?"

"Please stop singing, you're killing me."

Niner pushed forward, nearing a grate marking the end of the shaft. "So, back to your mama's hips. I've met your mama, she's got much nicer hips than yours."

"I agree," said Spock. "Much nicer."

"Can we please stop talking about my mama's hips? I'm going to have to crack some skulls if this keeps up."

Niner grinned as he reached the grate. "Now, your sister. She's definitely got your mama's hips."

"That's it, BD, I'm killing him when we get out of here."

"Use of deadly force is authorized," came Dawson's reply.

Niner peered through the grate and frowned. "That's okay, Spock will help me."

"I'm out of this. You're the one who brought up the man's sister."

"All I suggested was that she was a fine looking woman."

"Which means you think his mother is a fine looking woman," replied Spock. "Like I said, I'm out of this. Your skinny little ass is on its own."

"Yeah," rumbled Atlas, "a skinny little ass that I now own."

Niner pushed gently on the grate. "Again with the flattery. Now, if you two don't mind, I'd like to report."

"Please!" replied Dawson.

"Okay. I'm at the end of this shaft. Looks like some sort of mechanical room or something. There's a big ass fan in our way but it's barely moving."

"Can you shut it down?"

Niner examined the blades. There was no way he'd be able to do any real work, their spinning blocking access, though a small charge shoved into the right place would work. A big charge on the center of the blade would definitely work. "Yeah, but it could be loud. Give me a—" He froze, the sound of the fan's motor kicking into a higher gear sending his heart racing. "Shit!"

"What?"

"It's speeding up."

"Then stop talking about the Atlas family's hips and blow that thing."

"Roger that." He punched the corner of the grate, it popping loose, he catching it before it fell to the floor below. The fan was going full force now, almost taking his breath away. He reached behind him, feeling for a charge, gripping the smaller package, then paused.

Go big or go home.

He grabbed the larger device.

"It's gonna be loud!"

Control Center, Denier Installation, Iceland

"Advance another ten millimeters."

Laura's eyes were glued to the skulls overhead. She could recognize the one she had studied for years at the British Museum, its familiar grinning face almost comforting among the tension and excitement of the situation. Yes, they were here voluntarily, or at least that was what she had told herself. The reality was Chaney had insisted they come, then when they had protested, resorted to tempting them with being a part of history.

And it had worked.

She had to admit she was stunned that James had been the first to cave. The skulls had been part of her life's work, not his. The skulls had brought them nothing but pain since they met, and before that, for her, mockery and snickers behind her back. Her scientific papers on the skulls had all been discredited after the Triarii had substituted the genuine skulls for fakes before the BBC arranged testing, and ever since then, the entire field of study considered quackery. Even she had relegated the carving to a storage room, picking up the pieces of a nearly shattered career.

Yet she had persevered, the past now forgotten among her peers, she now occupying a prestigious post at the Smithsonian, a post that allowed her and James to share a life together, a life she wouldn't trade for the world.

She looked down at him in his chair, it clear he shared the excitement she felt, his hand, hovering over the kill switch, shaking from the adrenaline that fueled them all.

The needle jumped.

Her lungs burned.

She took a breath, not realizing she had been holding it, then pointed at the readout.

"Look!"

The needle had jumped then immediately settled back down.

Though not to zero.

Definitely not zero.

"Something's happening!" cried James, but the room knew it, the scientists shouting out numbers, pointing at displays, the entire room abuzz with excitement. She glanced over her shoulder at the security cameras covering the facility and noted not a sole were attending to their duties, everyone from guards to clerks standing, staring up at the nearest loud speaker or monitor, history in the making.

Thank God James made me come!

Her beliefs were being borne out, her secret beliefs that she had only ever shared with her husband, and even then only partially. She knew, she had always known, that there was something special, something unexplainable about these sculptures, and now their power was being revealed.

The scientist in her desperately wanted to know the reason, how these pieces of crystal were generating power, but the child inside wanted to simply enjoy the moment of wonder, the moment where a little magic, a little fantasy, a little science fiction, became real.

Her chest heaved as she stifled a sob.

"What's wrong?" asked James, staring up at her, taking her hand.

"I-I don't know," she whispered. "I'm just so…so"—she shrugged, wiping away a tear—"overwhelmed."

He smiled up at her, patting her hand. "I understand."

And she knew he did. This man understood her like no other, like none had before, and she was so grateful to the skulls that surrounded them for bringing them together. She stared up, picking out the skull he had discovered in Peru, the skull that had caused so much death and destruction, yet had united two people who would have never met otherwise, and closed her eyes, saying a silent prayer of thanks.

"Did you hear that?" asked James.

"Huh?"

"Ten kilowatts is being generated."

Her eyebrows popped. "Is that a lot?"

He shrugged. "I don't know, but they sure seem excited." He raised his voice. "Martin, what's happening?"

Chaney turned toward them, beaming a smile. "Ten kilowatts, and it's steady!"

Laura leaned over and hugged her husband, closing her eyes, fully committing to the excitement around them. There was no longer any shame in her beliefs, in her years spent studying the skulls, in her secret, childish beliefs that someday the secrets of the skulls would be revealed when mankind was ready.

Mankind *was* ready.

Today.

And the secrets of the crystal skulls were being revealed, once and for all.

She sighed, contentedly, the stress slowly easing as she watched the needle, steady, above zero, with no signs of a dangerous spike or buildup. But now the bigger questions needed to be asked. The fact they were generating power proved they were in fact genuine, not carved by conmen over a century ago to peddle to wealthy but naïve Europeans. And if they were genuine, then *someone* had created them.

But who?

Atlanteans, aliens, some pre-cursor civilization thousands or millions of years ago?

She believed in aliens, it simply unfathomable to her that life couldn't exist elsewhere, especially with so many planets already having been discovered so close to their own solar system, though she had a hard time believing they would drop thirteen skulls around a planet millennia ago then leave.

Some sort of alien reality show? Let's see how the stupid humans react?

She thought of the theory some scientists postulated that the entire universe as we knew it was an artificial construct, they actually designing experiments to prove whether we were in reality inside a Matrix style creation.

With the machines manipulating the events, the skulls nothing but simulated neurons firing in artificial brains.

Chaney suddenly hugged her, she not even noticing he had walked over to them, she so engrossed in her thoughts, staring up in wonder at the thirteen eerie faces that were about to change the world.

"We did it!" he cried, slapping James on the back as everyone in the control room exchanged hugs and high fives. "They *are* an energy source!"

She smiled, shaking her head. "I can't believe it!"

"I never doubted it!" Chaney returned back to the group, the woman from earlier planting a kiss on him that would melt the icebergs offshore.

Laura leaned over and delivered the same to the man she loved. "Thanks for convincing me to come."

He smiled at her. "Is that how it happened?"

The entire room shuddered, the revelry immediately halted.

"Report!" shouted Chaney as Laura glanced up at the skulls then down at the needle, still holding steady.

An alarm suddenly sounded and James slapped the kill switch. Her head quickly tilted back and she watched the arms the skulls were mounted to rapidly retract, the skulls disappearing into orbs that she assumed were the nonconductive holding chambers that Chaney had referred to before.

"Look."

She glanced down and saw James pointing to the readout.

Zero.

"The cooling plant just went offline!" shouted someone, pointing at a readout.

"That was no failure, that was an explosion," said Chaney. "Do we have cameras in that area?"

"Yes, sir."

Laura turned to see a large display switch from a view of the skulls to a CCTV image of a room filled with pipes, cables and other bulky equipment.

Along with men, dressed in black, dropping from an air vent.

"That's Bravo Team," whispered James, standing and putting a protective arm around her.

"Get security down there, now!" ordered Chaney. "Detain them if you can, kill them if you have to. And double the exterior guard. There's probably more outside."

James stepped forward. "Wait! You know these men. They're Bravo Team. They're obviously here for us."

Chaney spun toward him, rage in his eyes, the rage a zealot displayed when his plans were interfered with.

It was chilling.

Chaney pointed at the two guards manning the door. "Secure them."

The two men advanced, grabbing them both by an arm and hauling them back toward the door and away from any of the terminals.

225

James yanked his arm loose, pointing a finger at Chaney. "Hey, this wasn't our deal!"

"The deal is off. I can no longer trust that you'll do what's best for the experiment now that your friends have arrived." Chaney pointed at the screen. "*Nothing* stops what we are doing here tonight. Nothing!"

"Just hand us over and they'll leave, I guarantee it!"

"It's too late for that now." Chaney turned his back on them. "Resume the experiment from the previous position. Now!"

"Yes, sir!"

Laura stared up as the protective pods opened, the skulls reemerging, steadily advancing toward each other.

"Look!" hissed James, nodding toward the power readout. It was steadily climbing, higher than it ever had before. Laura felt her chest begin to tighten, her sense of joy and wonder from moments ago now lost.

Caution had been dismissed, panic had taken over.

Which meant mistakes could be made.

And James was no longer the source of reason, his kill switch now far out of reach.

"We have reached the pre-abort position."

Laura glanced over at the needle and saw it immediately drop, settling to where it had been before Delta had arrived. She turned to the security feeds, the Delta team advancing, another showing a large security detail rushing their way.

Be careful!

Mechanical Room, Denier Installation, Iceland

Niner dropped to the floor, raising his weapon and scanning the area from the new perspective, his perch from above already suggesting the room was empty, though it wouldn't be for long, not with the size of the explosion that had just occurred.

To his right, the fan blade still vibrated from the impact, it now embedded deeply in the concrete wall, several important looking cables severed, the mangled mess of the cooling system above him hanging on by a wire, ready to collapse at any moment. Dawson, Spock and Leather silently dropped from the duct above.

"We better book, I'm pretty sure they heard that," said Niner, pointing toward the only door in the room.

Spock cocked an eyebrow. "Ya think?"

Niner gave him a look then snap-kicked him to the chest before stepping back, spreading his arms out to herd Dawson and Leather out of the way as the rest of the cooling unit smashed into the floor, the lone cable above finally giving out.

Niner glanced at Spock. "Do you think they heard *that?*"

Spock grinned. "Ya think?"

Niner yanked him to his feet. "Is that mouth of yours still working? Seems to be stuck on repeat."

"Wouldn't you like to know."

"I guess it is." He lowered his voice. "We'll talk later."

Dawson pointed to the door. "Check it out."

Niner nodded and he and Spock rushed to the only exit as Dawson called for a comm check, the sniper teams outside reporting in. Niner peered through the small window to see an empty hallway lined with plain doors.

"Team Two, standby to detonate."

"Roger that, Zero-One," replied Atlas.

Niner frowned as half a dozen armed men turned the corner at the end of the hallway. "We've got company. Six hostiles, armed."

Using hand signals, Dawson ordered them to spread out. "Let's try to take them alive, we need intel."

"Copy that," said Niner as he took cover behind what appeared to be a large battery of some sort.

I wonder how this reacts to gunfire.

The door burst open and the six men poured in, fanning out.

"Halt!" shouted Dawson, popping up from behind his cover, his MP5 aimed directly at the new arrivals, the others doing the same. "Drop your weapons!"

The men hesitated.

Then one of them didn't.

The battle didn't last long, from the moment the first hostile fired, four MP5s opened up on them. Niner picked off the two in his arc within seconds, the others doing the same, it only taking two short bursts from each operator to eliminate the six hostiles.

Unfortunately though, eliminate indeed appeared to be the end result.

Niner emerged from behind the battery, weapon still aimed at the hostiles, when one suddenly gasped, beginning to writhe in agony. Spock and Leather checked for vitals on the others, headshakes indicating their status as Dawson knelt beside the one survivor.

"Where are the professors?"

The man stared up at him, his eyes filled with pain, his expression suggesting he wanted it to end, even if it meant his death.

But he said nothing.

Dawson leaned in, grabbing the man by the jacket and hauling him up so their faces were nearly touching. "I'll ask one last time before I tear this place apart looking for them. Any goddamned experiment you nutbars have going on here will be destroyed."

The man's eyes flared in panic, his pain momentarily forgotten. "N-no, you can't!"

"I will. Now where the hell are they?"

"Down the…"

The man's voice drifted off, his eyes fluttering as his head fell backward, the last spark of life gone, his suffering, and their source of intel, done.

"Well, I'm guessing he didn't mean down the rabbit hole," said Niner, watching the hallway.

"Might as well have," muttered Dawson as he laid the man gently back on the floor.

"Well, I guess we know whether or not they'll shoot first," said Spock as he took up position with Niner.

Dawson nodded, activating his comm. "Zero-One to all teams. Weapons free, repeat, weapons free. Just watch for our professors, over."

Control Center, Denier Installation, Iceland

"Advance another ten millimeters."

"Belay that!" snapped Chaney, eyeing the security monitors that had just shown the death of six of his men. Six good men, six brothers. "Twenty."

Dr. Melissa Cooper, the scientist running the experiment, spun toward him. "Excuse me?"

"Twenty."

"Why are we changing the parameters of the experiment?"

Chaney pointed at the monitors without looking. "Because we have hostile forces on the premises! We may not get another chance at this."

"But—"

"Do it!"

Cooper flinched, startled at the uncharacteristic outburst. "Yes, sir. Advance another twenty millimeters."

Chaney turned toward the readouts, his heart hammering as he glanced at the security monitors, the Delta team no longer contained to the mechanical room. And with their cooling plant now out of commission, he began to wonder whether the safety protocols they had in place were actually functioning should something go wrong.

But it didn't matter. They would proceed no matter what. They had to know. They had to know if the skulls truly were powerful, truly held the key to mankind's future. He had waited years for this, his entire life in fact, his own father a Denier. He had never dreamed he would actually become the head of the group. When much of the leadership had been killed by Delta not only in London but the West Bank as well, it had been decided a younger face was needed, one who the council would never suspect.

And no one would have ever expected him.

It had been a proud, terrifying moment for him when informed of the decision, he not even aware the leadership that remained was considering him. The shadow council still existed, safely ensconced somewhere else, though he was the Proconsul.

His word was final.

And he would use that power to make certain nothing interfered with their plans. Before this night was out, the world would know the power of the skulls, even if he had to die doing it. The time had come for their secrets to be revealed, for their power to be unleashed.

He had trained to be a doctor then switched his focus to law enforcement. But today he was a pioneer, an explorer, a descendent of the Thirteenth Legion, about to change the face of the world. Not a man or woman in this complex had any doubts that they were about to harness an incredible power source that would change the human species forever.

A free, unlimited power source of incredible proportions, would end man's reliance on all other forms of electricity, and with the expected abundance, would power the world for eternity, allowing man to focus on the future, of bettering the lives of those living in all corners of the planet, and eventually, moving toward the stars.

And eventually, discovering the origin of the skulls.

It was his belief that aliens had brought the skulls to Earth eons ago, in the hopes they would challenge whatever intelligent species arose to question their origin and attempt to tap their power, a power that would give the species the ability to leave this lonely rock and venture out into space to discover their benefactors.

This wasn't magic.

This was technology.

Handed them by the gods.

And he, Martin Chaney, was about to reach out and touch them, to see their power in all its glory.

The gauge spiked, passing the red line for a brief moment, then settled down, again higher than before.

A hum resonated through the room.

"What's that?" asked Cooper, searching about for the source.

"Didn't your scientists report a hum when the skulls were placed together in 1212?"

Chaney spun toward Acton, he and Laura still held at gunpoint near the door. He said nothing, though the man was right. There *had* been a hum. He placed his hand on the console and felt a slight vibration. He turned to Cooper. "Do we know the source of the vibration?"

Cooper shook her head. "Negative."

"Didn't that hum precede a massive explosion that levelled half of London?"

Chaney ignored Acton.

"Martin, please, you have to stop this, it's over!" cried Laura.

He turned toward her, pointing at the displays. "We're siphoning off the power easily, there's no risk at this point. London happened because there was nowhere for the power to go. Here there is. Now please, keep quiet and let us do our jobs!"

He turned to Cooper.

"Another twenty millimeters."

The needles spiked again before settling.

And the hum grew.

Outside the Denier Installation, Iceland

Atlas pulled away from his binoculars as bright lights suddenly bathed the entire area, the secret they were there apparently out.

"We've got activity."

Atlas looked toward where Moore was pointing, immediately spotting the new arrivals. "Welcome to the party, boys." He activated his comm. "Zero-One, Zero-Seven. We've got hostiles visible." He peered through his binoculars. "Two, make that four, no six and counting. Looks like they're trying to find us, over."

Dawson's reply was quick. "Anyone heading for the cables?"

Atlas watched the group for a moment. "Affirmative, two of them."

"Copy that. Do not detonate until they reach the charges. I want as many of them outside as possible. It will make our job inside easier."

Atlas rolled his eyes at Moore. "Gee, thanks."

"Don't say I never do anything for you. Zero-One, out."

Atlas reached for his pocket, a vibration having him thinking for a moment that his phone was ringing.

But it was everywhere.

"Do you feel that?"

Moore nodded. "If you mean the vibration, yeah. Started a couple of minutes ago."

Atlas looked over at the bright lights of the opened lab and a pit formed in his stomach.

Could these whackos actually be right?

Londinium, Britannia, Roman Empire
December 16th, 75 AD

Flavus sat beside the bed of the old man who had been with them for years now. He had become part of the family, part of the brotherhood that was the Thirteenth Legion. An odd fellow, a man of few words, he held a wisdom about him that Flavus had come to rely upon over the years. Though his counsel was rare, sometimes merely a smile or a nod, it was welcome, more so since Flavus had made the decision to plan for the future.

Atticus had found a wife and already had his first son, several of the others now with families. He too had just married with his first child on the way. A decision had been made not to inform the wives of their true purpose, and it would be up to the men to pass the legacy of the Triarii down to their sons when they were of age. The skull would remain a secret known only to those who bore the mark.

The old man held out his hand, the small tattoo on the inside of his left wrist revealed as his sleeve slipped higher, a tattoo he had been proud to receive a year ago after a symbol had been chosen for what would one day be more than just the few that had survived. All now bore the symbol, a symbol that represented who they once were.

The third and final line of the legion.

Two straight lines, representing the first and second lines of troops in a legion entering battle, the first the most inexperienced, the second, more experienced, ready should the first falter.

And a third, slightly curved line, the Triarii, the most experienced, seasoned troops, standing behind the first two lines of defense, ready to slaughter any who would make it through, any who would harm Rome.

Rome.

He closed his eyes, trying to picture it. It had been so long that now it was difficult. The bustling streets, the towering monuments. Word had arrived that Emperor Vespasian had begun a mighty coliseum in the center of the city, a monument that would certainly stand as a testament to the grandeur that was the Roman Empire.

An empire they all still served.

In secret.

He clasped the old man's hand in both of his. "How are you feeling?"

The old man smiled up at him. "I'm dying."

"Don't talk like that."

The smile broadened, the room beginning to fill with the others, word sent that the end was near. "It is time."

"Time for what?"

"For you to know the truth."

Flavus sucked in a quick breath, excitement surging through his body. He had known Ananias had secrets, secrets he refused to divulge. The man seemed to know something about the skull that no one else did. Flavus had asked him on innumerable occasions to share what he knew, the old man always refusing.

Could today finally be the day the truth was revealed?

"And what is the truth, old friend?"

Everyone gathered closer, saying nothing.

"I, and those of my kind, have been the keepers of the skulls for longer than you could possibly imagine."

Skulls?

His eyebrows rose slightly at the word, though he saved his questions, not wanting to interrupt what he hoped would be a steady flow of information now that the dam had finally been broken.

"I have been waiting to pass the torch, to hand the duty entrusted to me so long ago, to a new generation who would safeguard the skulls and continue our mission." He squeezed Flavus' hand. "It took me a long time to find the right people, but I die knowing I have. The task demanded of you by your emperor is more important than you could possibly imagine, and your responsibility extends beyond that of the Roman Empire, for it is merely a blip in what will be a long history for mankind."

"I don't understand," said Flavus. "You said 'skulls'. Are there others?"

The old man nodded. "Yes. Thirteen in total."

Everyone gasped, including Flavus. "Thirteen?"

"Yes. Thirteen that have over the years spread out across the land to the farthest reaches."

Flavus shook his head, still wrapping his head around the idea.

Thirteen?

One had been trouble enough, but thirteen sounded like a nightmare. With just the one causing so much trouble in the brief time he had been around it, from the fire in Rome to the restless Gauls and storms at sea, it could explain why much of the world outside the borders of the empire was so barbaric and troubled. If they too were being influenced by the evil contained within these cursed objects, there might be no hope for them unless they were found and destroyed.

"Are they the source of the evil that dominates so much of our world?"

This elicited a chuckle. "They are no more evil than the chair you sit in, or the child that plays outside this very door. But men will do evil things to possess them and harness their power."

"Power?"

"These are very special things, as I and the others like me have come to learn, and they do indeed have a power within them."

Flavus' eyes narrowed. "You refer to others. Who are they?"

Ananias shook his head. "They are no more. I am the last."

"Then who *were* they?"

"They were the ones chosen by those who preceded us. Just as I am choosing you. It has been a long journey, but I saw honor and sacrifice that day in Judea, and I decided it was time to reveal the skull I guarded to a soldier I knew had honor within his heart. It has been a journey of decades to see what would come of that fateful day when the Christian martyr died, but I knew, in the end, that men of good conscience would come, and you have." He closed his eyes for a moment, his breathing labored.

"What is this power you speak of?" pressed Flavus, fearing the old man may not be long for this world, and he needing to know the complete truth before Elysium claimed the tired soul that lay beside him.

"It is a power you are not ready for. But one day mankind will be, and when he is, the truth will be revealed, the power will be unleashed, and the dawn of a new age for the species will begin."

Flavus glanced at the others, excited and confused mutterings rounding the room. "I don't understand."

Ananias smiled, patting his hand. "You're not meant to."

Flavus felt his chest tighten in frustration, it replaced with concern when a coughing fit overtook Ananias.

"I need to see it, just one last time," he gasped.

Flavus turned to Atticus. "Bring it." Atticus nodded, leaving with several of the others to retrieve the skull kept in another room of Flavus' home. Flavus turned to Ananias, the old man having lived with him for years now. "What are we to do?"

"Protect it, seek out the others and protect them, but never bring them together until you know you are ready."

"Why?"

"The results could be disastrous."

"In what way?"

"In ways you cannot possibly understand. But in time, your descendants will."

Ananias smiled as Atticus entered the room carrying the chest, aided by another. It was placed on a nearby table and Flavus rose, unlocking it with a key held around his chest then lifting the lid, the original box revealed inside. He opened it, a shiver rushing up his spine as the skull grinned up at him. Removing it from the case, he returned to Ananias' bedside and the old man smiled, a shiver passing through his body as he reached up and placed a hand on the smooth cranium.

"Thank you." Ananias stared into the eyes of the skull, a tear forming. "Good bye, my old friend." His eyes closed and his breathing slowed, Flavus bowing his head along with the others. Suddenly Ananias gasped. "Wait!"

Flavus' heart slammed, startled. "Yes, what is it, my friend?"

"The skulls. They must not be hidden away. They must be allowed to continue their journey, to have their effect on man, to prepare them for the time when the secrets can be revealed." His hand left the skull and instead cupped around Flavus' cheek. "Promise me you will carry on."

Flavus held a hand against the old man's. "You have my word as a soldier, and as Legate of the Thirteenth Legion."

Ananias' eyes closed, a smile on his face. "My time has come. Yours is just beginning."

And with a gasp, he drew his last breath, the hand slipping from Flavus' cheek to rest on the skull that had meant so much to him.

Off the coast from the Denier Installation, Iceland
Present Day

Proconsul Kennedy stood at the prow of the boat, the cold of the North Atlantic going unnoticed as he peered through the binoculars at the bright lights in the distance, their drone having failed for some reason.

He sighed.

He had always wanted the position of proconsul he now occupied since he was a teenager and had learned the truth from his father, a member of the Triarii and the council member responsible for the British Museum skull. He had been ambitious, always done well in school and graduated from Oxford top of his class. A career in politics had given him the political and business connections he had felt would aid the Triarii in the future, and then he had made his bid to replace his father upon his retirement.

He had been granted the position, and the rest was history.

A history known only to those within the Triarii.

He rarely saw his old classmates now, but when he did he was forced to be vague about what he had done, having settled years ago on telling them he couldn't talk about it, it classified government work.

This always shut them up, and impressed them.

He had been proud of his work, of what he had dedicated his life to, but now it was all falling apart.

Under his watch.

He was just glad his father had passed before the troubles began in earnest with the incident in London.

As one was apt to do in these situations, he not only blamed himself, but also searched his memory for something he could have done differently.

He should have been tougher.

He should have rooted out the Deniers long ago so today would never have happened.

Why do they insist on being so reckless?

As he watched the lights glaring in the distance, reflecting off the clouds above, a small part of him wanted them to succeed in harnessing the energy, another part wanted them to fail, to have the entire area torn apart in a massive explosion, putting an end once and for all to this debate.

The truth would be discovered when ready to be revealed.

Of that, he had no doubt.

He had reread the digitized versions of the ancient scrolls referring to Ananias' final words, words he hadn't read since he was a boy. He believed the scrolls, they written as historic accounts, not opinions, and preserved over the millennia by his predecessors.

And Ananias had referred to thirteen skulls.

The legend of Ananias had been of an old man with the ravings of a lunatic, because for centuries there had been no other skulls found, and for over a millennia, housing the Oracles of Jupiter and Zeus together had resulted in no harm, unlike what Ananias had assured them.

Which was why when the third skull was found and brought to London, no one had thought twice about putting it with the others.

The result had been devastating, and with over a thousand years having passed, the warnings of Ananias had been forgotten, few reading the scrolls that far back as they were so fragile.

But the digitization effort he had pioneered when becoming Proconsul now afforded him that luxury, and what he had read was fascinating. All he had read before were references and copies, copies that were incomplete or incorrect, written by men influenced after the disaster, probably in an attempt to protect the legacy of the founders.

But Ananias knew too much to have been what was previously thought.

Thirteen.

He had predicted the number of skulls.

He had predicted disaster if they were joined.

And he had told the founders to seek out and protect the skulls, allowing them to pass through the hands of men until they were ready, at which point their power would be harnessed and the dawn of a new age would begin.

He sighed, the lights appearing to get brighter on the horizon, though it could just be his imagination.

Martin, don't screw this up.

He had faith in the skulls, had faith they were here for a purpose, and he couldn't believe they would wipe man from the face of the earth should something go wrong. Whoever or whatever had put them here had a purpose. What that purpose was, he didn't know, though it couldn't be to destroy. Not on a global scale.

Perhaps they merely destroy those who aren't ready.

He frowned.

We're not ready.

"Sir! We're experiencing some sort of interference on those bands you wanted monitored. Sounds like somebody is transmitting but it's encrypted."

Kennedy lowered his binoculars, returning to the warmth of the bridge. "Source?"

"No way to know, not with our instruments." The Captain nodded at the shore. "But if I had to guess."

Kennedy agreed, it the only logical answer.

"Do you think they know the professors' friends have arrived?"

Kennedy nodded. "Without a doubt."

"Should we join them?"

Kennedy shook his head. "No. We'll let them deal with the Deniers, and just pray the skulls remain unharmed."

"And the professors?"

"Are of no concern to us."

Lower Level, Denier Installation, Iceland

Dawson booted the door open, Niner stepping inside, he quickly following, his weapon raised as he scanned left to right, Niner the opposite.

"Clear!"

"Clear!"

He heard the same echo across the hall as Spock and Leather did the same. They had no idea where the professors were being held, which meant they couldn't bypass any of the nearly dozen rooms along the hallway leading from their entry point. It was slow work that meant more hostiles would be on the way, yet it was necessary.

It also prevented someone from coming up behind them.

Yet so far every room had been found empty, merely storage or office space.

Apparently everyone was watching the show.

Or pursuing Atlas and the others outside.

He hated having one of his men out there without Delta backup, but Leather's men were excellent, all ex-Special Forces, mostly British SAS, so they were good. Damned good. And they'd have the big man's back.

He smiled.

There was no way *he was fitting in that vent.*

"Company," hissed Niner, the sound of footfalls echoing in the hallway.

"Prepare to engage," whispered Dawson as he took a knee in the doorway, Niner just behind him, standing. Across the hall, Leather and Spock did the same.

And they waited.

The boots on institutional linoleum continued to get louder, the first black-suited guard appearing moments later, followed by three others.

They held their fire.

Until the first man spotted them.

"Open fire!"

A series of quick bursts and the four were down, not a shot returned.

"Let's clear this damn corridor."

He booted open the last door on the left, Niner rushing in, the room clear once again. Stepping over the bodies, they reached the end of the corridor, it splitting off in two directions. To the right were another half dozen doors and a dead end, to the left a corridor with several others branching off, and more doors.

With windowed rooms.

"This way looks more important."

Spock, covering their rear, spoke up. "Didn't the last intel suggest they went willingly?"

Dawson nodded. "That's what Fang relayed, yes."

"Then if they went willingly, they're probably not being held in a room as prisoners."

"What are you saying?"

"You know those two. They're always at the center of the action. I'll bet Niner's salary that they're in that control room we saw."

Dawson pursed his lips, thinking. Spock was right. If Acton had any say about it, he'd be right in the mix, trying to do something to either stop what was going on, or make sure whatever was going on didn't destroy the damned island.

And searching room by room was taking too long.

"Okay, let's find that control room."

He took point, the others staggered behind him, Niner covering their six as he headed toward a rather serious looking door at the end of the corridor.

Somebody stepped into the corridor, weapon raised, lead belching toward them. Dawson leapt to his left, the butt of his weapon leading, shattering the glass of one of the offices. He hit the floor hard on the other side, Niner landing on him a moment later as the distinctive sound of MP5s responding filled the air. Dawson jumped to his feet, leaning out the shattered window and adding his own fire.

Leather and Spock were prone, pouring on a steady stream at the junction ahead, the barrels from several guns making appearances around the corners as their opponents fired blindly.

And missed.

For now.

"Fire in the hole!" shouted Niner, pulling the pin on a flashbang, tossing it down the corridor. Dawson stepped back, his Sonic Defenders protecting his ears from the deafening explosion.

Those down the corridor weren't so well equipped.

Screams of agony erupted, Dawson leaping through the window as Leather and Spock charged forward, Niner on their heels. Short bursts from Leather and Spock silenced the cries and whimpers before Dawson had eyes on the targets.

"We need to thin these guys out a bit." He activated his comm. "Zero-Seven, Zero-One. Detonate, I repeat, detonate."

Outside the Denier Installation, Iceland

Atlas flicked the arming switch on the remote detonator. "Zero-Seven to all teams, fire in the hole." He pressed the trigger and a large explosion tore through the night sky to their right, the two hostiles about to reach the shore crying out in agony as their bodies were hurled backward. The security lighting flickered for a moment then returned, though dimmer than before.

Must have switched to batteries.

Which meant they had indeed just blown the primary power source.

"Open fire," signaled Atlas, the three sniper teams immediately eliminating the targets in their assigned zones, the bodies dropping, no shots fired, their positions still secure.

Something suddenly appeared to their right, thirty feet from their position.

Shit!

"Take cover!"

Atlas dropped behind the rock, flattening himself against the ground as best he could as sentry guns opened fire from all directions. He did a quick check on Moore who gave him a thumbs up, he impressively calm.

These SAS boys are the real deal.

Atlas listened, there at least half a dozen, if not more, distinctive sets of gunfire around them. He pressed his earpiece tighter. "Sniper Teams One and Three, report."

"Sniper Team One, we're good, over."

"Team Three good, over."

Atlas breathed a sigh of relief as he flipped onto his stomach, raising his head slightly. It was difficult to tell where the weapon positions were so close to ground, the sound echoing off the rocky landscape, the ricochets loud on the other side of the very rocks they were taking cover behind. He raised his head a little more, getting a view behind them.

"Looks like we're clear behind."

Moore pushed himself up, resting his back against the rock. "Agreed."

"We've gotta take these damned things out." Atlas poked his head up then immediately ducked. "Okay. One at our two o'clock, ten meters out." Atlas pulled a high explosive grenade from his ammo belt and loaded the M203 40mm grenade launcher attached to his MP5.

Moore smiled. "Good thing you brought those."

"BD was a Boy Scout. As soon as he heard about the automated systems outside London, he added them to the requisition order."

"Be prepared." Moore shifted position. "I'll spot, you shoot."

Atlas grinned. "Time for some fun." He activated his comm. "Sniper Teams, use your HE grenades and take those weapons out." He closed his eyes for a moment, picturing in his head exactly where the one weapon he had spotted was.

He popped up, fired then dropped, the explosion shaking the ground as he reloaded, a spray of pulverized rock covering the area around them, the sound almost a light rain. He poked his head back up then dropped, a smile on his face at the sight of the mangled wreckage.

"One down."

Moore smiled. "Nice shooting." He cocked an ear, trying to get a bead on another weapon as the sound of the other teams taking action were heard. Moore's head darted up, quickly scanning left to right before dropping back down. "Eleven o'clock, thirty meters, mounted on top of what I'm guessing isn't a genuine rock."

Atlas nodded, repositioning himself, bullets still spraying over their heads at random intervals as the weapons continued to unleash lead in all directions, whoever had activated them clearly setting them to go beyond simple motion detection. Atlas popped up, his eyes scanning his eleven o'clock, honing in on the weapon.

He dropped as it spun toward him, concentrated fire now on their position. Atlas crawled over the rocks, grunting as a sharp stone made its presence known. The gunfire continued on his former position, Moore hunkered down, tossing rocks in the air to keep the motion sensors entertained.

Atlas took a knee then raised his upper body, firing his round then dropping as the explosion silenced the weapon, Moore catching his last rock and giving a thumbs up.

And then there was silence.

Atlas slowly rose, quickly scanning the area then repeating, this time more slowly.

Nothing.

"Sniper Teams, report."

"Team One, secure."

"Team Three, secure."

"Keep your eyes open. They may have deactivated the weapons just to draw us out. Keep a watch for additional hostiles as well. They know we're here so they'll be more careful." He pointed toward where the guards had emerged and Moore nodded, rising. "Team Two, moving in. Teams One and Three, provide cover."

Control Center, Denier Installation, Iceland

"Advance another twenty millimeters."

Acton watched as Cooper glared at Chaney. "Sir, the power levels are reaching our capacity to bleed off! It looks like the wiring to the microwave bleeders has been damaged. There's nowhere for the power to go!"

Chaney ignored her. "Twenty millimeters. Now!"

"Martin, we've already proven our theory! There's no point in continuing!"

Acton gasped, pushing Laura behind him as Chaney pulled a gun and aimed it at Cooper, the poor women turning fifty shades of gray as she nearly collapsed.

"Another twenty, or I shoot."

Chaney's voice was cold, desperate.

Something was wrong.

All the readings clearly showed that something was happening. Energy was being generated, the hum in the room was now loud enough to be annoying.

His theory *was* proven.

So why is he so insistent on keeping it going?

Acton looked at Laura, her eyes holding the same questions he had.

Why, if the experiment had succeeded, was Chaney so desperate to keep going and risk all their lives?

He glanced at the security monitors, the Delta team still advancing.

Toward what, he had no idea, the layout of the facility a mystery.

He just hoped it wasn't a mystery to them.

Lower Level, Denier Installation, Iceland

Dawson came to a halt, peering around the corner of a four-way junction. It was clear, though again there was no way to know which way to go except forward.

Which hadn't worked so far, the facility a mystery.

"Okay, any suggestions as to which way to go?"

Niner pointed up at the ceiling. "I just assumed you were following those, like I was."

Dawson looked up and shook his head, large bundles of cables and piping evident. He followed them back to see them stretching the length of the hallway. They turned left at their current position. He deadpanned Niner. "Just testing you."

"Sure you were."

Dawson grinned then pointed up. "Let's assume these lead to the center of the action."

Spock crossed to the other side. "And that the professors are in the thick of it."

Dawson nodded. "If they're not, whoever is there will know where the hell they are."

He stepped into the hall, heading down the corridor to their left. He raised his weapon and took out a camera with a single shot.

No point making it too easy for them.

Control Center, Denier Installation, Iceland

"Sir! We only have five minutes on the generator!"

Cooper spun toward the tech who had just delivered what Acton sensed might be the final nail in all their coffins. If the control room were to lose power, there might be nothing that could stop the reaction occurring over their heads.

Cooper leaned over the tech's shoulder. "How is that possible? There should be hours of power left."

The tech shook his head. "I don't know. Something is drawing power at an incredible rate."

"What could be causing that?"

"I don't know. It shouldn't be happening. Beyond emergency lighting, all power is being directed to the control room."

Cooper shook her head. "No, we're generating power here, not using it. This makes no sense."

Acton watched the events unfolding in front of them, the jubilation of earlier gone, desperation now the rule of the day. Everyone knew the Delta team was getting closer and apparently something had happened outside as well.

There's only four on the monitor. More of them must be out there!

The more the merrier.

And the sooner the better.

Chaney was off his rocker, insisting they continue to proceed with an experiment that had proven they were right all along, everyone in the room clearly opposed.

Yet he continued to hold his weapon on them, pacing in silence to the side.

Which was odd.

Why isn't he questioning the latest thing to go wrong?

Acton watched their captor, their friend—former friend—as he fidgeted and paced, his eyes growing more desperate with each passing moment as he stared at the readings then the skulls overhead.

It's as if he's waiting for something to happen.

But what? It had *already* happened. The skulls had generated their power, of that there was no doubt, the gauges proved it. And the hum was exactly as described in the ancient texts.

What more does he need?

"Check the system," ordered Cooper. "See if there's anything running that shouldn't be. We need to find whatever's draining those batteries!"

Chaney spun toward her, his pacing halted. "Advance another twenty millimeters. Now!"

Acton turned to the readings on the monitor nearest him, the familiar reading showing the power being generated now accompanied by a new reading indicating the amount of draw on the batteries.

His jaw dropped.

Wait a minute!

Outside the Denier Installation, Iceland

The security lights rapidly faded then suddenly shut off, the bulk of the light now coming from the opened roof of the contraption housing the skulls and what Atlas assumed was some sort of control center. He was fascinated by science, always had been, though unfortunately he never had the opportunity when he was younger to pursue it.

Inner city schools were no place to learn.

They were places to survive then escape.

He had graduated, his parents insisting, he thankful they did. His uncle was army and his father had encouraged him to join, it the best way to escape the vicious cycle repeated all too often on the streets he grew up on.

It was the best decision he had ever made.

He loved his job.

Loved it.

And he couldn't imagine himself doing anything else. He had the best friends one could imagine, a job that actually *meant* something, and he got to fire guns and blow shit up every day, while learning things he never knew he was capable of learning. If someone had told him when he was seventeen that he'd be an expert hacker one day or that he'd speak several languages, he'd have asked for some of what they were smoking.

Though no one could have prepared him for some of the incredible things he had been involved with over the past few years. Ancient crystal skulls? Two-thousand-year-old cults? Tombs of Cleopatra? Kidnapped Popes?

It just never seemed to end.

And he wouldn't have it any other way.

He spotted what appeared to be a seam in the rock wall facing him. He pulled out his flashlight and played it along the crack, it quickly clear the seam extended all the way around, forming a rectangle.

Got ya!

He activated his comm. "Zero-One, Zero-Seven. We're secure out here, over."

"In the middle of something! Could use a hand if you're done doing your nails!"

Atlas waved for the other teams to join him, it evident they were now alone and the weapons systems apparently destroyed. He stepped back from the door and launched a shell into it, taking cover behind a large boulder. The explosion shook the ground under his feet, it suddenly clear this wasn't rock he was standing on, but something artificial. Peering out from behind his cover, he smiled at the door hanging off its hinges.

"Zero-One, Zero-Seven. We're on our way!"

Vehicle Bay, Denier Installation, Iceland

Dawson leapt behind an SUV as gunfire sprayed at them from across what seemed to be a large underground parking area, at least a dozen vehicles of varying types and sizes parked in two neat rows, a ramp at the far end appearing to lead to the outside.

This would probably be their means of eventual escape, now that they had found it, but for the two dozen guards they now faced.

He rolled behind the rear tire, Niner taking up position at the front, Spock and Leather still in the doorway, exchanging turns providing covering fire. He looked over his shoulder at the others. "Conserve your ammo, choose your targets! We don't know how many more we're dealing with."

He stretched out, prone on the cold concrete, peering through the scope on his MP5, spotting feet behind a vehicle on the other side of the large vehicle bay. He squeezed the trigger. Someone cried out and dropped to the floor, writhing in agony.

Exposing their upper body.

Dawson squeezed again, silencing him.

Another dropped, Niner's weapon spurting disciplined shots across the way, Spock and Leather delivering short bursts to keep their opponents' heads down.

Dawson searched for more feet, finding two pairs huddled together. A quick shot then another had them both on the ground. Two additional shots thinned the herd some more. He continued to scan, but found nothing.

They'd wised up.

"Flashbangs!"

Niner pulled one off his belt, Dawson doing the same. He looked over at Spock and Leather, who both nodded. Dawson popped the pin. "Three... Two... One..." He lobbed the grenade over the SUV and against the far wall, it hitting with a satisfying clang before rattling to the ground, Niner's landing a moment later.

The dual eruptions were deafening in their concrete enclosure, the screams of the victims echoing all around them.

"Let's go!"

All four of them quickly advanced, Niner and Dawson taking the left, Spock and Leather the right. As the smoke cleared, their opponents could be seen stumbling around, hands over their ears, moaning in agony. He immediately squeezed the trigger, clearing his arc of targets as the others rained hellfire on those who remained.

"Behind you!"

Dawson spun at Leather's warning and cursed, at least a dozen hostiles streaming into the vehicle bay.

This is what happens when you don't have proper intel.

Control Center, Denier Installation, Iceland

"Advance another twenty millimeters."

The hum was now a whine, high-pitched and approaching painful. The guards were staring up nervously at the skulls, their weapons lowered, their duty forgotten as they watched the objects they had coveted their entire lives deliver upon their fabled promise.

Unlimited energy.

But it was all bullshit.

And Acton could hold his tongue no more.

"It's fake!"

Everyone in the room spun toward him, Chaney's jaw dropping slightly, his eyes wide.

But nobody said anything.

Acton stepped forward, past the guards, pointing at the main display showing the energy generated by the skulls and the draw on the batteries. "It's fake! Look! Don't you see it? The battery power is being drained at almost the same rate the energy is being generated! We never noticed it before because whatever energy source you were using was enough to maintain the illusion, but now you're using the batteries to keep it going." His eyes met Chaney's. "It's all fake! The skulls are doing nothing!"

"That's a lie!" shouted Chaney, looking at the others. "Don't listen to him! He doesn't know what he's talking about!" He pointed at the guards. "Get them the hell out of here!"

"Oh my God! He's right!" It was Cooper that said it, the guards freezing in their tracks, the entire room's focus now on the woman examining several displays, her fingers flying over a keyboard. "The numbers match almost exactly. The battery draw is equal to the amount of power being generated by the skulls plus the expected draw from our equipment. Every time the skulls have moved closer since the power failure, the drainage rate on the batteries has increased!"

Chaney stabbed the air with his finger. "You're relieved!" He motioned to the guards. "Take her!"

The guards remained still, staring at each other, not sure what to do.

But Cooper did. She pointed at Chaney. "Seize him!"

The guards hesitated, though only for a moment, before they marched toward Chaney. Chaney leapt for a control panel to his right, slamming his hand down on the kill switch several times then holding it in. An alarm sounded and he looked up at the skulls, all eyes following his.

Acton gasped as all thirteen skulls steadily advanced toward each other. "What the hell did you just do?"

"What needed to be done!"

They all watched in horror as the skulls continued to advance, the high-pitched whine ear piercing. Acton covered his ears, Laura doing the same as he squinted, trying to see what was happening through tearing eyes.

They touched.

All thirteen in a circle, each touching the skulls beside them.

And there was no explosion.

No disaster.

No calamity.

Nothing.

The high-pitched wail faded to a whine then a hum then nothing. The needles all zeroed out, the draw on the main battery dropped to nearly nothing, the remaining power estimate leaping.

And a room filled with believers, suddenly didn't know what to do.

"What just happened?" asked Laura, taking Acton's hand.

But Acton knew. There was only one explanation for what had just occurred, and why. He watched a defeated Chaney as the man dropped into a chair, the gun clattering to the floor. "Why don't you explain yourself?"

Chaney stared at him then the others, Cooper standing in front of him, a mixture of shock and anger on her face. "Please. What have you done?"

"What needed to be done." Chaney's shoulders heaved and his head dropped as he bent over. Cooper knelt in front of him, putting a hand on his shoulder.

"Martin, please, tell us what this is all about."

Chaney drew a deep breath and nodded, sitting up and wiping the tears from his cheeks. He rose, squaring his shoulders as he looked at those that surrounded him, those that he led. "You all deserve an explanation. This was a failsafe."

"A failsafe?"

Chaney nodded at Cooper. "Yes. As Proconsul, I knew that if the skulls didn't react as we expected, everyone had to think they had. I had a failsafe designed into the system that would kick in if nothing happened after the first few tests. I didn't want us to lose our resolve, perhaps stopping out of fear there might be a sudden, large explosion, so I had the system designed to slowly ramp up the readings, just in case."

"And the hum, the vibrations?" asked Cooper.

"All part of the failsafe. I had hoped that eventually the skulls would begin to generate their own power, and they might have, but we weren't given the chance to find out"—he turned to Acton and Laura, jabbing a finger at them—"because your Bravo Team destroyed the tidal generators!"

Acton pointed at the skulls pressed together in a circle. "They're touching now, so wouldn't we be seeing something?" His eyes narrowed. "And what was that you did that triggered them moving together?"

Chaney glared at him then his expression softened. "If was the final failsafe."

"What do you mean?" asked Cooper.

"It was the only way to ensure we could reunite the Triarii and try again in the future."

Acton suddenly felt a pit form in his stomach. "What did you do, Martin?"

Chaney looked at him. "You're too smart for your own good, Professor. Now that the experiment has failed, and the deception has been discovered, no one can be allowed to live." Laura's grip tightened on Acton's hand. "The others are out there, I know they are. This facility will be destroyed, and we will all die."

"What's the point of that?" asked Laura, fear in her voice, a voice also laced with a hint of anger.

"I've shaped the blast so that it will appear the skulls are once again responsible. It will inspire future generations to try to succeed where we failed."

Acton shook his head in frustration. "But they'll fail too! It didn't work!"

"No!" cried Chaney. "There was obviously a flaw in our experiment, a misunderstanding of some sort." He pointed at the skulls overhead, rising from his chair. "The skulls have power, just not one that we understand yet. We had assumed it would be some sort of energy we could measure and tap, but it wasn't. There's something else at play here." He lowered his voice, approaching them. "Jim, you know that. Laura, I *know* you do. You've felt its affect on you every time you shiver. There's something there, but we're obviously not ready to understand it."

Acton sighed, nodding toward the skulls. "Shouldn't they have exploded?"

"Yes!" exclaimed Chaney, whipping around and striding into the midst of his stunned brethren. "Yes! There should have been a massive explosion, even if we weren't able to tap their power. We know that from our own history." He looked at Cooper. "It means what we did here worked somehow, we somehow were able to prevent that explosion. It means we're getting closer to discovering the answers to the questions we've had for two thousand years." He placed a hand on Cooper's shoulder then moved on to the next person, patting their cheek, surveying the room. "I can see it in your eyes. You think we've failed, but search your hearts. You know we haven't. You know our history, you know why we're here, and you still have your faith.

"Do Christians say God isn't real just because they're prayers aren't answered? No! They realize that not all prayers are answered, and they continue on, their faith remaining strong knowing that the day they truly need that prayer answered, the day they are truly worthy, it will be.

"And the same is true for us, for the Triarii. One day our prayers, our questions, will be answered." He frowned, his head bobbing slowly. "But not today. And not for us." He paused, putting an arm around the woman who Acton had sensed some history with. "We failed here today, and if word were to get out, it would shake the faith of the entire legion, just as it has shaken our own faith. It could mean the death of the Triarii, the death of the descendants of the Thirteenth Legion that sacrificed everything. I refuse to believe that it was all for nothing! I refuse to believe that I dedicated my entire life to nothing!" He spun, staring at Acton. "And I refuse to let *my* failure here today destroy two thousand years of tradition."

Chaney lowered his voice, taking a more comforting tone. "My friends, we will die here today, and the mystery will continue. Our brothers and sisters will come and collect the skulls, they will see the evidence I want them to see and assume the skulls are indeed the cause, and things will continue with the knowledge that mankind is still not ready to harness their power. This is something we know, for we weren't able to do it today. And in the future, someone, somewhere, will make the courageous decision once again, like you all did, to unite and try again." He smiled, everyone now huddled together in the center of the room, arms around each other, heads pressed together, almost a mirror image of the skulls overhead. "The Triarii will live on. The Thirteenth Legion will live on. And we will never be forgotten for our sacrifice."

To hell with this.

Acton grabbed the gun Chaney had dropped on the floor and aimed it at the guards. "Deactivate the bomb. Now!"

The cult turned toward him, though no one advanced, even the guards standing with their hands to their sides, their weapons draped across their chests, untouched.

Chaney smiled, shaking his head slowly. "That's not going to happen. I am prepared to die here today, as we all are." Murmurs of agreement accompanied by the bobbing heads of indoctrinated psychos sent a jolt of panic through Acton.

There's going to be no reasoning with them.

"Professors." Chaney paused, his smile broadening. "Jim. Laura. We knew the risk when we came here. We knew something could go terribly wrong and that we could all die. We were prepared for that. Now we die for another reason. We die to preserve the legacy so that future generations may try again where we failed."

Acton looked at Cooper, who he had thought was a true scientist, motivated by a thirst for knowledge, not proof in the supernatural. "Surely you can't agree with him! You're willing to die to cover up the fact you failed?"

She stepped forward, stretching out her hand toward Chaney, who took it. "He's right. The Triarii *must* go on, the skulls *must* go on." She stared at Chaney, a smile spreading across her face. "I happily sacrifice myself so the Thirteenth can live."

"Well, we don't."

Chaney motioned toward the guards who immediately advanced. "I'm afraid you must, Professors. You are aware of our secret."

Acton aimed at the chest of the approaching guard, firing two rounds, the large man dropping in a heap as Acton fired two more rounds into the second guard, returning his aim to the group of scientists.

"Nobody moves."

Laura grabbed one of the guard's weapon and they backed toward the door.

"You're too late, Jim."

"We'll see about that."

Chaney pointed toward the display showing the energy generation and the battery draw. Acton looked, the first readout still zero, though the draw on the batteries was higher than earlier. "When the batteries run out of power, this facility will be destroyed. There's no stopping it."

Acton grabbed the door handle and pulled it open, Laura stepping through. He glanced back at Chaney.

"Martin, sometimes a shiver is just a shiver."

Exterior Entrance Stairwell, Denier Installation, Iceland

Atlas charged down the stairs, the others behind him, the sound of gunfire getting louder, his concern growing. He came to a halt at a door, waiting for Moore and the others to gather at the bottom. "Ready?"

Everyone nodded and he pulled open the door slightly, the din of gunfire suddenly deafening. He peered through the crack, quickly assessing the situation, the distinctive sounds of MP5s coming from the far right, FN P90s pretty much everywhere else.

He stepped back so the others could hear him. "It's some sort of large garage. Half a dozen vehicles close to us, another half dozen on the other side. We're at the one-two corner. Friendlies are to the right, near the one-four corner, hostiles concentrated on the opposite side on the number three and four walls." He activated his comm. "Zero-One, Zero-Seven. Friendlies at your nine o'clock, over."

"About time you arrived. Join the fun, try not to shoot Niner."

"No promises." Atlas pulled the door open and stepped out, weapon raised toward the far wall. He held his fire, the hostiles apparently not yet noticing them.

Flanking opportunity.

He ducked behind the nearest vehicle, some sort of large loader, the others joining him, the door closing behind them. He pointed at two of Leather's men, indicating they should remain and provide covering fire, the others to follow him. He peered out from behind the front of the vehicle then sprinted across the way, diving behind the row of vehicles on the far side, clearing the thirty feet unnoticed. He took up a covering position and Moore followed.

The MP5 fire from Dawson's position had increased, the intense distraction working, Moore clearing the distance easily, the remaining of Leather's men following, again unnoticed.

Atlas peered around the vehicle and saw at least a dozen Triarii hiding behind vehicles about a hundred feet away.

All in plain sight from his angle.

He motioned for Moore to take a position on the floor, under the rear bumper, giving him a clear shot from a low angle. He looked at the others and they all indicated their readiness.

"Now!" he hissed, stepping out and taking a knee, the others leaning on the trunk of the vehicle, using it as cover. Lead belched at the unsuspecting men at the far end of the vehicle bay, bodies dropping quickly. The sound of the MP5 fire shifted, Dawson apparently pressing the momentary advantage.

Moore was firing below him, Atlas noting that the man was taking out targets trying to hide behind the vehicles, giving them no quarter as their numbers dwindled from dozens to a dozen, then half, then none.

Then silence.

Atlas rose, rushing toward the enemy position, the others on his six. Reaching the downed hostiles, there was little movement. A few moaned and he quickly kicked the weapon away from one, Moore doing the same.

The threat had been eliminated.

He looked over to where Dawson had been. "You boys can come out now!"

Niner poked his head up. "Am I still on your hit list?"

"I'm saving it for the ring."

Niner's eyes flashed.

Hmm. Fear?

He smiled.

Nobody talks about my mama's hips.

Dawson and the others approached and Atlas motioned toward the dimming lights. "Looks like they're running out of power."

"Batteries must be dying quickly," agreed Dawson. "Doesn't make much sense for a facility this size to have less than fifteen minutes of backup power."

"Must be that experiment they're running."

"Must be."

Atlas looked about. "Any idea where the professors are?"

Dawson shook his head. "Nada." He pointed at the ramp. "That looks like it leads outside, so I'm guessing those doors over here"—he pointed to a set of doors nearby—"lead somewhere important, since they're the only doors one of us hasn't come through already."

Suddenly the doors burst open and eleven MP5s were directed at it.

"Hold your fire!" shouted Dawson as Acton and Laura emerged, skidding to a halt as they raised their hands in the air.

Atlas shook his head with a smile, the two of them armed.

How the hell do they do it?

"Hello, Professors, good to see you," said Dawson, stepping toward them.

Acton waved him off, pointing at the rapidly dimming lights.

"We've gotta get the hell out of here, now!"

Control Center, Denier Installation, Iceland

"Has the transfer been completed?"

The tech nodded. "Yes, sir. All the funds have been successfully transferred back into accounts controlled by London."

"And the data streams?"

"Wiped. There will be no record of what happened here tonight."

"Excellent work." Chaney smiled at his people then sat down on the floor beside Annette, a woman he had wished he had more time to get to know. She had been fantastic this past year, a friend who had grown into much more, though only recently. Perhaps it was a relationship built purely on adrenaline, yet at the moment it was the only one he had. He put his arm around her shoulders and she rested her head on his.

The Triarii had their money back, so they would survive and thrive when he was gone.

He sighed.

The Proconsul had been right. They weren't ready, though not for the reasons the old man had thought. They simply had completely misunderstood the power.

Or maybe we didn't.

His eyes widened slightly at the thought. Perhaps they hadn't misunderstood the power, perhaps they truly simply weren't ready. Could the skulls themselves have withheld the power? There had been no explosion as there should have been. They had read no power being bled off from the skulls beyond what his ruse had fed into the system, a ruse he had designed himself, he ever the prudent one. It was amazing what could be accomplished with enough money and compartmentalization, nobody knowing what anyone else was doing, having no idea how their tiny bit fit into the entire picture. One person designed a shunt, another a piece of code, another a coded failsafe, another yet some additional piece to the puzzle, that when all put together, created something that would save the organization he had dedicated his life to, the organization he loved.

"I'm sorry it had to end this way, my friends, but we die for a purpose. We know the mission of the Triarii is pure and is for the good of all mankind. We failed here today not because we have been misguided in our beliefs, but because we were not ready. Whoever or whatever gave us the gift of the skulls has deemed us not ready for the secrets they possess." He smiled, squeezing Annette against him. "But future generations will be, I am certain of that, and by sacrificing ourselves here today, we will preserve the wonder that are the skulls so that our descendants can fulfill the destiny handed to them two thousand years ago."

He rose, the others joining him, and he gazed up at the skulls overhead. He raised his fist in salute to not only the skulls, but to everyone that had sacrificed for this day over the millennia, and who would sacrifice themselves for the millennia to come.

"We are the Thirteenth Legion! We are the Triarii! We shall know the truth!"

The others cheered, their fists pumping the air before they clasped their hands over their hearts.

Then silence as the lights flickered.

He lowered his gaze, smiling at those gathered.

"Goodbye, my friends."

Vehicle Bay, Denier Installation, Iceland

Acton rushed toward Dawson and the others, relieved to see them, but there zero time for pleasantries. He pointed at the lights. "The entire place is rigged to blow the moment they run out of power."

"How big?"

Acton shook his head. "No idea, but it's meant to destroy the entire facility and kill anyone inside."

Dawson pointed at three SUVs nearby. "Check for keys!"

Niner raced toward the nearest one, two of Leather's men the others, all three roaring to life almost immediately, the keys apparently kept inside.

"Okay, let's go!" shouted Dawson. "Professors with me!"

Acton helped Laura into the backseat of Niner's SUV then climbed in after her, Dawson getting in the passenger side, Spock and Atlas taking the third vehicle as Leather's team filled the remaining spaces. Niner hit the gas and they rushed toward the ramp at the far end, the front angling up as they hit it, racing toward a rapidly approaching exit.

That was closed.

"How the hell do we open that thing?"

Acton tried to remember how they had got in before when Laura pointed at a fancy garage door opener clipped to the visor. "Press that!"

Niner reached up and pressed the button, the doors slowly beginning to part as Dawson pressed his earpiece.

"Control, Zero-One! We need evac now! Make sure the choppers don't travel over the complex, it's rigged to blow!"

Off the coast from the Denier Installation, Iceland

"What's going on?"

Kennedy shook his head as he peered through his binoculars. What were once bright lights were now barely visible, the brilliant display a shadow of its former self. "I don't know, but the lights are definitely continuing to get dimmer."

"Maybe they finished?" suggested Simmons, the excitement clear in his voice. "And there was no explosion so it must have worked!"

Kennedy nodded slowly, not willing to give in to the excitement he so desperately wanted to feel. He believed in the skulls, he believed in their power. Not only the danger of that power, but the potential. And if Martin Chaney and his Deniers had indeed succeeded, succeeded in safely harnessing the energy he knew was within, it was indeed a great day.

An incredible day.

The world would forever be changed from this moment forward. An unlimited, clean, free power source, provided to mankind by the gods, humanity finally ready to receive the gift bestowed upon it untold millennia ago.

He thought of Ananias and his prophecies, and how he had suggested he was the last of a long line of keepers, a line that had succeeded those before them, and it made him wonder for just how long these skulls had kept their secrets hidden.

And how one bold, brash move, by a younger generation, had finally unlocked them.

He owed Chaney an apology, apparently, though there was no excuse for the blood spilled to get to this moment in history.

270

The sky suddenly lit up, a fireball racing toward the heavens, it unlike anything he had ever seen before. He rushed to the deck to get a better view, the explosion rapidly retreating in on itself, the light of the flames dying as he peered through the lenses. He turned to the Captain, still on the bridge, and pointed at the Denier facility.

"Get in there! Now!"

The engine roared to life and within moments they were racing toward the fading fires, fires suggesting not only that he had been right to fear what Chaney had attempted, but that mankind was still not ready for the secrets of the skulls to be revealed.

Route 1 Ring Road, Iceland

Acton gripped the handhold as Niner raced toward the rock wall blocking their access to the road. He pressed the button overhead but nothing happened.

"We're getting a little close," commented Dawson, his voice straining to remain calm.

"Patience, my dear, there's another button." Niner pressed it and the rock in front of them quickly lowered into the ground, their SUV bouncing as the tires hit the top, it not having had a chance to retract completely. "See, nothing to worry about." Niner cranked the wheel to the right, sending Laura sliding into Acton. He helped her back to her side.

"Get your seatbelt on."

She reached for it, her hands shaking as she tried to push it into the buckle. Acton reached over and put his hands on hers, steadying them, allowing her to finally insert the tongue with a click. He pulled his own on as he was pressed into his seat, Niner stomping on the accelerator.

Dawson pointed to a bend in the road ahead. "We need to get around that bend! That'll put the hill between us and the blast!"

Acton turned in his seat, staring back at the complex, the garage door they had exited still visible, a dim light inside flickering.

Then nothing.

"It's too late!"

A massive fireball shot into the night sky and outward, racing toward them. Acton grabbed Laura and pushed her down, undoing his seatbelt as he threw himself over her, his only thought now of saving her. He felt Niner press harder on the accelerator, the engine protesting.

272

Then everything changed.

He turned his head to see what was happening, sounds muffled, a screech of evil unleashed surrounding them. The entire vehicle glowed as flames licked at the windows.

And there was heat.

Something popped and suddenly they jerked to the right.

Heading straight off the highway.

He gripped Laura tighter, regretting he had ever agreed to come along.

Operations Center 2, CIA Headquarters, Langley, Virginia

"Oh my God!"

Leroux dropped into his chair as Sonya's outburst turned to whimpers, the entire op center in shock as the satellite feed showed a mushrooming eruption of fire and rage filling the entire screen in an eerie green and black. They had just spotted three vehicles turning onto the road but they were nowhere to be seen now, the fireball having almost immediately overtaken them.

Nobody could survive that!

He felt his chest tighten as he thought of the brave men he had dealt with on various ops in the past, of the professors he had never met yet felt he knew, and of his friend Kane, who had just lost comrades-in-arms he had fought and shed blood with on countless deployments.

He's going to take this hard.

He pushed himself out of his seat, watching the explosion quickly dissipate. He turned to Child. "Get the choppers back there, now! We need to know if there are any survivors."

"Yes, sir." Child was unusually subdued. Leroux wasn't sure if his newest team member had ever watched a friendly die before, and he felt for him. He remembered his first time.

He'd never forget it.

Don't give up.

He activated his comm. "Zero-One, Control. Come in, over."

Nothing.

"This is Control to any Bravo Team member. Do you read, over?"

Again, nothing.

Nothing but the static of dead air.

Route 1 Ring Road, Iceland

Niner jerked the wheel to the left, setting them back on track as the heat and flame suddenly dissipated. Acton lifted himself off his wife as Niner continued to struggle for control, three more loud bursts heard before they ground to a halt, their tires blown.

"Everyone out!" ordered Dawson as he threw his door open. Acton helped Laura from her seatbelt then followed her out her door and onto the scorched pavement. He stared, eyes wide, at their vehicle. Anything that wasn't metal was melted or still burning, the paint job flaking off, the rubber tires smoldering goo.

"I can't believe we survived that." He looked back at the other two vehicles to see them in even worse shape, the third actively burning, the men inside shouting for help.

"Oh my God!" cried Laura.

Acton sprinted toward the rear vehicle, the others following, flames licking up the sides. Dawson smashed the driver side window with the butt of his MP5, the others doing the same. Acton pulled his leather jacket off and threw it over the melted doorframe, momentarily smothering the flames, allowing Dawson to reach inside and haul the driver through as Leather did the same on the other side. Acton helped pull the driver to safety, glancing back to see Niner reaching through the shattered rear window and pulling Spock free, Atlas tumbling out after him.

Dawson rose. "Is that everybody!"

"Yes!" shouted Leather, dragging his last man from the vehicle, the interior now engulfed in flames. "We've gotta get out of here, there's ordnance in there!"

Dawson hauled the driver to his feet. "You good?" The man nodded. Dawson turned to Spock and Atlas. "You guys?"

Spock patted himself down. "I'd feel at home in a bucket of the Colonel's finest, but I'll live."

"I'm good," replied Atlas who then looked at Niner. "And my hips fit through that window just fine."

Niner grinned, Acton not getting the joke.

"Then let's go! Everybody, move!"

Acton helped the still weakened driver as they all began to sprint toward the bend in the road that would provide them cover. He glanced back at the complex, engulfed in flames, black smoke billowing into the night sky, and said a silent prayer for the poor misguided souls who had given their lives for nothing.

Hugh!

His chest tightened as he remembered his forgotten friend in all of this. Reading and Chaney had been best friends, and he had been heartbroken when Chaney had disappeared. If Delta was here then Reading certainly knew what was going on, which meant he would know his friend had betrayed them all.

And now he'd have to deliver even more bad news to the man.

His best friend was dead.

For no reason other than idolatry.

How much more bad news can Hugh take?

Reading was strong. The strongest man he knew. But the death of Kinti had killed him inside, and Chaney's disappearance had left an even deeper hole, he losing his best friend when he needed him most. Yet at least there had been hope, hope that one day his partner would return.

And now that hope was gone.

The angry roar of ammo and grenades ripping at the interior of the rear vehicle had them all ducking as they pressed forward. Acton reached back for Laura's hand, the driver now running on his own. She grabbed hold and he hauled her ahead, putting himself between her and the danger behind them, when suddenly there was a massive screeching sound as the fuel tank ignited. The blast of heat and air pressure nearly knocked him off his feet but he regained his footing and continued forward, checking to his left and right to see the others still pressing on and around the bend.

Dawson raised a fist and they all slowed to a halt, turning back to stare at the devastation they had just escaped. The flames at the Denier facility had died down dramatically, the smoke having thinned. Much of what Acton had seen was concrete, glass and steel, materials that didn't burn well, which probably meant most of the fireball was the explosives themselves.

"Choppers," said Spock, pointing to the waters.

Acton turned and spotted two choppers, their searchlights on, racing toward the area. Dawson pointed down the road where it was slightly wider and looked at Niner. "Have them land there."

Niner nodded, activating his comm as he ran down the road to direct their evac. Dawson turned to Acton.

"Is there anything worth going back for?"

Acton shook his head. "There's no way they survived. They designed it that way."

Dawson's eyes narrowed. "What do you mean?"

"They sacrificed themselves so the mystery could live on."

"What about the skulls?"

Acton shook his head. "I don't see how they could have survived that blast, but I'm guessing they did. Chaney mentioned a shaped charge or something. Even if they did, I couldn't give a shit. It was all faked, the

278

entire thing. They killed themselves and made it look like it was the skulls that caused it so that the fact nothing happened would never get out."

Dawson stared at the smoldering complex then at Acton. "They're not going to want that secret getting out. Did you just survive one problem to worry about another?"

"No. Besides us, no one knows it was faked. If the Triarii go in there, they'll think Chaney's crew died because the experiment succeeded but they weren't able to control it. It's the Great Fire of London all over again."

Dawson pointed to the first chopper as it landed. "Let's get you two home. There's a lot of people worried about you." Dawson turned when Acton reached out and grabbed him.

"BD, I never got a chance to thank you." Acton extended his hand. "Again."

Dawson smiled, shaking his hand. "I think we're going to start charging for the service."

Laura hugged him and gave him a peck on the cheek. "You just name your price."

Niner bounded toward them. "I see kisses are being handed out!"

Acton grabbed him and planted a wet one on his cheek then shoved him away. "Good for you?"

Atlas and Spock roared as Niner wiped his cheek dry. "I get no respect."

"Aww, poor baby. Come here." Laura reached out and pulled his head closer, planting a gentle, tip of the lips kiss on the pouting operator. She gently pushed him away. "All better?"

Niner threw his arms in the air, fists pumping. "Oh yeah!" He jabbed a finger at Atlas. "*That's* what you can enjoy when you're single."

Atlas smiled at him. "Enjoy it while you can, little man, you and me got a date in the ring when we get back."

Acton laughed. "What did he do this time?"

"Talked about his mama's hips *and* his sister's hips," replied Spock.

Acton winced. "Really, Niner? And I thought you were an intelligent man."

Niner shrugged. "So did I. Apparently I was wrong." He lowered his voice slightly. "Umm, so Laura, if I needed to make a quick getaway, could I borrow one of your jets?"

Laura laughed. "For you, Niner, anything."

Niner winked at Acton. "Watch her, Doc, I think there might be love here."

Acton laughed. "I'm thinking it's more a pity thing."

"Oooh, burned by the Doc!" laughed Spock, punching Niner in the shoulder. "Let's get you to safety before the lovely lady's husband wants to join Atlas in the ring."

Spock led Niner away, Leather approaching.

"Good to see you two are okay, mum."

Laura smiled at him. "And your men?"

"A few are singed, but they'll be okay."

"If they need anything, you just let me know."

Leather smiled. "I'll send you the bill."

Laura laughed. "You do that!" She gave him a hug. "Thank you, Cameron. You and your men have always been there for us, and I appreciate it immensely."

"Just doing our job, mum." Leather nodded at them both then rejoined his men as they boarded the second chopper.

Dawson helped Laura and Acton into the first chopper, the other Bravo Team members following, Dawson the last boot off the ground.

"Take us over the facility!" shouted Dawson to the pilot, the man nodding then banking toward the smoking debris. Acton leaned against the window, staring down at the devastation below, and gasped.

It was a crater.

A near perfect crater, radiating out from the center of where the skulls had been.

Preserving the illusion that the skulls truly did have power, a power Acton now had no doubt was purely myth. He looked at his wife and thought of how she must be feeling now, then remembered her words when they had first met and she had described what sculptors using ancient methods would have had to go through just to polish the surface.

It would have taken over three hundred years to complete.

He closed his eyes as they banked back toward Reykjavik and sighed.

If no one knew how to make them today, then who *did* make them?

And why?

Denier Installation, Iceland

Proconsul Kennedy leapt to the shore and rushed through the obstacle course that was the rock-strewn landscape. The flames were mere flickers now, the smoke continuing though blowing gently inland. As the others swarmed around him, all eager to see the aftermath of the disaster, he found himself slowing, his heart heavy with the thought of what he was about to find.

They'd be dead.

Of that, he had no doubt. No one could survive this, though someone had. They had spotted two choppers landing briefly then leaving, obviously having picked someone up. He hoped it was the professors and their friends. They were innocent in all this and didn't deserve to die for the beliefs of the Triarii.

He would know shortly, a simple phone call when they returned to London would be enough, though the first phone call would be to give notice to the new tenants at their Fleet Street headquarters.

The Triarii would be coming home.

He reached the edge of what turned out to be a large crater and gasped. It was easily a hundred feet across, and almost perfectly circular, it as if a meteor had just hit.

In the center was the wreckage of what must have been the lab, shattered and melted terminals and displays evident.

He gagged.

And bodies.

Charred, blackened bodies, some strewn about, some just parts tossed about, torn away by the explosion, but the majority clustered in the center of the facility, as if they had been huddled together to comfort each other in the end.

They must have known something was going wrong and there was nothing they could do about it.

His eyes burned as he pictured these people, these people who were still Triarii, despite betraying the organization. They all believed. They were all descendants of the original Thirteenth Legion.

They were all family.

Family had died here today, it a horrible thing that would be mourned when the time was right.

But for now, they had a job to do.

A duty.

"Sir!"

Kennedy looked down in the pit, Simmons waving up at him. "What is it?"

"The skulls, sir! You have to see this!"

Kennedy stumbled down the edge, his arms out to his sides as he tried to keep his balance. "Are they okay?" he asked as he rushed up to where Simmons and several others stood, tearing away at some sort of orb. He peered inside and gasped.

All thirteen skulls were together, unharmed.

He breathed a sigh of relief.

And shivered.

"It's a miracle!" cried Simmons.

Kennedy looked around him, the perspective entirely different from inside the crater. Everything around them was broken concrete, twisted metal and melted glass and plastic, save this one spot.

"Just like London."

It was almost exactly as described in the ancient texts. The skulls had been found at the center of a blast zone, untouched.

Just as today.

May the gods be praised.

He closed his eyes for a moment, remembering those who had been lost, then opened them. "Get them into the boat, now. And keep them as far apart as possible. We have irrefutable proof that they are indeed powerful. I want footage of everything before you touch them though. Let's document this so there can never again be any doubt."

"Yes, sir!"

The team scrambled, phones out taking HD video of everything as he stepped back and stared at the charred remains of Chaney and the others who had joined him. He placed his hand over his heart and bowed his head, speaking to no one but the spirits of the departed.

"Your sacrifice will not be forgotten. We will protect the skulls as we always have, once again united in our beliefs, knowing that we are not yet ready for their gift to be revealed." He looked up at the remains, focusing on one with an arm around another beside it, getting a sense that this darkened mass was a man he once considered his prize pupil. "I promise you, Martin, that in time we will discover the truth."

He smiled.

"After all, you were right. It has been our mission all along."

Laura climbed down the steps of the Gulf V and onto the tarmac at the private terminal, Acton holding her hand before they both rushed toward their friends. Reading stood, shaking his head at them as if he were their father; Milton and Sandra just seemed extremely relieved to see them.

Acton gave Milton a thumping hug as Laura gave Reading a long one, he almost a father figure to her.

"Glad to see you guys are safe," said Milton. "We've been worried sick."

"We're so sorry for that," said Laura as she gave Milton a hug, Acton and Reading exchanging a hearty handshake, he knowing the man hated hugs from other men.

"How are you holding up?" he asked, there happiness yet gloom in the man's eyes.

Reading grunted. "I'll survive. Just happy you two are okay." He looked toward the plane. "They're not with you?"

Acton shook his head. "No, they took a separate flight. Can't be seen coming in with us."

Reading nodded then shivered. "Let's get inside, it's freezing out here."

Acton shrugged. "I was just in Iceland. *Ice*-land."

"Show off."

They entered the toasty warm terminal and Acton smiled, Laura rushing forward as they spotted an old friend.

"Fang!" cried Laura, grabbing the startled woman in a hug. "How are you?"

The shocked Chinese woman bowed her way out of the embrace, her cheeks flushed. "I am well. I'm happy to see that both of you are okay."

"We are. I understand in part thanks to you."

A rapid headshake of disagreement. "No no no! I merely acted as liaison."

"Well, you played your part, and you protected our friends. For that we thank you," said Acton, bowing. Fang gratefully returned the familiar gesture, bowing deeply.

She motioned toward a nearby doorway. "I have arranged a private lounge for you to rest in while the final arrangements are made for your return home."

"Thank you, Fang." Laura stepped through the door, Acton and the others following. Laura hadn't seen Fang since her near rape in Africa, Fang having a far worse experience than his wife. She never spoke of it, and he could only imagine what the poor Chinese soldier had gone through. He had seen a lot of death over the past few years, though he'd be hard-pressed to find a group of bastards that had deserved to die more than those that had kidnapped those poor women.

He shook away the memory, this a happy time. Sitting beside Laura, he draped an arm over her shoulders as the others sat down across from them, Fang hanging by the door, still providing security. He debated inviting her over, but knew that would just make her more uncomfortable.

"I received a phone call a short while ago."

Acton felt his chest tighten at Reading's words. "From who?"

"The Proconsul of the Triarii."

Acton closed his eyes for a moment as he heard Laura inhale quickly. He looked at Reading. "And what did *he* have to say?"

"He expressed his relief that you were both safe."

Acton grunted. "Whatever. And the skulls?"

"He said they were recovered, unharmed."

"How the hell did they manage that?" asked Milton. "I thought there was a massive explosion that destroyed everything?"

Acton crossed his legs. "Niner said it was probably a shaped charge, designed to focus the blast wave away from the skulls. It would make it look like the source of the explosion was the skulls themselves, and leave them untouched. Get it wrong though, and there'd be nothing but dust."

"Unless they truly are magic," murmured Laura.

Acton smiled at his wife. "You still believe, don't you?"

She shrugged. "I don't know. Maybe they don't have the powers the Triarii thought they had, but we still don't know who made them or how. And then there's the shivering."

Milton grunted. "Probably just a planted subconscious suggestion. They asked you about it, didn't they?"

Reading, Acton and Laura all replied at once. "Yes."

"So the idea was planted in your head. Then you *remembered* experiencing that same thing, even though it might never have happened. Then, from that point on, you were programmed to shiver every time you saw the skulls because you thought you had the first time, and there was some significance to it."

Acton's head bobbed slowly as he considered his friend's words. "You know, you could be right. I can't honestly say whether or not I shivered when I first saw them. I *think* I did, but you could be right." He shrugged. "What the hell, I'll never see the damned things again, so I guess it doesn't matter."

Laura raised a finger. "Umm, actually, we might."

Acton groaned, letting his head drop back on the couch. "Why?"

"Well, one of the skulls belongs to the Smithsonian. It was stolen by the Deniers over a decade ago, remember?"

Acton's eyes closed as he let out a heavy, frustrated sigh. "I remember."

"So, I'm guessing the Triarii are going to return it."

Acton lifted his head. "With my luck, you're probably right."

"And since I now work at the Smithsonian…"

Acton looked at Sandra. "Do you know a good divorce lawyer?"

She grinned at him and Laura pinched his leg.

"Oww!" he cried, laughing as he gave her a hug. "Would you consider finding another job?"

She elbowed him.

Acton stared up at the heaven's, wagging a finger. "What do you have against me?" He gave Laura a squeeze. "Well, I guess there's no way to keep a girl and her skulls apart, and thanks to Martin, perhaps one day you'll figure out where they actually came from."

"Clever bastard," muttered Reading, shaking his head. "He thought of everything, right down to the end."

Acton agreed. "He believed it would work, but knew it might not, though not for the reasons you and I would think. He planned for the possibility that mankind wasn't yet ready to receive the secrets of the skulls, but rather than risk a failure that might cause the Triarii to lose faith, he created a failsafe that would preserve the mystery."

"Well, it appears to have worked," said Reading. "That nutter on the phone sounded just as enamored with the skulls as he ever did. More so probably. He spouted off about continuing their work, returning the skulls to their rightful owners and carrying on as if nothing had happened, promising that one day Martin's sacrifice would pay off, the secrets of the skulls revealed to all." He made a spooky sound while waving his fingers in the air.

Acton got the distinct impression Reading didn't believe.

He smiled at his friend. "Well, as long as they leave us out of it. I've had my fill of crystal skulls."

"Hear! Hear!" Milton raised an imaginary glass. "From your lips to God's ears."

"I'd drink to that if there was a Scotch about," agreed Reading.

Sandra cast some gloom on the situation. "Can we be sure they truly are out of our lives, though?"

Acton shrugged. "No, I guess not, but the Deniers are dead, the Triarii, for the first time in history, have all thirteen skulls, and they believe in their power more now than ever before. There should be no reason we ever have to deal with them again." He glanced over at Reading who had just let a deep sigh escape. "You okay buddy?"

"Just thinking of Martin."

Laura rose, walking over to Reading and sitting on the arm of his chair, giving him a hug. "You poor dear."

Acton leaned forward. "Listen, Hugh, you should know that Martin died for something he truly believed in, and that he was surrounded by his friends."

Reading nodded, his eyes glistening.

"But not his best friend."

EPILOGUE

Niner climbed in the ring, the muscled Atlas in the far corner. He smacked his gloves together as a large crowd surrounded them, cash exchanged as bets were laid.

"You ready for an ass whoopin'?" he asked, showing off some fancy footwork à la Rocky 3.

"I am," rumbled Atlas. "Your ass. My whoopin'."

The bell rang, Jimmy clicking the stopwatch. "So, what rules are we playing by? Marquess of Queensberry?"

Atlas smacked his gloves together, channeling Mr. T's eye of the tiger. "No rules. I beat you until you can't even picture my mama's hips."

Niner jerked a glove over his shoulder. "You mean these hips?"

Spock yanked on a rope and a long banner unfurled, a picture of Atlas' mom and sister, hips jutting out, suddenly on display.

Atlas froze. "What the—?" His gloves dropped. "How the hell—?"

"I called them up and they sent the pictures. Spock—"

"Leave me out of this!"

"—had the banner made." Niner stared at their handiwork. "They *are* nice hips."

Atlas began to laugh, the rest of the crowd joining in once they knew it was safe to do so. He shook his head and walked over toward Niner. "I don't know why, but I can never stay mad at you."

He embraced Niner, Niner returning it, slapping the big man's back with his gloves, breathing a sigh of relief, when suddenly he was scooped up off the floor, raised feet first over Atlas' head, then vertical-suplexed onto the mat.

Atlas regained his feet and pointed at Niner. "*Nobody* talks about my mama's hips."

Niner weakly raised a hand. "Never again," he groaned, the hand dropping to the mat.

And the Triarii were true to their word, following Ananias' instructions not to hide the skulls away. In Saudi Arabia, a skull was returned to Faisal's family, in Nepal, the Crystal Oracle was presented to the Lama, in Paris, Henri delivered a skull to his museum, recommitting himself to a life with the Triarii after watching the footage of the crater, and as others were returned around the world, in Hope Trailer Park, New Mexico, Leroy arrived home to find his safe opened once again, his precious skull returned.

And he fell to his knees, thanking the crystal gods.

THE END

ACKNOWLEDGEMENTS

The Triarii is where I got my start. The Protocol was the first novel I ever wrote, it based upon a conversation my late friend Paul Conway and I had, where he told me about the crystal skulls he had seen on a documentary. "When you decide to write a novel, you should write about that!"

I did. Good advice from an old friend. It was accepted, a contract was signed, and now, fourteen books later in this series, and eight more in spin-offs, I think it is safe to say it was a good thing my friend had been flipping through the channels that night.

The Triarii also featured very prominently seven books later in The Venice Code, Book #8, and now seven books later in this book, Book #15, and everything, I think, is all wrapped up.

Or is it?

Who knows? This time there are no major loose ends left dangling, but there seems to be a pattern there, so maybe Book #22 will have them returning. I literally shrug as I type this. Who knows? They're still out there, and maybe someday I'll want to revisit them and see what new nightmares they can put Jim and Laura through.

Fun fact: In the original novel, The Protocol, there is the escape tunnel used by Laura to lead them to safety. Pulling up Google Maps while working on this novel, I looked at Fleet Street and found, exactly where I needed it, the Bride Lane described in this book. Then using Google Street View, I saw there was a garage door exactly where I needed it, and lo and behold, there was a camera under a balcony. The fun part? I had written the scene, not knowing this lane existed, let alone that it had the garage door I needed or the camera placed exactly as I had described.

And for my next trick…

As usual, there are people to thank. My dad for all the research, Brent Richards for some weapons and tactics info, Ian Kennedy for some military terminology help, Greg "Chief" Michael for some navy info (and yes, there's no navy reference in this *because* of the info!), Richard Jenner for some Britishisms, and Kenny Johnson for some wrasslin' info. And of course, my wife, daughter, parents, friends, and my loyal readers who are the reason I'm able to do this for a living.

To those who have not already done so, please visit my website at www.jrobertkennedy.com then sign up for the Insider's Club to be notified of new book releases. Your email address will never be shared or sold and you'll only receive the occasional email from me as I don't have time to spam you!

Thank you once again for reading.

ABOUT THE AUTHOR

USA Today bestselling author J. Robert Kennedy has written over twenty-five international bestsellers including the smash hit James Acton Thrillers series, the first installment of which, The Protocol, has been on the bestsellers list since its release, including a three month run at number one. In addition to the other novels from this series including The Templar's Relic, a USA Today and Barnes & Noble #1 overall bestseller, he writes the bestselling Special Agent Dylan Kane Thrillers, Delta Force Unleashed Thrillers and Detective Shakespeare Mysteries. Robert lives with his wife and daughter and writes full-time.

Visit Robert's website at www.jrobertkennedy.com for the latest news and contact information, and to join the Insider's Club to be notified when new books are released.

Available James Acton Thrillers

The Protocol (Book #1)

For two thousand years the Triarii have protected us, influencing history from the crusades to the discovery of America. Descendent from the Roman Empire, they pervade every level of society, and are now in a race with our own government to retrieve an ancient artifact thought to have been lost forever.

Brass Monkey (Book #2)

A nuclear missile, lost during the Cold War, is now in play--the most public spy swap in history, with a gorgeous agent the center of international attention, triggers the end-game of a corrupt Soviet Colonel's twenty five year plan. Pursued across the globe by the Russian authorities, including a brutal Spetsnaz unit, those involved will stop at nothing to deliver their weapon, and ensure their payday, regardless of the terrifying consequences.

Broken Dove (Book #3)

With the Triarii in control of the Roman Catholic Church, an organization founded by Saint Peter himself takes action, murdering one of the new Pope's operatives. Detective Chaney, called in by the Pope to investigate, disappears, and, to the horror of the Papal staff sent to inform His Holiness, they find him missing too, the only clue a secret chest, presented to each new pope on the eve of their election, since the beginning of the Church.

The Templar's Relic (Book #4)

The Vault must be sealed, but a construction accident leads to a miraculous discovery--an ancient tomb containing four Templar Knights, long forgotten, on the grounds of the Vatican. Not knowing who they can trust, the Vatican requests Professors James Acton and Laura Palmer examine the find, but what they discover, a precious Islamic relic, lost during the Crusades, triggers a set of events that shake the entire world, pitting the two greatest religions against each other. At risk is nothing less than the Vatican itself, and the rock upon which it was built.

Flags of Sin (Book #5)

Archaeology Professor James Acton simply wants to get away from everything, and relax. A trip to China seems just the answer, and he and his fiancée, Professor Laura Palmer, are soon on a flight to Beijing. But while boarding, they bump into an old friend, Delta Force Command Sergeant Major Burt Dawson, who surreptitiously delivers a message that they must meet the next day, for Dawson knows something they don't. China is about to erupt into chaos.

The Arab Fall (Book #6)

An accidental find by a friend of Professor James Acton may lead to the greatest archaeological discovery since the tomb of King Tutankhamen, perhaps even greater. And when news of it spreads, it reaches the ears of a group hell-bent on the destruction of all idols and icons, their mere existence considered blasphemous to Islam.

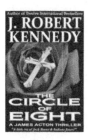

The Circle of Eight (Book #7)

The Bravo Team is targeted by a madman after one of their own intervenes in a rape. Little do they know this internationally well-respected banker is also a senior member of an organization long thought extinct, whose stated goals for a reshaped world are not only terrifying, but with today's globalization, totally achievable.

The Venice Code (Book #8)

A former President's son is kidnapped in a brazen attack on the streets of Potomac by the very ancient organization that murdered his father, convinced he knows the location of an item stolen from them by the late president. A close friend awakes from a coma with a message for archeology Professor James Acton from the same organization, sending him on a quest to find an object only rumored to exist, while trying desperately to keep one step ahead of a foe hell-bent on possessing it.

Pompeii's Ghosts (Book #9)

Two thousand years ago Roman Emperor Vespasian tries to preserve an empire by hiding a massive treasure in the quiet town of Pompeii should someone challenge his throne. Unbeknownst to him nature is about to unleash its wrath upon the Empire during which the best and worst of Rome's citizens will be revealed during a time when duty and honor were more than words, they were ideals worth dying for.

Amazon Burning (Book #10)

Days from any form of modern civilization, archeology Professor James Acton awakes to gunshots. Finding his wife missing, taken by a member of one of the uncontacted tribes, he and his friend INTERPOL Special Agent Hugh Reading try desperately to find her in the dark of the jungle, but quickly realize there is no hope without help. And with help three days away, he knows the longer they wait, the farther away she'll be.

The Riddle (Book #11)

Russia accuses the United States of assassinating their Prime Minister in Hanoi, naming Delta Force member Sergeant Carl "Niner" Sung as the assassin. Professors James Acton and Laura Palmer, witnesses to the murder, know the truth, and as the Russians and Vietnamese attempt to use the situation to their advantage on the international stage, the husband and wife duo attempt to find proof that their friend is innocent.

Blood Relics (Book #12)

A DYING MAN. A DESPERATE SON.
ONLY A MIRACLE CAN SAVE THEM BOTH.

Professor Laura Palmer is shot and kidnapped in front of her husband, archeology Professor James Acton, as they try to prevent the theft of the world's Blood Relics, ancient artifacts thought to contain the blood of Christ, a madman determined to possess them all at any cost.

Sins of the Titanic (Book #13)

THE ASSEMBLY IS ETERNAL. AND THEY'LL STOP AT NOTHING TO KEEP IT THAT WAY.

When Professor James Acton is contacted about a painting thought to have been lost with the sinking of the Titanic, he is inadvertently drawn into a century old conspiracy an ancient organization known as The Assembly will stop at nothing to keep secret.

Saint Peter's Soldiers (Book #14)

A MISSING DA VINCI.
A TERRIFYING GENETIC BREAKTHROUGH.
A PAST AND FUTURE ABOUT TO COLLIDE!

In World War Two a fabled da Vinci drawing is hidden from the Nazis, those involved fearing Hitler may attempt to steal it for its purported magical powers. It isn't returned for over fifty years.

And today, archeology Professor James Acton and his wife are about to be dragged into the terrible truth of what happened so many years ago, for the truth is never what it seems, and the history we thought was fact, is all lies.

The Thirteenth Legion (Book #15)

A TWO-THOUSAND-YEAR-OLD DESTINY IS ABOUT TO BE FULFILLED!

USA Today bestselling author J. Robert Kennedy delivers another action-packed thriller in The Thirteenth Legion. After Interpol Agent Hugh Reading spots his missing partner in Berlin, it sets off a chain of events that could lead to the death of his best friends, and if the legends are true, life as we know it.

Available Special Agent Dylan Kane Thrillers

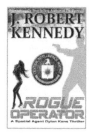

Rogue Operator (Book #1)

Three top secret research scientists are presumed dead in a boating accident, but the kidnapping of their families the same day raises questions the FBI and local police can't answer, leaving them waiting for a ransom demand that will never come. Central Intelligence Agency Analyst Chris Leroux stumbles upon the story, and finds a phone conversation that was never supposed to happen but is told to leave it to the FBI. But he can't let it go. For he knows something the FBI doesn't. One of the scientists is alive.

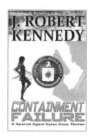

Containment Failure (Book #2)

New Orleans has been quarantined, an unknown virus sweeping the city, killing one hundred percent of those infected. The Centers for Disease Control, desperate to find a cure, is approached by BioDyne Pharma who reveal a former employee has turned a cutting edge medical treatment capable of targeting specific genetic sequences into a weapon, and released it. The stakes have never been higher as Kane battles to save not only his friends and the country he loves, but all of mankind.

Cold Warriors (Book #3)

While in Chechnya CIA Special Agent Dylan Kane stumbles upon a meeting between a known Chechen drug lord and a retired General once responsible for the entire Soviet nuclear arsenal. Money is exchanged for a data stick and the resulting transmission begins a race across the globe to discover just what was sold, the only clue a reference to a top-secret Soviet weapon called Crimson Rush.

Death to America (Book #4)

America is in crisis. Dozens of terrorist attacks have killed or injured thousands, and worse, every single attack appears to have been committed by an American citizen in the name of Islam.

A stolen experimental F-35 Lightning II is discovered by CIA Special Agent Dylan Kane in China, delivered by an American soldier reported dead years ago in exchange for a chilling promise.

And Chris Leroux is forced to watch as his girlfriend, Sherrie White, is tortured on camera, under orders to not interfere, her continued suffering providing intel too valuable to sacrifice.

Black Widow (Book #5)

USA Today bestselling author J. Robert Kennedy serves up another heart-pounding thriller in Black Widow. After corrupt Russian agents sell deadly radioactive Cesium to Chechen terrorists, CIA Special Agent Dylan Kane is sent to infiltrate the ISIL terror cell suspected of purchasing it. Then all contact is lost.

Available Delta Force Unleashed Thrillers

Payback (Book #1)

The daughter of the Vice President is kidnapped from an Ebola clinic, triggering an all-out effort to retrieve her by America's elite Delta Force just hours after a senior government official from Sierra Leone is assassinated in a horrific terrorist attack while visiting the United States. As she battles impossible odds and struggles to prove her worth to her captors who have promised she will die, she's forced to make unthinkable decisions to not only try to save her own life, but those dying from one of the most vicious diseases known to mankind, all in the hopes an unleashed Delta Force can save her before her captors enact their horrific plan on an unsuspecting United States.

Infidels (Book #2)

When the elite Delta Force's Bravo Team is inserted into Yemen to rescue a kidnapped Saudi prince, they find more than they bargained for—a crate containing the Black Stone, stolen from Mecca the day before. Requesting instructions on how to proceed, they find themselves cut off and disavowed, left to survive with nothing but each other to rely upon.

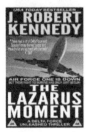

The Lazarus Moment (Book #3)

AIR FORCE ONE IS DOWN.
BUT THEIR FIGHT TO SURVIVE HAS ONLY JUST BEGUN!
When Air Force One crashes in the jungles of Africa, it is up to America's elite Delta Force to save the survivors not only from rebels hell-bent on capturing the President, but Mother Nature herself.

Available Detective Shakespeare Mysteries

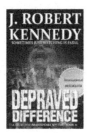

Depraved Difference (Book #1)

SOMETIMES JUST WATCHING IS FATAL

When a young woman is brutally assaulted by two men on the subway, her cries for help fall on the deaf ears of onlookers too terrified to get involved, her misery ended with the crushing stomp of a steel-toed boot. A cellphone video of her vicious murder, callously released on the Internet, its popularity a testament to today's depraved society, serves as a trigger, pulled a year later, for a killer.

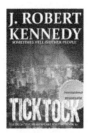

Tick Tock (Book #2)

SOMETIMES HELL IS OTHER PEOPLE

Crime Scene tech Frank Brata digs deep and finds the courage to ask his colleague, Sarah, out for coffee after work. Their good time turns into a nightmare when Frank wakes up the next morning covered in blood, with no recollection of what happened, and Sarah's body floating in the tub.

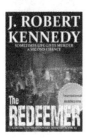

The Redeemer (Book #3)

SOMETIMES LIFE GIVES MURDER A SECOND CHANCE

It was the case that destroyed Detective Justin Shakespeare's career, beginning a downward spiral of self-loathing and self-destruction lasting half a decade. And today things are only going to get worse. The Widow Rapist is free on a technicality, and it is up to Detective Shakespeare and his partner Amber Trace to find the evidence, five years cold, to put him back in prison before he strikes again.

Zander Varga, Vampire Detective

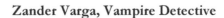

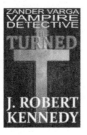

The Turned (Book #1)

Zander has relived his wife's death at the hands of vampires every day for almost three hundred years, his perfect memory a curse of becoming one of The Turned—infecting him their final heinous act after her murder.

Nineteen year-old Sydney Winter knows Zander's secret, a secret preserved by the women in her family for four generations. But with her mother in a coma, she's thrust into the frontlines, ahead of her time, to fight side-by-side with Zander.

Made in United States
Orlando, FL
11 May 2023

33048361R00189